Books in The Newto

Because of You

Out of my Depth

# Broken *and* Lost

*To Christine*

*"Love, Joy and Peace..."*
*Galations 5 v 22*

*by*

## GWENYTH CLARE LYNES

*Gwenyth-Clare Lynes*

**Grosvenor House
Publishing Limited**

All rights reserved
Copyright © Gwenyth Clare Lynes, 2017

The right of Gwenyth Clare Lynes to be identified as the author of this work has been asserted in accordance with Section 78 of the Copyright, Designs and Patents Act 1988

The book cover picture is copyright to Gwenyth Clare Lynes

This book is published by
Grosvenor House Publishing Ltd
Link House
140 The Broadway, Tolworth, Surrey, KT6 7HT.
www.grosvenorhousepublishing.co.uk

This book is sold subject to the conditions that it shall not, by way of trade or otherwise, be lent, resold, hired out or otherwise circulated without the author's or publisher's prior consent in any form of binding or cover other than that in which it is published and without a similar condition including this condition being imposed on the subsequent purchaser.

A CIP record for this book
is available from the British Library

ISBN 978-1-78623-963-1

The characters, events and places in this book, other than well established towns, are entirely fictitious and any resemblance to actual persons, events and places is purely coincidental. Any mistakes are the author's entirely.

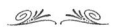

All Scripture quotations are taken from the Holy Bible, New International Version Anglicised Copyright @1979, 1984, 2011 Biblica.

Used by permission of Hodder & Stoughton Ltd, an Hachette UK company. All rights reserved. NIV is a registered trademark of Biblica UK trademark number 1448790.

# Acknowledgements

So many have encouraged me to complete this book in what has been a challenging year. It would be difficult to name you all but I thank you for your continued support. Your prayers and Christian love have been a great source of comfort and strength.

I particularly express my appreciation to Jon for his meticulous proof reading and editorial skills ensuring the script stays on track as well as to Andi and Oliver for so willingly giving their technical knowledge and guidance to the project.

My grateful thanks to all the Staff at Grosvenor House.

*Dedication*

For my dearly loved husband
TREVOR GEORGE LYNES JP MA
4-6-1943 – 3-6-2016
'He chose us in Him before the foundation
of the world...'
Ephesians ch1 v 4

# Glossary

Newton Westerby has been placed just south of the Norfolk/Suffolk border in East Anglia, England. The local inhabitants, who are native born, speak with a Suffolk dialect. However, only a few families and some of the older residents, have been depicted as using such in the text.

Suffolk people have a tendency to use double negatives i.e. won't be no more/not no more.

They also pronounce 'ing' endings as en' i.e. keepen', growen', headen', thieven', somethen', builden' ect.

Frequently an 'a' is added to these words i.e. a-sayen', a-sorten' ect.

Ow/ou pronounced ew i.e. snow – snew, you – yew.
O/ow pronounced oo i.e. so – soo, go – goo.
Afore – before.
Aloan – alone.
An' Oi int gorn-a dew e' – And I'm not going to do it.
A-tween – between.
Bin – been.
Bor – boy.
Dew – do.
Doan't – don't.

E' – it.
Fule/fewell – fool.
Funny – odd/strange.
Fust – first.
Git/gits - get/gets.
Gor – got.
Gorn – going.
Hen't – haven't/have not; hasn't/has not.
Hum - home.
Int – not/isn't.
Lorst – lost.
Mardle/mardling – to chat/chatting.
Niver – never.
Noo – no.
Oi/oi'l/oi'm – I/I'll/I'm.
Ole/owd – old.
Putter – complain.
Roite – right.
Rud – road.
Rum ole do – strange happenings.
Sin – seen.
Soo – so.
Squit – nonsense.
Stuff – things of an uncertain kind.
Taak – take.
Tew – to.
Thass – that's/that is.
Thowt – thought.
Ul – I'll/ I will.
Wholly – really.
Worsent – worse.
Yew – you.
Yewsel' – yourself.
Yow'n/yourn –your/yours.
Yup – yes.

# Prologue

A smile of happiness radiated from RK's face when she awoke on Tuesday morning. She stretched her arms above her head, threw off the duvet then gracefully rose from the bed, her long legs sprinting effortlessly towards the east facing window. Eagerly she drew back the bedroom curtains her eyes enticed to gaze through the glass towards the distant view where the rolling sea met the far horizon before flinging open the large windowpane. She rested her elbows on the sill as she absorbed the fragrance and sounds of the sea. It was a scene of breathtaking beauty as the waking sun bathed the moving ocean with its early morning brilliance, a panorama that constantly captivated her landlubbing nature.

The charm of the ever changing vista that extended beyond her cottage garden never ceased to fascinate RK despite her unpleasant experience in that spot a number of weeks earlier. The remembrance of that nail biting night still triggered shivers down her spine even though the scoundrels who had scaled her garden wall and caused such a fright and subsequent havoc in her life were now apprehended. *Obnoxious intruders!* RK shuddered then looked across to the dancing waves as the sunlight kissed their peaks before they tumbled onto the shore. She lifted her eyes to the heavens.

"Good morning, God. I guess you're there, somewhere, even though I can't see you. Thanks for this lovely day."

Her heart knew such a feeling of contentment; it was indescribable. "I finally know the real meaning of joy. It bubbles up inside until there's so much it can't be contained; like whisking egg white for meringues, the foam froths up then spills over the brim of the bowl, add sugar and the mixture gains substance. Thankyou, God, for filling me up with so much effervescent joy I can hardly contain it. I guess I'll find the substance will come as I get to know You."

RK wrapped her arms around her mid-riff as if to keep the euphoria to herself as she looked out across the seascape which had in recent months become so precious to her.

"For years I didn't believe You existed and now, the moment I acknowledge Your presence, You turn my life up-side-down. I hardly dare think what the folks at home will have to say about all this. Dad, I am sure, will go ballistic. He doesn't agree with this Christian thing. The girls will probably side with him and Mum tag along because that's what she always does."

Actually, for the time being, RK was glad she was still in her own home, albeit temporary, and not on her parent's farm a hundred miles or so away in rural Lincolnshire. The seaside cottage at Newton Westerby which she rented from the village housing trust had become a blissful haven.

So much had changed in her heart and life in the last two weeks the re-direction would certainly cause ructions in the family. *I really don't want to get into a heated spat with them at the moment.* She had needed the quietness and calm of her home in its coastal location to sort out her thoughts and feelings. The hustle and bustle of the farm would not allow for moments of contemplation.

RK's annual holiday had been scheduled to commence on the second Saturday in May but her employer, Laura Catton, had an appointment to see a consultant in Norwich the following Monday. So, when Laura's husband, Adam, asked RK if she could delay her departure in order to look after the children she willingly agreed to change her plans to accommodate the Catton family's requirements. She had been nanny to the Catton's children ever since their young mother's stroke the previous year.

"I can leave sometime on Tuesday, Adam, if that fits in better with your schedule, then should Laura's appointment run late on Monday, I will still be here to attend to the children's needs."

So, having fulfilled all her duties, the day had arrived.

She was now packed and ready to go yet, reticent to leave.

Over the past few months RK had frequently been challenged in her own mind on the atheistic stance she had stubbornly held to in discussions with her new friends in Newton Westerby. Never once had they tried to dissuade her from the dogma she had imbibed from her parents, her father in particular. However, the manner in which some of the people from the village conducted themselves and went about their affairs made an unseen impact upon RK. At first she thought they seemed too good to be true till she became the recipient of their kindness and generosity and realised the faith they lived by and the friendship offered to her was genuine.

When she accepted the tenancy of Ferry Cottage fully aware it lacked mod-cons, Jennifer Pedwardine, the retired primary school headmistress, graciously opened up her home, known as 'Bakers', to RK for bathing facilities. She had given RK a key so that she could come and go as she pleased.

Others, such as Emma Cooper and Miranda Durrant, as well as, Rachel and Ben Durrant freely offered hospitality and friendship, no strings attached, completely knocking on the head her father's philosophy that "you don't give unless you get something in return".

P.C. Dan Prettyman's conduct also surprised her; he treated everyone with such consideration and courtesy, it was hard to believe he was a policeman. A timely quiet word was his style of policing rather than a dogmatic 'laying down of the law' particularly when dealing with boisterous youngsters from the village or stroppy, mischief-making visitors. He seemed to be a friendly young man but because of a number of incidents at her cottage RK also had occasion to see the official side of him at work adhering strictly to the letter of the law.

Numerous helping hands had also reached out with assistance when RK first moved into Ferry Cottage, foremost among them had been Tessa Jenner, owner of the Mill B&B where RK had stayed when she first visited the village the previous year, and Trixie Cooper, wife of Doctor John.

"But why?" RK asked.

"Because we help our own," was the response from the willing helpers.

"But I'm not local."

"Oh, but, if it's in the Lord's plan, you will be."

"I don't believe that!"

"We do."

During the time RK worked as nanny to Adam and Laura's children she witnessed first-hand the young couple's unwavering faith and perseverance throughout the trauma of Laura's untimely stroke and subsequent slow recovery. Seeing the outworking of faith in action in their home was an eye opener and inspiration but still RK argued it was not for her. She repeatedly pushed aside the nudging that sometimes churned within her heart, obstinately stating, "My life's perfectly fine as it is, thankyou very much." That is, until last Sunday week. It seemed God Himself had other plans and used the Vicar to catch her attention.

"Jesus said, 'I am the way.' It's here recorded in John's gospel but hundreds of years before, Isaiah wrote, foreshadowing the coming of God's Son, 'This is the way walk in it.' Today, there is no other way for you and..."

"There is no other way." Rev Hugh's words on that Sunday morning lingered in RK's mind. They also reached into her heart. RK hadn't intended to stay to the worship service but the children's Sunday Club classes were overrunning so, instead of standing in the church foyer to pass the time while waiting for her young charges to finish, RK allowed Emma Cooper, the junior Doctor's wife, to usher her into the service to sit with herself and Roger.

Throughout the time that RK had been looking after the Catton children, Daniel, Kirsten and Poppy, she had accompanied them to many activities held at the church but always successfully managed to shut out any personal involvement that might influence her thinking of the Christian faith. RK frequently stressed she wanted nothing to do with religion. Her father's anti-religious dogma had put her off for life.

"I don't believe in Church, God or the Bible!"

Nevertheless, after months of seeing members of Newton Westerby church fellowship care for the Catton family following Laura's stroke, RK said to Penny Darnell, the vicar's wife, "For the first time in my life I understand what the church is really meant to do. You all demonstrate love and care in action quietly, but also, with genuine compassion not with empty words, pomp and show as per my father."

The personal God Adam and Laura knew and spoke to, as well as many of the other friends she had made since moving to Newton Westerby, amazingly, became real to her. The experience came as a surprise because she had been so against the idea that God even existed let alone remotely interested in her. Dad was emphatic in his outlook; "The God thing is for the weak. It's a crutch for the spineless." All her life she had accepted and lived by his belief; never deviating from what he had taught her.

In spite of this, in the service that Sunday morning RK had repeated, with conviction in her heart, the words spoken by Rev. Hugh, "I believe in Jesus Christ, God's Son. I believe He died and rose again for me, to bring me redemption. Having, today, asked God for forgiveness I will, from this moment, trust Him to save me and teach me to grow in His grace."

However, the declaration was not accompanied by bright lights or fireworks and at first RK wondered if anything at all had happened. She felt the same; there was no significant difference; she hadn't changed. RK looked around the church and began to feel a sense of disappointment until she heard Hugh say, "Remember, this is not about how you feel. It's about trusting, with mind, as well as heart, in the promises God has made to you, His child. When Satan tempts you to doubt, respond with the little phrase, 'I believe in Jesus.'"

"Yes, I believe in Jesus," RK whispered.

"Tell someone what you have done. Don't keep it to yourself. It will help strengthen you in your faith."

Emma sensed the significance of the moment for RK, so sat quietly, praying for her friend. When RK started to fidget Emma asked, "Are you OK?"

"Oh, yes, Emma, I believe in Jesus." RK glowed and the glory of the presence of the Lord was still with her on Tuesday morning when she finally departed from Newton Westerby, on her Harley-Davidson motorbike, to commence her long overdue holiday on her parents' bulb and flower farm in the heart of Lincolnshire. On the point of departure P.C. Dan stopped by to wish her Godspeed.

"Have a safe journey and a restful holiday, Robyn." Dan never abbreviated her name.

"Thanks, Dan. I'll be back before you can blink," RK quipped, a grin spreading across her face.

"I'll look forward to that. Maybe we could go to the barbeque Miss Pedwardine is hosting at 'Bakers', together."

"What a treat! I can't wait," she teased. She enjoyed the relaxed friendship with the young policeman. *Maybe now I'm a Christian he'll be less guarded perhaps...* Her heart skipped at the thought of a closer relationship developing with Dan and her eyes sparkled. Dan picked up on it and smiled. *Father God, watch over her as she travels, she's so special.*

RK switched on the motor-bike engine. Just before she set off she looked at Dan over her shoulder and called, "I believe in Jesus, Dan."

An overwhelming sense of joy and wellbeing accompanied her as she travelled. Glad she had left early to avoid heavy traffic RK was amazed at the number of lorries and commercial vehicles already choking up both the A47 and the A17 as they travelled across north Norfolk into Lincolnshire.

RK negotiated the numerous roundabouts with ease and kept up a steady speed for many miles, sandwiched between a motor spares van and a blue Ford Fiesta; on the single carriage-way passing places were few and far between. A few miles west of King's Lynn the van pulled away leaving a gap between himself and RK's motor-bike.

As she approached the acute A1357 Moulton turning RK was vaguely aware of a large vehicle approaching on her left hand side travelling at an angle towards the main road. However, the driver didn't stop when he reached the A17, but pulled out straight in front of RK leaving no time for her to brake or overtake. As the lorry impacted with the Harley-Davidson its attached trailer swung round on to the main road as RK somersaulted over the handlebars. She hurtled through the air and landed upside-down on her helmet to a cacophony of hooters, horns and crashing metal imploding in her head.

# Chapter One

❖

"Mic, six pallets mixed tulips required for Manchester, Wednesday," shouted Phil.

"Br...r.r.Br...r..." the telephone shrilled.

"Dickinson-Bond Nursery, can I help you?" Phil manipulated the phone under her chin as an email came in on the laptop. "Please, can you hold?"

"Mic," she yelled, adjusting the mouth piece against her shoulder as she speed read the email. "Two pallets each of 'King Alfred', 'Winston', 'Cheerfulness' and 'Queen of the Night' are needed for the Covent Garden run tomorrow."

Phil returned to the telephone caller, "Sorry to keep you, how may I help you?"

The office door clattered open forcefully.

"Where's your mother?" Mr Dickinson-Bond demanded curtly.

Phil gesticulated towards the house.

"I might have guessed she'd be with Wounded Winnie." He slammed his hand heavily on the desk.

"I need her, now!" He repeatedly pounded the desk top to emphasize his words as his voice crescendoed in decibels. "Neil's brought in a batch of bulbs from the east field. I've trimmed and put the load through the sorter but I need your mother to check the quality of the batch already in the grading shed, now!" The din from the tractor engine reverberated across the yard and in through the open door.

Phil put her hand over the mouth piece, "Dad, calm down, can't you see, I'm on the phone – a big order. Close the door."

His face screwed up with rage.

"If your Mother doesn't come and do quality control now there won't be any goods ready for orders and consequently no money for your fancy wages!"

"Please, Dad!"

Mr Dickinson-Bond stomped irritably towards the house slamming the office door behind his bulky frame. As he left the printer rattled out another order.

"Amy, Amy," he yelled as he kicked open the back door of the farm-house. "Come and do your proper work. Stop babying the girl."

"I'll be there shortly, George," a harassed voice called out. Amy Dickinson-Bond, a small, bird-like woman scuttled into the kitchen a few minutes later, all of a fluster and wringing her hands. "Now, George, what is it you want?"

"I want you to come and do some work," he bellowed rudely. "The hoppers are full in the sorting shed, Phil has more orders coming in than she can cope with and Mic is short of stock required for the pallets for the early run to London and quality checks need to be done on the batch in the grading shed."

"Where's Davi?"

"Doing accounts."

"She'll need to pack, too."

"THAT girl ought to get off her back-side and come

and bag." George tossed his head crossly in the direction of the closed door that led into the sitting room. "I can do it with my eyes closed so I'm sure she can, if she put her mind to it, instead of sitting around doing nothing all day but mope. She needs to earn her keep!" he snapped irritably.

"George, she's not well."

"Serves her right! If she's not man enough to take the medicine of her actions, she'll have to bear the consequences. Stop mambi-pambying her. We can't afford to carry passengers. Sh..." He stopped speaking as the back door was flung open.

"Dad, Al's back. In which order do you want the load putting into the lorry?" Davi shouted from the yard. George turned to exit the kitchen in response to his daughter's query but briefly looked back and wagged a finger in his wife's direction.

"Mark my words, Amy. She's got to pull her weight. I'll give her till the end of next week; then, she's out."

"But...George!" Amy continued to wring her hands.

"We've kept her for nigh on two months. What's she given in return?"

"George!"

"Nothing! Absolutely nothing!"

"Dad! Al's waiting!"

"If she won't work I'm not keeping her a day longer. She's had more than enough time to get sorted out," George shouted and shook his fist furiously in the direction of the closed farmhouse door. "That girl's just bone idle and you're encouraging her!" Purple faced George strode back to the packing shed to give instructions to Al, his eldest daughter Phil's husband and his driver for the week. Al and Neil, Mic's boyfriend, had negotiated with Mr Dickinson-Bond some while back to share the long distance deliveries by doing alternate weeks, that is, driving one week and farm work the other. Their willingness to be flexible contributed tremendously to the well running of the farm but this action was neither appreciated nor acknowledged by their curmudgeonly boss.

Amy scurried towards the packing shed in George's wake calling into the office to speak with Phil. "I'm just about at the end of my tether, what with seeing to Our Kay's needs and meeting your Dad's demands. I don't think I can take much more."

"Perhaps these new friends of hers who are calling in this afternoon will come up with some ideas."

"Oh, I'd forgotten about them coming and we've so much to do," said Amy wringing her hands.

"Not to worry, hopefully they'll see we're busy and not stay long or we could give them a job to do. They might even take her off your hands for a few days," Phil suggested sarcastically.

"That would be a relief she could scream all day at someone else for a change."

"Amy! Amy, come on! Wasted time means lost money yet you still expect housekeeping at the end of the week," George roared from the yard.

"And you expect a meal on the table at the end of each day," Amy muttered.

"Phil, can you print some more labels?" Mic called out as she rushed up the steps almost bumping into her mother. "We've also run out of medium bags."

"Medium sized bags are in the second drawer down on the right."

"Thanks."

"What labels do you need?"

"'Cheerfulness' and 'Princess Caroline'."

"Look in the third tray on the middle shelf for one and sixth tray on the bottom shelf for the other."

"Great! This should be enough," Mic rushed out clutching the bags and the labels.

"Amy, do come on!" George's voice boomed impatiently across the yard. "Neil's in with another batch. We'll be up till midnight at this rate. You really must get that girl to use her hands. She can still feel, can't she?"

"George, give it time."

"I'll be bankrupt if I give it much more time."

"George!" Amy ran her bony fingers through her hair in despair.

"She's contributing nothing to the coffers. It's all take, take, take! And you're encouraging her!" George stormed off to assist Neil unload the trailer of bulbs.

"It's true, Mum, Our Kay's doing nothing to help and she's taking you away from the work you do on the farm. We all have to pull together or the business will fail. Then where'd we be?"

"It's alright for you, Phil, to sit in the office and issue judgements, but I'm torn in two ways either I please your Dad or I see to Our Kay."

"She ought to be seeing to herself, by now, so that you're not placed in this dilemma."

"That's easy for you to say but..."

"Amy!" George belted out.

"...you're not in her situation." Amy twisted her fingers repeatedly around themselves.

"Amy!"

"Coming!"

"If I were, I'd find some way round it, not shut myself away and scream for attention all day," Phil muttered to herself as Amy ran to the sorting shed mumbling under her breath, "If only George would trust one of the girls, with quality control, it wouldn't all fall on my shoulders."

A van drew into the car park. Amy looked up. "Oh, no, it's Spriggs from Lincoln. I hope his order's ready. He can be so short tempered if he's kept waiting."

"Good morning, Mr Spriggs," Davi, ever alert to incoming traffic, walked to greet the new arrival. Amy breathed a sigh of relief. "Your order's ready if you'd care to come and check it, then we'll help load the van."

"I'll do my own loading and then I'll know I've got the right amount," he sneered.

"Right-o, but we'll check together then you can settle up with Phil in the office."

"Humph!" he snorted.

Spriggs was a sly customer, had a sleight of hand, and would always swear the order was not correct. His fuse was as short as George's and Amy had long ago learned to keep the two apart. So, when Spriggs was due in, Davi was assigned to deal with him. With her business acumen she was able to be civil and yet outsmart him and pick up on his little wiles. Every time he called at the farm Spriggs felt he was being overcharged as he tetchily complained, "I'm paying money for petrol to collect my order so I should be entitled to a discount." Davi painstakingly pointed out that, "Customers, who have orders delivered pay carriage charges in addition to the charge for the goods." Thankfully, he was unable to run rings round her.

George was beginning to see that allowing Davi to attend college was starting to pay dividends. Her expertise also ensured that, not only were orders delivered to time, but they were paid for on delivery. From the moment Davi had assumed responsibility for business management of the farm there had been no defaulters. This pleased George, who would never admit that his business acumen was somewhat lacking, and his overbearing, threatening letters to non-payers rarely achieved the required results. At least ever since Davi took on the helm in that department no accounts had been surreptitiously pushed under the carpet and forgotten. He had expertise of a different kind. George knew about soil, seeds and seasons and how each interlinked to produce quality plants and stock.

He just needed Our Kay to play her part then all the cogs in the family concern would be in place. George believed that growers by sheer hard graft and tenacity survived in the ever changing world in which they lived. The rich, black alluvium Lincolnshire soil on the farm had been worked by his predecessors for more years than he cared to remember but the family business was more than a tool for making a living. An ancestral business like theirs, which had traded for many generations, was very special. George was one of those who would always endure in order to carry on the family tradition. It seemed as though survival was bred into him even as he had a reputation to maintain.

Whilst disappointed that his girls were not boys he was determined to instil in them the same work ethic his father had drummed into him. He was relieved, too, that Phil and Mic had young men who were willing to join the family firm and work hard to ensure the farm succeeded.

Our Kay was his thorn in the flesh. Why, oh, why couldn't she have been a boy? Standing over 6 feet tall in her stocking feet she would have made a fine strapping lad. Robin Keith, George had chosen and what did Amy do but produce another girl. Robyn Keitha she named her. From a tiny tot the child knew her own mind and wouldn't be moulded into subjection like the other three. How she'd dug her heels in about getting the qualifications she wanted and not following the path he intended for her. However, George wouldn't let her have all her own way but insisted, alongside her chosen course, she also study motor mechanics with emphasis on agricultural machinery. She became a good mechanic and a brilliant, safe driver; someone he could trust. But she wanted none of it. A children's nanny she wanted to be!

Now look at her! Useless!

---

Following the fall from her motor-bike RK had been released from hospital into her parent's care with a number of broken bones and a sore head. The manner in which she landed on her head caused her open-faced crash helmet to crack and as a consequence the impact brought about nasty facial injuries and blindness. This condition caused both RK and her parents to despair; RK because she was locked into an unknown state of darkness, the senior Dickinson-Bonds because they hadn't the time to spend looking after an invalid, the farm demanded every waking moment. The doctors were reticent to say whether the condition was permanent or only temporary.

Mr Dickinson-Bond was suspicious of their diagnosis and Mrs Dickinson-Bond felt it was an unsatisfactory prognosis but RK suspected it was because they were unsure of the eventual outcome of the accident on her sight. The doctors had initially ordered rest but, on her parents Lincolnshire farm life was chaotic, demands and schedules had to be met and orders fulfilled to time. There was always busyness on the farm. Her parents and sisters, Philipa, known as Phil, Michaela, called Mic, and Davina, shortened by all to Davi, Phil's husband, Al and Mic's boyfriend, Neil, were all involved in the day to day running of the farm. Their tasks encompassed growing, packing and distributing bedding plants and bulbs as well as seasonal salad and root crops.

At certain times of the year the seedlings and plug plants for the home and continental markets, housed in the six huge nursery greenhouses, required constant attention. The new hydroponics plant also exacted tremendous time and energy but anticipated returns were considerable. To ensure a creditable yield from the produce grown on the farm necessitated the input of many man hours. Her father, driven by the need to succeed, had no time for sickness or shirkers. Throughout her life it had been deeply ingrained in RK, and her three sisters, that the survival of the family business was of paramount importance. They were all expected to be involved in the farm and willing to endure enormous sacrifices and, at times, hardships to secure its continuation.

However, for RK the family yoke chafed too long and she reached a point where she needed to be released from her father's stranglehold. Although she loved country life working for ever with the soil was not her life's ambition. She eventually managed to persuade her parents to allow her to attend college in Lincoln to obtain NVQ qualifications to work with children and she subsequently acquired a post in the nursery attached to the local primary school with the proviso that she work on the farm at weekends and school holidays.

When her contract with the education authority was not renewed, because of government cutbacks, RK took private short term nannying posts. Then, she accepted a more permanent position with a family in the seaside village of Newton Westerby situated on the Suffolk/Norfolk border. At first this decision created enormous problems for the rest of the family members because she was no longer available to do certain long haul lorry delivery runs. Then Mic started going out with Neil. He became part of the family firm when they became engaged and was willing to do the lorry deliveries which relieved the pressure on RK. Al, Phil's husband, subsequently volunteered to share the driving during their busiest periods so that with ungracious reluctance Mr Dickinson-Bond was forced to accept RK's work choices.

However, Davina, the youngest of her older sisters, also wanted to break from the family concern but like RK she learned that survival of one's rights and independence came at a price.

Davi had done exceptionally well at school in Maths attaining A* in O and A level grades and had won a place at Durham University to take Business Studies but her father refused to let her go.

"Too far for you to come home to help out at weekends!" he'd adamantly stated.

Determined to succeed Davi compromised and enrolled at Lincoln University, lived in during the week and came home at weekends and holidays. This was to pacify her father. However, having been allowed to take her chosen course achieving the highest grades for her degree, George demanded that Davi put her learning to use in the business. "You owe it to your mother and me," he insisted.

Their father persisted in his philosophy that, "only by hard work and total commitment will growers, like us, survive in this ever-changing world in which we live." George reiterated again and again to his daughters, "I'm not afraid of hard work and I expect you to be of the same mind." He firmly believed his success came about because he had the wit to act sooner than his immediate competitors and diversify before the economic slump could bite but there was no letting up.

"If we're to remain the best we've all to put in the effort. It's the duty of each family member to shoulder responsibility of work on the farm." George constantly reminded them of his dogma. "Your value to the firm can only be measured by the conscience of each of you. This will be evident in your daily commitment. Your forebears gave their lives for this farm and I expect the same from you."

Great grandfather, Richard Dickinson, was one of those who pioneered the cultivation of tulip bulbs on his Lincolnshire farm.

When George Bond married Amy Dickinson their adjoining farms, as well as their names, were amalgamated and so created a sizeable holding. Thus, history and current life continually interweave and colour daily activities on the farm.

Peace and tranquillity are impossible.

# Chapter Two

At the farm RK was made to feel useless and a tiresome burden by everyone in the family. The bulbs and some of the root crops were ready for harvesting simultaneously and it was a race against time to lift them from the ground, get them graded, packaged and marketed whilst in prime condition. Each member of the family team was working flat out and didn't have time to give attention to RK so she was left alone for many hours at a time. At first, the enforced darkness frightened her and she constantly screamed out for someone to help her, chiefly her mother but frequently God, though to her emergent faith He seemed somewhat elusive. As the days in the dark became weeks RK's normal self-reliance seemed to desert her and the sense of helplessness brought about an uncharacteristic nervousness.

"Please, don't leave me," RK pleaded on one occasion as she reached out to hold on to Mic's arm but Mic roughly shrugged her off.

"Do you know how pathetic you sound?" Mic asked sarcastically.

"I'm sorry it seems that way but I feel very vulnerable on my own."

"You'll just have to get used to it, then, won't you," Mic continued callously.

"I'm finding that rather difficult, Mic."

"Well, you've got yourself into this fix; you'll just have to learn to deal with it."

"I didn't cause the accident."

"That may be so, but if you'd been here, where you belong, instead of gadding off to goodness knows where, you wouldn't have been in the wrong place at the wrong time, would you," Mic spat out.

"I was doing a jo..."

"There's a job here for you to do. When you go skiving to other parts of the country we're run off our feet with all the extra work."

"It was always understood that when I qualified I would no longer be available to work on the farm. My skills are in other directions that is why I trained to work with children."

"You're just a shirker with no loyalty to the family firm. Dad depended on you to do the driving and servicing of the vehicles and machinery. You've let us all down. You deserve all you've got."

RK was shaken at the venom in her sister's words. The silence lengthened till RK was unsure if Mic was still in the room or if she had been left alone. Quietly she asked, "Could you pass my coffee?"

"It's there on the table. Get it yourself. You're not a helpless baby, are you?" Mic got up and stalked out angrily. She bumped into Davi as she came into the house, rolled her eyes up at her younger sister and with an exaggerated sigh groaned sarcastically, "She'd try the patience of a saint! She's such a wimp!"

Davi refrained from comment and made her way cheerfully into RK's room.

"Hi there, Our Kay, how're you doing?"

RK promptly burst into tears.

"Hey there, I came to cheer you up not to turn on the water works."

RK smiled wanly as she brushed the tears from her cheek. "Do you know you're the first one to ask me how I am since I came home from the hospital?"

"I've missed you since you went off to East Anglia so am pleased to see you home, that's why, but I'm truly sorry all this has happened to you, ducky." Davi drew close to her sister and put her arms around her shoulders and gave her an affectionate hug.

"I'm here to assist you to the bathroom or has Mic already done that?" When RK gingerly shook her head Davi helped her on to her feet, handed her the crutches and then steered RK carefully round the furniture obstacles.

"She wouldn't even pass my coffee although she'd made it."

"First things first then I'll make you another one, OK?"

"Thanks, but I'm so afraid that I'll knock it over or smash something."

"Not to worry, if you do I'll sort it, and you." The girls giggled together.

A short time later, ablutions attended to, RK settled, coffee made, the sisters sat to chat.

"Why do the others hate me, Davi?"

"Hate's a bit strong. They don't hate you, ducky, but they are piqued with jealousy."

"What do you mean?"

"You've broken free of Dad's stranglehold. Phil and Mic need jobs but haven't the wit or the skill to try anything different so they're tied into Dad's regime."

"But they're both so very good at what they do".

"That's not the point. Although they're competent and qualified in their respective jobs they resent the fact that, because you are no longer here to do the driving, it's fallen on Neil and Al to do it, and they are away from home such a lot. The girls don't like that. Phil in particular feels the boys don't see enough of their Dad and that Al is wasting his degree sat for hours on end in a lorry cab."

"We both know the answer to that problem."

"True, but Dad will still not consider joining the consortium."

"Surely it would cut down costs?"

"It certainly would, but his pride won't let him. He wants to keep the business in the family at all costs, so he has something to pass on to Phil's two lads, which is why he won't employ anyone else, apart from the locals who help at bunching time, and to be honest, they're slow and past it."

"I think if he sticks with that viewpoint he'll ultimately lose the business."

"I'm sure you're right. We're struggling to keep our heads above water as it is. *'There's none so fickle as folks'* is a favourite saying of Dad's because an individual's choice creates fluctuation in the demand for plug plants each season. So, if Dad gets his calculations wrong in the quantities and varieties of seedlings to grow we suffer serious losses which ultimately lead to cutbacks. The bulb market is holding its own but more and more we rely on a good beet and potato crop to keep us solvent."

"So it would make sense to go with the consortium particularly for transport and deliveries?"

"Yes. Our neighbours have done it successfully as have White and Taylor and both have retained their own packaging and company logo."

"Why don't you write up a business plan where Dad can keep face? Present it in such a manner that he can't fail to be impressed, for instance, where he saves money instead of losing it, like the deliveries. Have you considered employing students or linking up with the local horticultural college and offering work experience?"

"No, I haven't but that sounds a good idea. I'll give it some thought." Davi rose to return to work, looked around cautiously and then said quietly, "I am in negotiation with a supermarket chain to supply the tulip hydro cuts but don't say anything to Dad. He's anxious for this new venture to succeed, and I think it will, but I'll break it to him when the deal's signed, sealed and settled."

"Of course I won't. He's barely speaking to me at the moment, anyway. Perhaps handing Dad a fait accompli may be the best way to win him over. Thanks, Davi, for spending time with me and treating me as normal."

Tears welled up in Davi's eyes as she knelt down by RK's chair and flung her arms around her sister.

"Of course you're normal, ducky, just a bit broken in a few places, which given time will heal."

"The other's treat me as though I'm a freak and a skiving one at that."

Davi burst into laughter.

"I'm glad you've not lost your sense of humour." She jumped up. "I must get on or Dad will be after me. Don't worry about the others. Keep smiling m'duck, see you." Within seconds Davi was out of the door and on her way to the office.

RK's head remained partially bandaged and persistently ached. With her broken arm in plaster it made so many actions awkward. She was pleased Davi had stopped by to chat and helped with her coffee but, after she had returned to work, the attitude of the other family members played on RK's mind causing her head to ache even more. They were adamant they were not giving her assistance of any kind. They made it clear she didn't deserve it. They couldn't wait for the healing process to end but were unwilling to help RK achieve that goal.

Back-slab plaster splints were still on both legs, hindering movement. Lack of sight thwarted attempts at physiotherapy because she was unable to see where she was going or what she was doing, though the greater hindrance was the family's distinct lack of understanding, refusing to move or relocate furniture to accommodate RK's temporary immobility.

"For goodness sake, Our Kay, make an effort," Phil frequently shouted at her as though she were deaf as well as blind. "We're too busy to run around after you."

So, frustratingly, her father had no patience with her, and two of her sisters had no time for her, they were all too busy working on the farm and occupied with their own interests in life. Her mother's loyalties were sorely tried divided as they were between her husband and the success of their livelihood and the adult child who so desperately needed her attention all the time. As a result, RK's relationship with her mother was becoming increasingly more difficult. RK was not pliant and conforming like her sisters. Thus it was that after seeing to RK's personal needs first thing in the morning Amy locked her in a downstairs room in the house, for her own safety, so she said. Then she set about her own tasks on the farm.

When someone remembered they came to check that RK was satisfactory, attended to her toilet needs and banged food and drink down on the table regardless of whether she could reach or locate it.

Being cooped up, in what seemed something akin to solitary confinement, was proving very difficult for RK.

*God, where are You in all this mess? We were only just getting acquainted. Now look at me, blind, inept and a nuisance, I'm utterly broken, lost and useless,* RK wailed despondently one morning after her mother had left for work. *I wish I knew how much longer this was going to take, and then I could get on with my life.*

RK loved the Lincolnshire countryside. The wide open, fenland spaces, where the horizon stretched for mile upon mile, had been an idyllic place in which to grow up. Whilst they were each given responsibilities and tasks to perform on the farm from an early age the girls had still been allowed a certain amount of freedom as children to explore and enjoy the flat land that was their heritage.

The many straight, level droves that were built alongside the drains and dykes Vermuyden and his like had designed to drain the land, were ideal for learning first of all to cycle bikes along, and then progress to driving cars, and for RK, riding motor-bikes. Ramrod flat roads stretching ahead, as far as the eye could see, also enabled easy movement between the farms and villages, and in her grandparent's day, access to the railway station, a vital link to the home markets for their valuable but perishable merchandise although a mode of transport long since gone under Mr Beeching's axing plans.

Outside the window RK could hear many different noises, the tractor engine mingling with Phil's shouts from the office, appropriate loud responses from her father, Mic or Davi, banging doors and clattering implements, other vehicles pulling into the yard as well as unidentifiable voices and the fork lift truck moving pallets around. The blindness gave her a sense of claustrophobia and a desperate desire to break through the black curtain that engulfed her. Panic frequently overwhelmed her when repeated clawing at it would not tear the darkness down.

*How I miss the spaciousness and freedom of the countryside*, RK bemoaned the limitations her condition placed upon her. *I wish I could stroll along the beach, or the clifftop, or even sit in my little cottage at Newton Westerby and absorb the peacefulness. Will I ever smell the sea and feel the wind on my face again, or hear the squawking of the gulls as a fishing boat comes into harbour?* She hardly dare think of that scenario. *I wonder what the children are doing and how Adam and Laura are coping in my absence. How I miss them.*

In frustration RK banged her good fist on the arm of the chair angrily. *Instead of helping them, here I am cocooned in these four walls, confined in a living tomb of blackness. God, they never once blamed You for Laura's illness. In fact, their belief in You seemed to get stronger. That always mystified me. I don't know You very well, God, but their experience has taught me that You must be someone special. I wish I could talk to them right now, I have so many questions about You and there's no one here I can ask. I dare not mention You in front of the family Dad would explode and the others give me short shrift. Yet there, in Newton Westerby, I know I could speak to one of any number of people about You and they would answer my queries and concerns without hesitation.*

Across RK's mind's eye flitted cameo pictures of the many new friends she had made over the months she had spent in Newton Westerby; Emma, Miranda, the Jenner family, Jennifer, Adam and Laura and their children, Ben and Rachel, Justin, Annette, Dan...Her heart plummeted when she thought of Dan. She so enjoyed his company. RK wasn't one to spend time in idle daydream but she did find him interesting and attractive. *I'm sure he wanted to build on our friendship when I returned from my holiday. Now look at me, God, my life's a shambles and my body's a wreck. What man is going to look at me twice or consider me a worthwhile prospect as a marriage partner?*

In no time at all her mood changed from the cheerfulness she had earlier shared with Davi to one of despair and despondency when she recalled the happy times she had enjoyed in the East Anglian coastal village and contrasted them with the situation she currently found herself in. With anger she reflected on the bad judgement of the lorry driver who was the cause of her present condition and had denied her a more reasonable sojourn with her family as well as an opportunity to find out more about the God thing when she had returned to Newton Westerby.

The darkness that shrouded her eyes seemed to descend like lead to her heart. The callous attitude of the family towards her following the accident signified a denial that there was anything wrong with her that a bit of 'mind over matter' wouldn't put right. *Pointing out the problem of broken bones and blindness is not worth the effort. They simple won't listen.* In her enforced, isolated seclusion RK became morose and depressed.

Her condition became a challenge for herself and to those around her. On the few occasions when Davi had attempted to give RK a little more attention she had incurred her father's wrath. "You needn't think you're joining the idler's club, too, ducky," he jeered.

So, RK remained alone in her room for days on end and gradually withdrew into herself. She refused to listen to the family bickering over her incapacity and what they called her 'health issues'. Frustration overwhelmed her because she was unable to acknowledge letters from her friends in Newton Westerby who remained unaware of her situation. Her father would not permit the family to inform them of the true nature of her condition. "We're too busy to spend time acting as your secretary," he retorted brusquely.

RK had received notes from the Catton and Jenner families, postcards from Dan Prettyman, letters from Emma Cooper, Rachel and Ben Durrant and Penny Darnell, plus numerous get well cards from other members of the village community. All remained unanswered. Staff at the hospital had kindly read the early ones to her, which Davina had delivered on the one and only occasion a member of the family had visited her, but since RK's arrival back at the farm no one had the time or the inclination to read to her or offer to correspond for her. They simply slapped the mail on the table and stated, "Your post!"

Her mobile phone had been damaged in the accident and the one occasion she had tried independently to use the landline she had got into a hopeless muddle so, as a consequence, abandoned further attempts.

Vexation at her futile efforts to try the simplest of tasks caused RK to call out to the empty room, "I can't stand this. How much longer?" Her voice crescendoed with impatience. "God, if You can hear me, tell me how much longer do I have to wait before they take off the bandages and I can see again? I can't take much more." Her shouting was such that it nearly drowned the noise of the tractor and fork-lift truck in the yard.

Almost at once RK was ashamed of her churlish outburst and sat wondering how she could better her own situation knowing that perhaps it was unreasonable of her to have expectations of the family when the farm demanded every waking moment from them. As she sat in her isolation RK recalled the words of the physiotherapist on the day of her discharge from hospital, *'While the breaks heal we need to keep the muscles supple with gentle movements. Then we'll gradually build them up again with more intense physiotherapy.'* RK took a deep breath. Gingerly she tried to move her splint clad legs.

"Have patience, my child, and trust me, for I have plans for you."

Startled by the voice because she had believed herself to be in the room alone RK called out, "Hello, who's there?"

When there was no reply RK called again, "Hello! Dad...? Al...? Neil...?"

She waited and listened. "Stop messing about. Who's there?" The clock ticked its relentless rhythm and the regular farm noises could be heard beyond the closed window but RK could not pick out any other noise in the room apart from her own heart which suddenly started to beat as loud as a big base drum.

"Trust me, my child." The silence became elongated as the truth gradually dawned on RK.

"It's You, isn't it, God?" she whispered breathlessly, shaken by an overwhelming awareness of the presence of God.

# Chapter Three

"Well, my dear, this has been a most refreshing few days." The Rev Hugh Darnell picked up his wife's hand and tucked it affectionately through his arm. As they walked away from the cathedral and strolled carefully down Steep Hill towards the car park Hugh looked tenderly at Penny. "Thankyou, my dear, for coming with me; the sessions have been good, well constructed and meaningful in content. I feel quite invigorated. That final service was a fitting finale and such a blessing. I hope the days have been enriching and restful for you, too." They had just shared in an ecumenical retreat hosted by the Lincoln dioceses.

Penny turned and smiled up into his earnest face locking with Hugh's piercing, clear hazel eyes as he continued, "I know we haven't spent too much time together but I've been glad of the moments we have had on our own and I trust you've thought it all worthwhile." Penny pressed her hand tightly on her husband's arm.

"It's been a little like those early days of marriage when it was bittersweet being apart from one another but oh, so precious, when we came together again." They shared a sweet intimate smile.

"I'm so glad you agreed to accompany me."

"It's been strange to be without the children."

"I'm sure they've managed very well without us and probably had the time of their lives with Trixie and John. I know the young people had a barbecue planned, amongst other things, and I agreed Ellie and Gareth could go as long as behaviour and homework allowed."

"That will please Ellie she so wants to be accepted by her peers."

"And yet she is such an individualist."

"I'm pleased with the way she's applied herself to her course work this last year."

"That's because she's studying something she's really interested in."

"Thankyou for trusting her judgement, your backing gave such a boost to her confidence. Interior design has been her choice for quite a while and so far her results have proved exceptional."

"Only time will tell." Hugh stopped walking, the aroma of coffee emanating through a doorway tantalizing his taste buds. "Shall we have coffee before we leave?"

Penny nodded. She was not averse to lingering for additional moments with her husband. With a hand beneath her elbow Hugh guided her up the step into a coffee shop. Before long, they would be travelling on their way home and, in no time at all, swathed in the busyness of church affairs. Their plan was to make a detour to the Dickinson-Bond farm, on their return to Newton Westerby, to see how RK was progressing. They, along with many others from the village, were surprised not to have received any communication from RK since her departure from the village in order to commence her holiday. Her mother's one contact with Adam Catton had been brief and uninformative.

The phone call Penny made to the farm to explain their intent met with a very terse response from the person who answered the phone. So, as they drew closer to the farm an hour and a half later they were unsure of their welcome.

But, when they eventually made their approach to the farm, neatly trimmed hedges that bordered the fields on either side of the open entrance gates made quite an impact on both the Darnells.

"Oh, this is delightful," commented Penny as Hugh drove into a pristine yard that had tidily stacked pallets alongside orderly parked farm implements and vehicles, enhanced by colourful hanging baskets adorning the farmhouse as well as the office and one of the packing sheds. "It is so inviting!"

"Mmm! RK always spoke with pride of her father's meticulousness on the farm," said Hugh.

"Maybe this bodes well for our reception," Penny replied with more confidence than she'd felt earlier.

However, the cool, indifferent reaction to their arrival left them in no doubt at all that their presence was unwelcome.

They were escorted across to the farmhouse in a manner that had Penny wondering if this was something akin to being frogmarched to a prison cell. *Oh dear!* The clutter inside the house was such a contrast to the orderliness outside in the yard and across the farm it was hard to believe both properties belonged to the same people.

Penny and Hugh shared a swift questioning glance when a key was produced as they stood in the entrance hall beside a closed inner door. Penny swallowed hard when a stale stench emerged from the room even as Mrs Dickinson-Bond unlocked the door. What is more, as the door was slowly opened, they were totally unprepared for the sight that greeted their eyes.

The gloom, disorder and dust at first reminded Penny of Miss Havisham's room described in Dickens's 'Great Expectations', then as her eyes adjusted she gasped, clapping her hand involuntarily across her mouth. The pathetic creature huddled in a chair was unrecognizable as the tall, bright, witty RK they knew and had grown to love. Hugh and Penny were shocked beyond belief at the state RK was in, eyes bandaged, arm in plaster, legs in splints, hair lank and straggly, clothing in disarray and, worst of all, was the generally unkempt appearance accompanied by a grey, unhealthy pallor that seemed to totally engulf her.

Hugh recovered his equilibrium first. As Mrs Dickinson-Bond, for whatever reason, seemed disinclined to make any introductions RK was unaware of their presence so he walked decisively towards their friend and said, "Hello, RK, it's Rev Hugh and Mrs Darnell. We've called to see how you're getting on."

Penny, still shaken, moved more gradually towards the chair and carefully placed a hand on RK's shoulder, "My dear RK, I'm so very sorry. We had absolutely no idea you were so badly hurt."

Mrs Dickinson-Bond hopped from one foot to the other then said brusquely, "While you talk to her I'll get on with my work. Perhaps you'll knock some sense into her. If you want to see the farm, Reverend, George is in the packing shed next to the office waiting for you." She then retraced her steps walking out of the room with haste leaving the Darnells astounded that the mother had completely ignored her injured child.

Penny caught Hugh's eye and nodded.

Hugh reached forward and took hold of RK's hand that lay limply in her lap.

"I'll go see your father, RK, while you and Mrs Darnell catch up on news. I'll be back shortly." Hugh exited the door and made his way to find Mr Dickinson-Bond.

RK had not said a word during the entire exchange.

As Hugh strolled around the packing shed and chatted to members of the family he saw first-hand how hectic work was to meet customers' expectations. Then, when Neil took him on a whistle-stop tour of greenhouses and various sheds he realised how strapped for time they were. However, George made time to proudly show off his recently developed hydroponics greenhouse and cold store, "This is the way forward in this industry, growing the bulb in water."

"I see," said Hugh, "so, no more colourful tulip fields to delight the eye in spring?"

"I've kept a small field to satisfy the tourists but no, this is the way to go, saves money," he said, rubbing his hands together in satisfaction.

There was a lull in conversation so Hugh took the plunge and asked, "What happened to RK?"

"Fell off the bike."

"What's the damage?"

"Oh, it's a right-off."

"And RK?"

"Costing me money."

"How long before she can get back to work?"

"She could start today. I've a full hopper that needs packing but the lazy good-for-nothing won't get off her backside and do a thing."

Almost at once, Hugh realised he had asked the wrong questions so, rather than allow Mr Dickinson-Bond to pursue his angry tirade against RK, decided to make a speedy exit. "Thankyou for your time, Mr Dickinson-Bond, I won't detain you any longer. I appreciate you're very busy so I'll just see how Mrs Darnell is getting on with RK, and then we'll be on our way." Hugh ambled across the yard to the farmhouse hoping that Penny had made better headway than he had with regard to the true nature of RK's injuries and state of health.

When Hugh departed for his jaunt around the farm Penny sat quietly with RK.

"Are you comfortable with this, RK? Did you know we were coming?"

RK slowly shook her head.

"Are you able to speak? I have no wish to embarrass you but I'm unsure of the nature of your injuries. May I ask you some questions?"

"Yes. I'm just overwhelmed that you're here," RK replied with a break in her voice.

Penny leaned forward and squeezed her free hand.

"My dear RK, if we had but known the true state of things we would have been here sooner. Adam received only the briefest of messages that you had had an accident and would not be returning as planned following your holiday. We didn't have a contact number, other than your mobile, and only a vague idea of the location of the farm. As no one received a reply to letters or cards we assumed the address was incorrect or correspondence had gone astray. None of us anticipated you'd be away this long or we would have made a greater effort to be in touch sooner. Hugh and I have been in Lincoln on dioceses' business and looked up the farm's number in a local directory while we were there. Can you tell me what happened to you?"

In a faltering voice RK explained in detail the day of her departure from Newton Westerby, her stay in hospital and her days at the farm since her discharge.

"Oh, how awful for you, I guess it's taken some while to adjust to the restrictions placed on you."

"Mmm, it has been hard."

"How long have you been home?"

"I'm not sure, but I think it's about five or six weeks, could be more and I was in hospital for about a month. I've lost track of time. I don't even know what date it is."

"I see. I think you've been away from the village since the May Bank Holiday and it's now the 15th of August. So many people miss you and send their love and best wishes. I'd better read them to you or I'm bound to forget someone." Penny pulled out a list from her bag and proceeded to pass on messages from RK's friends in Newton Westerby. "They are all anticipating your return."

"Thankyou, and Dan? How's Dan?" RK asked tentatively.

"Like everyone else very concerned about you. I think he texted your mobile, or wrote you a note, almost every day."

"Which I didn't receive because it was smashed in the crash and the notes are probably somewhere..." RK wafted her good hand to indicate they were in a pile, unopened, in an indeterminate place.

Penny spied them on the corner of the sideboard. "Would you like me to read them to you?"

"Yes, please." So, for the next few moments RK revelled in the pictures in her mind that the messages Penny read conjured up. Some, like those from Keir and Lily, caused her to smile while others, such as the notes from Adam and Laura, brought an ache to her heart.

"It is wonderful to have such good friends."

Penny then updated RK on Laura's situation and explained her encouraging progress and Adam's new role as village window cleaner in order to be near at hand to attend to Laura's needs and look after the children, Daniel, Kirsten and Poppy. "They miss you. Like us they are totally unaware of your true state of health. They will be saddened to learn of your situation. This must be so difficult, RK."

RK grimaced. "That is an understatement. If you must know, it is an absolute nightmare. My family blame me for the predicament I'm in so will do nothing to help me."

Penny was flabbergasted at this disclosure but did her utmost not to convey this to RK.

"Have the doctors given any indication how long everything will take to heal?"

"I don't know. I haven't seen any doctors since I came out of hospital. No one in the family has time to take me to keep appointments. The farm occupies every waking hour."

"Can't you have hospital transportation?"

"I don't know. It hasn't been mentioned in my hearing. That's not to say other's have been told about it but refused it on my behalf because they don't want the hassle of getting me ready to go."

"How do you feel about that, RK?" Penny gently probed to discover RK's true state of mind.

"If you must know, frustrated! I know I should do exercises to strengthen the muscles in my legs but I can't read the sheet I was given so don't know what they are and the family think it's a waste of their time."

"When are the dressings coming off your eyes?"

RK slowly shook her head. "Again, I don't know. If I could use the phone properly I would contact the hospital and make arrangements myself but as you see I am hampered."

"Yes, my dear, I appreciate your difficulty. Seeing you like this is such a shock and I'm trying to think, as we speak, how best we can help you."

"Can I ask you something?"

"Of course, RK, fire away."

"Have you got a Bible with you?"

This was not at all what Penny was expecting. "A Bible?"

"Yes, I...I prayed the prayer that the Rev Hugh prayed for new Christians when I came to the service on my last Sunday in the village. I was going to ask him what I do next when I returned from my holiday but ... well... that never happened."

"Oh, my dear RK, so many of your friends have been praying for you since that morning but if you can't see to read how do you think a Bible can help you?"

"After all this happened to me I had to repeat over and over again, 'I believe in Jesus,' to convince myself the experience of that morning was still real. I know so little about this Jesus. I thought if you could read something about Him I would be able think about what I hear and learn a little about the One I'm talking to."

"Right, RK, I understand where you're coming from. Hugh has one in the car, I'll ask him to fetch it when he gets back."

"Thanks, Mrs Darnell. Do you know the God person spoke to me?"

"He did?"

"I thought it was Dad or one of the boys messing about but when the voice spoke a second time I knew it was God."

"What did he say?"

"'Have patience, my child, trust me, I have plans for you.'"

"Dear RK, what wonderful words of encouragement. There are words similar to those in the book of Jeremiah in the Bible."

"Really! I find that hard to believe!"

"It's true. When Hugh comes back I'll ask him to read them to you."

"That would be helpful. At the time I really needed them. I was getting pretty irate with God about the length of time the healing process was taking. At times the blackness really gets to me. It feels like an insurmountable wall and I just want to tear it down."

"I can't pretend to understand your desperation RK, but I can sympathize and pray that God will give you the grace and strength to cope with every difficulty, one step at a time."

"That's a good thought; one step at a time. I tend to want to run ahead of myself and I get impatient because I don't seem to be mending as quickly as I would like to and, as a consequence, experience dreadful bouts of low spirits."

"Oh my dear, RK," Penny laid a hand affectionately over RK's good hand. "We'll continue to pray for you. We have a clearer picture of your situation, now."

When Hugh returned Penny explained RK's desire to have something to focus her mind upon concerning Jesus and the Christian faith.

"I'll step out again and fetch my Bible from the car then I'll read some verses which I trust you'll find helpful, RK, afterwards we'll share a prayer before Penny and I take our leave."

"Darling, could you bring the spare mobile phone out of the glove-compartment?"

Hugh raised his eyebrows at Penny.

"My mobile," she mouthed nodding her head in RK's direction. "There's also a small reel of tape in the recess of the passenger door."

Hugh nodded in understanding.

"We'll devise a way of raising the answer button, RK, so that when I call, you will know what to press in order to speak with me."

Both Penny and Hugh were appalled by the harsh manner the Dickinson-Bond family spoke about RK and the cruel way they treated her. It was only when Davina came into the room to check on RK's toilet needs that she drew Penny aside and begged her to take RK with them that Penny saw a hint of kindness in her tone. "Our Kay may be broken in body and lost inside herself at the moment but she'll simply perish if she stays here."

Then, when Davina escorted RK to the bathroom, Mrs Dickinson-Bond, who had slipped in for a moment, pleaded desperately for any help Penny could give that would benefit RK Penny recognized the plea for what it was; a release from the draining responsibility of caring for a physically injured adult child. At that point, Penny determined to do everything within her power to get RK away from the oppressive situation she found herself in. *No wonder she felt she had to get away from here in the first place.* Penny recalled her first conversation with RK on her arrival in Newton Westerby nearly eighteen months ago. *I needed a break from the demands of work that would send me home refreshed.*

As they left the farm Rev Hugh and Penny promised to pray and look at all possibilities that would improve the quality of life for RK.

They travelled for a few miles in total silence both stunned by the appalling state of affairs they had encountered at the farm.

Penny broke the silence, "Whatever can we do to alleviate that poor girl's suffering?"

"I take it you're referring to RK's mental and physical state not her medical condition?"

"Even that's not being attended to."

"I would think keeping company with two hypercritical parents, such as the Dickinson-Bonds, is enough to cause anyone depression without the complications of broken limbs and temporary blindness."

"I think the situation is further compounded by the unspoken disappointment RK feels, but does not express, at having the needs of the farm constantly thrust upon her while her own needs remain unacknowledged."

"Oh, I believe it's worse than that, RK's needs are totally ignored. Her father was more concerned about the damage to the bike!"

"That poor girl, I don't know how parents can be so heartless."

"They're driven by greed and a burning desire to succeed."

As they journeyed home Hugh and Penny discussed all possible scenarios in which they could offer practical help to RK.

"We've plenty of room in our spacious home but with two lively teenagers it's certainly far from peaceful. The stairs, too, would be a problem at the moment."

"Yes, I agree, it wouldn't be ideal but it would get RK away from the enforced claustrophobia she's tied into at present."

"Those closest to RK in age and had most interaction with her when she lived in the village, such as Ben and Rachel and the other young married couples, have young families or are young singles still living at home with their parents, like the Cooper girls, or Annette and Annelie. Emma and Miranda are very tied up with work. An incapacitated young woman needing a lot of assistance would not fit easily into their households."

"I agree. It's not simply having a place where she can recuperate; RK requires rehabilitation, therapy, and possibly the impetus to build a new life."

"Whatever do you mean?"

"Reading between the lines, I'm sure she fears her sight loss is permanent."

"That does put a different slant upon the matter."

"Yes, the older members of the village may feel unable to deal with RK's current incapacity even though they might have room and time."

"The cottage RK made her home whilst she was looking after the Catton children following Laura's stroke is still available, isn't it?"

"Yes, it is in the process of being upgraded in her absence. Ben has designed a sun room, which is being added to the rear of the property with a much needed bathroom built over the top of it. However, if RK elected to return to Ferry Cottage someone would have to live in with her, at least, till she learned to cope on her own."

"It's not an easy dilemma to solve."

"Might be easier if RK could be cared for in a villager's home where someone was on hand to assist her."

"Dear Bernice Durrant and 'Green Pastures' would be ideal but Bernice has become so involved in helping out at the Village Stores when needed and looking after her niece Alex's little girl, Bethany, she is no longer free and available."

After further deliberation, Hugh and Penny decided to put RK's predicament before the church family on their return home and also to make it a matter of fervent prayer.

# Chapter Four

A few days after their return to the village Rev Hugh called together a meeting of RK's closest friends. They met in the sitting room at the vicarage to listen as Hugh and Penny explained the situation they had found at the Dickinson-Bond nursery farm. The group were stunned into silence and one could have heard a pin drop. Deeply perturbed by the revelations that were shared regarding RK's state of health Dan Prettyman decided to take a few days holiday in Lincolnshire with immediate effect. He shot up from his chair, "I've got 12 days owing to me so I'll go pack a few things and make a couple of calls..."

"Dan, don't be too hasty," cautioned Penny.

"Why ever not, Mrs Darnell? Clearly if things are as bad as you say Robyn desperately needs help and support from her friends, now." Dan paced up and down the room.

"Yes, you're right, Dan, but surely it's important we give careful thought to what those needs are. Please stay and help us plan." Penny could see that the young policeman was shaken by their account of RK's appalling injuries and the manner in which she was living. Without doubt he was as disappointed as they had been that the

Dickinson-Bond family had felt unable to pass the details of her accident on to her friends in Newton Westerby.

Dan slumped back into a chair and wrung his hands together in frustration as deep emotional pain scored his brow. Penny admired the young man's self control as he sought to keep his feelings in check. He had got as close as anyone to RK during her stay in the village and couldn't understand why he hadn't received replies to any of the notes and texts he had sent to RK. The Darnell's disclosures explained how this had happened.

Penny walked to where Dan was sitting and put a motherly arm around his shoulders. "We've all come this evening because we're concerned for RK's wellbeing. So, before you go racing off to Lincolnshire like a bull in a china shop let's talk together about the constructive ways we can do something practical for RK."

Dan sat quietly for quite a few minutes digesting Penny's words of advice.

"You mean pinpoint the vital problem areas then decide what we can do in each situation to alleviate her suffering?"

Penny nodded, "I think we need a definite plan of action in place, don't you, before anyone travels to see RK." Her eyes moved slowly around the room. Others in the group, who had been invited to the vicarage to hear about RK's plight, were of the same mind and inclined their heads in assent at Penny's suggestion. Now that contact had been made with RK all those privy to the news Hugh and Penny had imparted felt it was important to maintain the link and do something positive to eliminate the wretchedness which seemed to engulf RK.

"You mean things like care, meals and appointments," Dan stated thoughtfully.

"And where she can live safely," Penny added.

"I see!"

"How long did the journey to Lincolnshire take you, Hugh?"

"I think about two and a half hours," Hugh looked across at Penny for confirmation. She nodded, "Depending on the volume and speed of the traffic."

"No motorways then?"

"No, just lots of lorries, tractors and other farm vehicles clogging the single carriageway roads greatly impeding movement of traffic."

"So, a visit that needs to be planned," said Trixie.

"I would say so."

"Not a call that can be squeezed in between appointments in a busy schedule, then?" commented Doctor Roger thoughtfully.

"Not really."

"Apart from the very obvious neglect by her family what would you identify as RK's greatest area of need, Hugh?"

"As I see it, from the brief time we spent with RK, there are three main matters that need addressing; Firstly, medical, second, physical and I'd put the final category under the dual heading of social/spiritual. Would you agree, my dear?" Hugh looked across to Penny for approval of his brief summary of RK's situation.

"Yes, that is a simple but succinct list of RK's needs. Broken down the areas of need are far more complex but in this room alone we have expertise that can match those needs and in our wider village community, I believe, we have skills necessary to give a quality of life back to RK."

"I think I'd like to see her for myself then I'll be able to make a more informed assessment of her requirements. Is there an available window in my schedule?" Roger looked across to Miranda who made a note on her pad. "I'll check your diary the moment I get in to work in the morning, Doctor."

"Thanks, Miranda," Roger acknowledged his receptionist's response as his eyes sought Emma's. His wife read his intent and inclined her head in agreement.

"I believe a visit may need to be sooner rather than later, Miranda."

"I'll see what I can arrange, Doctor."

"One thing that hasn't been mentioned, which may have considerable bearing on any decision making we engage in," interposed Jennifer Pedwardine, who had been unusually quiet for most of the evening, "is RK's families' reaction to strangers taking over her care and RK's response to our assuming that role on her behalf."

"W..e..ll," replied Hugh and Penny in unison as they glanced at one another.

"I think her family would welcome our 'interference' with open arms. Without judging him too harshly I can just hear her father saying 'good riddance' and rubbing his hands with glee."

"Vicar! I am surprised at you."

"Don't be, Jennifer, I'm afraid what Hugh says of RK's father is all too true and her mother and sisters would also heave a great sigh of relief." As Penny spoke a number around the group shook their heads in disbelief so she added, "I think RK would welcome any assistance that would aid her recovery. She's hampered at present because she's not in a physical position to help herself which is further exacerbated by the lack of correct medical care."

"On that note, let's get some ideas on paper. Miranda, perhaps you would keep us on track and get us organized."

"Hey! Just a minute," Adam waved his arms vigorously. "Before we get bogged down with rearranging RK's life as we see fit don't you think we ought to pray. You know Jeremiah 29 verse11." He looked directly at Ben. Ben smiled remembering the occasion when he and Adam were making plans for Laura's future and he had quoted scripture to Adam.

"'I know the plans I have for you.....to give you hope and a future,'" Ben murmured softly.

Penny mouthed a prayer of thanks as she recalled RK's comments and experience surrounding those words.

"Quite right, Adam," Hugh affirmed "We so wanted you all to have a picture of RK's true situation our focus has been on what we can do about it but we do need to pray; for clarity of mind and purpose, and for wisdom to follow the right course of action. Before we start our discussions let us pray."

A hush fell upon the company. As Hugh voiced a prayer each one present had an image of RK in the picture of their mind. A gentle breeze came in through an open window. Afterwards someone said, "It was as if the Holy Spirit was hovering upon each of our heads, moving amongst us with his benediction of approval, giving us a clear indication of the way we should go."

After the prayer, while Penny served refreshments, the gathering broke up into smaller groups in order to thrash out practical issues involved in RK's possible care and their implications. Miranda collated all their responses into a chronological table showing what might be required and who could provide it and when or how.

Dan felt he was probably best placed to take time off from work and initiate the first move towards RK's rehabilitation. Most in the room agreed but Ben spoke a word of caution, "Dan, you must act with your head and not your heart." *But it's my heart that's driving me to go.*

"Right, Ben. Tomorrow I think I'll book in to a B&B nearby, plan to explore the countryside around Robyn's home and call in to see her; perhaps offer to take her out for a drive in the car and ascertain how she would like us to help her."

Penny laid a hand gently on Dan's arm, "Dan, I must warn you, she is not the same person we knew when she lived in the village."

"What on earth do you mean?"

"Dan, I don't want you to be disappointed but RK has experienced devastating trauma which she is struggling to come to terms with. It has changed her. For some reason her family have difficulty supporting her and helping RK through these awful circumstances."

"You mean Robyn is finding it difficult to cope with her injuries?"

"Yes, amongst other things."

"I'll bear that in mind, Mrs Darnell and act with caution and sensitivity."

"I would advise, too, that you contact the family first rather than turn up unannounced, and for RK's sake, don't be deterred by their offhand manner. This is the number we were able to reach them on." She handed a piece of paper to Dan.

So, first thing the following morning, Dan telephoned Mrs Dickinson-Bond to acquaint her with his intentions, "I'm on holiday in the area and wondered if I could call in to see Robyn?"

"Let me tell you, constable, I'm at my wits end. It will be good to have someone else to take the flack of Our Kay's temper. We can't put up with her idleness much longer. Her father has given her till the end of next week or she is out." Dan was quite taken aback by Mrs Dickinson-Bond's curtness. She continued to rant for a further five minutes or so as though RK's predicament was his fault. "I'll happily take her out for a drive if you think that would help," he said ingratiatingly, hoping to curb the lady's angry outburst.

But instead Mrs Dickinson-Bond snorted disparagingly and stated in response, "We need Our Kay to start pulling her weight and stop idling around, constable. I was hoping you could lay it on the line about where her loyalty and responsibilities lie not encourage her in her idleness."

When Ben called by, later in the morning, to see how his holiday plans were going Dan explained about his conversation with RK's mother. "It really seemed to me as though Mrs Dickinson-Bond wasn't coping with Robyn's condition and was anxious for someone else to step in and put up with what she called 'her moods'. She struck me as someone who didn't have very much patience."

"Oh dear, Dan, I don't envy you this visit."

"The lady's attitude certainly mirrored Rev and Mrs Darnell's assessment of the situation."

"You will keep in touch, won't you?"

"Yes, I promised to contact Mrs Darnell on a regular basis and she will liaise with all who need to be aware of what's happening."

"OK, my friend, I won't pester you unduly but remember I'm always available at the end of a phone if you need a listening ear."

With that Dan clapped his friend on the shoulder, "Thanks owd boy."

When Ben was gone Dan switched on his lap-top and Googled Lincolnshire B&B's. However, finding somewhere to stay in the vicinity of the Dickinson-Bond farm proved far more difficult than he imagined. The nearest B&B seemed to be six miles away in Moulton or even further away in Boston, Holbeach or Spalding. Dan opted to take the Moulton accommodation and if he found somewhere else more suitable when he arrived in the area he would rebook.

Dan stepped outside, lifted the boot of his car and threw in his holdall. He set the postcode of the Dickinson-Bond farm into his satnav, checked that he had his mobile phone and patted his jacket pocket to ensure his wallet and bank cards were inside. He opened the driver's door.

"Dan! Dan!"

He looked around.

"Dan! Wait, Dan!" Running down the road waving an arm in the air and carrying a package in her other hand was Rosie Jenner. "Oh, please wait, Dan."

She finally reached him and stood for a few moments to catch her breath before explaining her mission.

"Hi, Rosie, can I help you? I'm just off on holiday. I'm going to Lincolnshire and hoping to call and see Robyn."

"Yes, I know." Rosie thrust the parcel she was carrying at Dan.

"Mum has baked RK's favourite quiche. Please, will you take it to her, with our love? I've made some other bits and pieces and Jilly's also sent some pasties for your lunch. Bye." As quickly as she had come so Rosie returned up the lane hardly giving Dan a moment to proffer his thanks for such kindness. He placed the bag carefully on the back seat and prepared to drive away. He reached forward to put the key in the ignition when he felt vibrations from the mobile phone in his pocket.

"Dan, are you still here?"

"Where would here, be?"

"Sorry, Dan, what I meant to ask is, are you still in Newton Westerby?"

Dan smiled when he recognized his caller. "Yes, Miss Pedwardine, but I'm on the point of departure."

"Good! Will you call at 'Bakers' as you leave the village? I've cut some flowers for you to take to RK. They will be a happy reminder of the evening strolls she took in my garden."

"On my way."

Dan graciously accepted Miss Pedwardine's offering for RK and placed the flowers on the back seat opposite the food parcel. While the gift was ideal for RK Dan found the flowers' scent overpowering so left the back window slightly open. He deftly performed a three point turn in order to leave the village via the city road because it linked up with the A47 on the outskirts of the city of Norwich.

He had almost completed the manoeuvre when he spied Daniel and Kirsty Catton dancing perilously close to the edge of the lane wafting papers high above their heads.

Dan pulled up by the side of them and rolled down the window.

"Hello, you two. What can I do for you?"

"We have drawn some pictures for RK. Please will you take them to her and tell her we miss her and to get better quickly and come back and see us as soon as she can."

"Oh, and Dad has sent these chocolates for RK from him and Mum."

Dan reached out to receive the further gifts for RK. As he placed them on the passenger seat he said to the children, "That's really thoughtful of you. I'll make sure they are delivered safely into the hands of Robyn."

"Thanks, Dan. Bye!" Before he had chance to turn the ignition on Daniel and Kirsty had scampered back into their garden, and his mobile rang again.

"Hi, Dan, before you set out for Lincolnshire can you collect a hamper for RK from the Store?"

"Sure, Emma, but, though her family may not be very good at looking after her I think they are still managing to feed her."

Emma laughed, "Trust you to think of things for your stomach, Dan. In fact, I've put together a hamper of girlie things that I'm sure RK will appreciate."

Before long the car will be so full of presents there won't be enough room for the messenger, Dan murmured to himself as he clambered from the car to walk across the road to the Village Stores.

"This is Roger's Blackberry number, Dan. Please don't hesitate to call any time of the day or night. RK is still registered as his patient." Emma handed to him a slip of paper as he closed the boot having put the hamper next to his hold-all.

Eventually, Dan and his car left Newton Westerby an hour and fifteen minutes behind schedule but carrying very certain evidence of the goodwill of her village friends towards RK.

However, Mrs Dickinson-Bond didn't tell RK of Dan's impending visit. So, RK was totally unprepared for her visitor, particularly someone whose company she had enjoyed when she lived in East Anglia, after the initial mistrust between them had been sorted out. Her leathers and Harley-Davidson coupled with a keen interest in boats and activity around the harbour had created a mystique in the village about her persona but Dan had sussed it out. Later on RK had helped Dan and his colleagues in the apprehension of trespassers to her garden who later proved to be wanted for drug handling. From then on the two had shared some first-class conversations together when they had met at village social gatherings and RK was beginning to get quite fond of the young police constable. They were good friends on the brink of becoming something more or so she had thought.

"Hi, Robyn, how you doing?" Dan blurted out in an enforced jovial manner. He was shaken at the change in his friend.

"Dan?" RK whispered in disbelieve. Totally unprepared for this encounter she turned her back on him in embarrassment.

In spite of the pleasant memories it was a shock to hear him in her parents' home. RK felt at a distinct disadvantage because Dan could see her but she couldn't see him. She was mortified that he should find her in such a dishevelled and broken state. Her anger at her mother for bringing him in when she was so totally unprepared to receive visitors, and this visitor in particular, bubbled up inside her.

Dan, too, was appalled at RK's physical and medical state despite the forewarning of Mrs Darnell. The unkempt, pathetic being before him was hardly the vibrant young woman he was used to seeing striding around the village or the confident leather clad cyclist riding off on a Harley- Davidson.

*Oh Lord, how do I handle this situation?* Dan prayed in his heart.

The answer came just as silently, *Be yourself.*

Dan pressed into RK's hands all the gifts that had been sent from her friends in the village and passed on every message he had been entrusted with. When RK didn't respond he continued to speak of the people and positive aspects of life in Newton Westerby to Robyn, as he called her, and had done so ever since their encounter on the cliffs above the village when he learned she was female and not male as so many villagers had believed initially when RK first visited Newton Westerby.

Realising RK was as overwhelmed by the encounter as he was Dan deliberately cut short his first visit. Rev Hugh and Penny Darnell had warned him of the terrible condition RK was in but it still came as a shock to actually see her like this, encased in plastercast and bandages, and her neat sculptured hair style replaced by what could only be described as lank, unkempt rat's tails!

"I'll be back tomorrow. See you then. Be ready to go out. I have the car not the motorbike so you can take me around your countryside." Before she had opportunity to contradict him he was gone. A deliberate ploy and one he had prearranged with Mrs Dickinson-Bond who knew if RK was given a choice would object.

# Chapter Five

The following day dawned bright and fair. Dan called at the farm house to take her out as planned but RK refused to go. So, he came the next day and the next. His visits did a little more each time to break down her obstinate resolve not to go out of the house. Sensing the embarrassment of her sister in the presence of a visitor Davi offered to assist RK with her morning ablutions and dressing routine. Knowing her hair was brushed and she was better presented helped to ease the awkwardness RK displayed in front of Dan; also wearing clean, freshly pressed clothes helped to restore some of her self esteem.

Initially, it was difficult for either of them to re-establish their friendship on its former footing. RK's mortification that Dan should have seen her at her inelegant worst caused her to withdraw more deeply into herself, and Dan's heartache at the drastic change in RK coupled with his incensed feelings at the cavalier treatment her family meted out to her, created a barrier to normality. *Dear Lord, this is tricky. I need help handling this situation, please guide me,* Dan prayed as he drove towards the farm on the fourth day of his holiday. *Quietness and confidence, patience and perseverance*, was the response to his heart.

The mid morning sun was welcome as it broke through the autumnal nip that had greeted the day even though it was only late August and the sky presented a cloud free canopy of blue as he negotiated the long, straight droves alongside un-fenced dikes between his B & B and the Dickinson-Bond nursery and farm. For as far as the eye could see crops had been harvested and many fields were now dotted with tractors ploughing in readiness for autumn sowing.

*I am with you always. Who will separate us? No one and nothing.* Dan's lips mouthed a prayer of thanks for the assurance of God's presence as he approached what he felt to be a very uncomfortable situation. The words of the psalmist came unbidden to his mind.

*Where can I go from your Spirit?*
*Where can I flee from your presence?*
*If I go up to the heavens, you are there;*
*If I make my bed in the depths, you are there.*
*If I rise on the wings of the dawn,*
*If I settle on the far side of the sea,*
*If I go to an inhospitable farm,* Dan added,
*even there your hand will guide me.*
*Your right hand will hold me fast.*

*Father God, thanks. I'm not on my own!* His heart lifted and his spirit soared as he started to sing. *I will sing of the mercies of the Lord for ever...* Relief flooded through his being. *Thankyou, thankyou Father, wherever I travel and whatever I have to face today You are going to be with me.*

Dan punched the air with one hand whilst guiding the steering wheel with the other. He sat up straighter in the driver's seat. *Bless you, Rev Hugh, for encouraging us to memorize scripture. It sure came to mind just when*

*I needed it.* Hugh would be delighted with this accolade. In the Bible fellowship he constantly advised committing verses and even longer passages to memory for those occasions when it wasn't physically possible to access a Bible.

*My dear Robyn, with God's help, we'll face this thing together.*

Dan prepared for his time with RK in a more buoyant mood. On arrival at the farm his reception was cool. Mrs Dickinson-Bond greeted him poker-faced and RK gave him the cold shoulder. Nevertheless, Dan approached her cheerfully.

"Good morning, Robyn, I'd like to explore your Lincolnshire countryside today but I will need your help."

RK did not move. No matter how much Dan cajoled RK refused to budge.

"OK, Robyn, if you don't wish to go out today we will postpone our jaunt until tomorrow."

RK did not flinch but remained absolutely rigid.

"Maybe you would prefer to hear news about your friends in Newton Westerby. Although I seem to remember you left the village to commence your holiday about the end of May I can't precisely pinpoint the sequence of events so I may repeat information with which you are familiar." Still, there was no response from RK who continued to sit huddled in her chair. Undeterred, Dan drew up a chair to sit beside her.

"If you're quite comfy, I'll fill you in on some of the happenings in the village. Do you remember Billy Knights, the deck hand on Laura's cousin Mark's boat? Well, he has finally been apprehended for drug smuggling. You know, that was a brilliant deduction on your part putting him in the frame for drug dealing. Who would have thought when you saw him exchanging packages with those chaps in your garden at Ferry Cottage it would lead to a big breakthrough for the police in solving the drug problem in our area. He was a slippery customer but his greed eventually led to his downfall and when the drug squad caught up with him they unravelled quite a network. My bosses suspected you when you first came on the scene. How wrong they were!

"The matter of the silenced shopkeeper, that you overheard Billy mention, is an ongoing investigation so I'm unable to give you an update on that. But the other guys you saw with Billy have been identified as doctors from the hospital in the city."

Dan expected some sort of reaction to this news from RK but she continued to sit in stony silence and appeared not to have heard a word he said.

Undeterred Dan proceeded to tell her of Jansy Cooper's innocent involvement in the drug transactions of Doctors Hollis and Stead on the paediatric ward. "Following your report of the garden incident my colleagues in Norwich were able to identify a thread of evidence that linked the two investigations. The discovery of her colleagues' duplicity really shook Jansy so she came home to her Mum and Doctor John for a break."

Dan further explained about Jansy's accident in the harbour and her subsequent reconciliation with Dave Ransome and their pending marriage.

As he proceeded to give an account of further village activities RK sat hard faced and unmoved. Dan stifled a sigh and wondered if he was doing the right thing then, as he closely watched RK's face, he saw an almost imperceptible shake of the head or the slight incline of a nod and sometimes the barest twitch of a smile on her lips as he mentioned friends and incidents from Newton Westerby. Suffice it to say, this reaction encouraged him to continue.

With each succeeding hour Dan introduced further topics from RK's life at the seaside. He spoke of Laura's recovery and the antics of the Catton children and mentioned how much they missed her. Dan described in detail the additional renovations that Ben and his team were planning to carry out on Adam and Laura's home to open up space for the children to play and a study for Adam. He recounted the excitement generated by Laura's find of an unclaimed premium bond in Adam's name. This information necessitated an explanation of Laura's increasing involvement in the care of Daniel, Kirsten and Poppy and also her gradual participation in tasks about the house.

Knowing how much RK had enjoyed life in Newton Westerby Dan proceeded to enlighten her about the expansion at the Village Stores and the creation of the coffee shop that most people in the village welcomed.

"Young Maxine Cook seems to be shaping up very well as an assistant in the shop. You may remember she went there for her work experience in her last year at school and is now doing shop management at college and working in the Stores on day release twice a week.

"The conversion of Emma's flat is almost complete. Everyone says it will be a most attractive venue for locals and visitors. Now she and Roger are living in the delightful cottage on Main Street, that was once Alex and Graeme's home, Emma's working and private life won't be so entwined with one another."

If it was possible to see bandaged eyes light up Dan was seeing it now for a definite spark of interest showed on RK's face as he continued to regale her with happenings from the village.

"Someone, I believe Lord Edmund under the auspices of the PCC, has instigated a mammoth clearance operation in Kezia's Wood. You wouldn't recognize the place. Right at the heart they've discovered some tumbledown buildings and believe it or not Doctor John bought one for Stephen's twenty-first birthday gift. He has really gone to town on the restoration in between finishing his degree and setting up a carpentry business. In fact, the whole village seems to have got involved in one way or another. Loads of stuff has been unearthed in the cupboards of one of the rooms less derelict than the others, remarkably preserved although water damaged and faded in some instances. Adam has had a fine time trying to decipher the ledgers and documents."

"I seem to be missing so much," RK murmured.

"Don't you wish you could be there to see it all?"

Dan could have kicked himself the minute he had spoken, for his insensitivity, but RK's immediate response was, "Oh yes."

Dan quickly resumed hoping to divert her attention from his blunder by narrating tales about Jenner's Mill and the family living there who had first welcomed and hosted RK in Newton Westerby.

"Nathan is about to commence his final year at the Agricultural College in Easton, on the outskirts of Norwich. He's studying all aspects of farming but I believe he's particularly interested in animal husbandry."

"Yes, I remember him enthusing about pig farming."

"However, he's made it clear that he doesn't want to cater solely for the popular meat market but intends to specialize in rare breeds and he also dreams of one day expanding Tessa's free range hens' project by introducing more exotic varieties."

"I'm not sure that will go down well with his mother considering her strong vegetarian views."

*Thankyou, Lord, she's talking to me and taking an interest in someone else.* Dan breathed a prayer of thankfulness.

"Knowing Tessa and Stuart's policy of discussing things thoroughly with their children I think they will have thrashed out that issue before making it public knowledge."

"I'm sure you're right."

"Rosie's continuing to work with Jilly Briggs in the Stores kitchen and has almost completed her NVQ course in catering."

"She always loved cooking and experimenting in her baking."

"Well, that is ongoing under the direction of the college and Jilly's watchful eye. The selection of pastries in the box I gave you the other day was Rosie's creation."

"They were delicious; just melted in your mouth. Do you know, even my mother approved."

Dan grinned glad RK couldn't see his face. He steeled his features before allowing himself to continue.

"Dan Prettyman, don't you dare laugh at me," RK scolded.

Dan couldn't hold the grin in any longer and with a bellowing laugh asked, "How did you know?"

"You left too much time before you answered me."

"Aah! Robyn, how perceptive you are."

"During my enforced blindness I've learned to depend more on my ears and listen to not only what people say but also to interpret their silences. What about the other children, how are they?"

"Keir is still full of fun and mischief and Gil as studious as ever, but I don't see so much of Lily and Pansy."

"I do miss them."

"Tessa is expanding the market garden with a view to Nathan taking it over when he's qualified. She has plans to produce more veggie stuff and preserves for the Stores and also the coffee shop."

"Some of Tessa's dishes were so tasty she even won over many deep-died, anti-vegetarians; me, for one."

"They're certainly very well-liked in the Village Stores."

"What did you say Dave and Jansy are doing?"

"Dave has diversified with a new venture which is proving very popular."

"Surely Jansy's not persuaded him to work on shore?"

"No, he's still at sea, but running day excursions and sea fishing cruises aboard the 'Sunburst', throughout the summer months and his Dad, Doug, is manning the booking kiosk which is based on the quay. On the longer charter trips both Doug and Christina accompany him, Doug as first mate and his Mum as cook," Dan elaborated.

"That sounds exciting," RK laughed, and then added, "if you're in to that sort of thing."

"You're not?" Dan teased.

RK shook her head, "You know I'm not."

"Of course, you and hooks don't mix." Dan remembered RK had quite an aversion to wriggly worms on hooks. "Though as a variation Dave sometimes demonstrates trawling and as an added attraction he's acquired a net from the Holy Land to show how the disciples would have cast their nets on the Sea of Galilee."

"I don't know anything about that," RK shivered. "Let's change the subject. How's Jansy?"

"Jansy is adjusting to life as her father's practise nurse and preparing for her wedding day."

"So she's back in the village permanently?"

"Oh yes, you'll be surprised to learn they're going to live in the lovely cottage you persuaded them was a good buy."

"Really?"

"Mmm, Dave went ahead and bought it at the time, believing it was the right thing to do, even though they went their separate ways for a while."

"Actually, that was a pretty cottage and so perfectly placed. I'd have been tempted to purchase it myself if I'd had the wherewithal. I hope all goes well for them this time."

"I think everyone is praying that for them."

"When is their wed...Oh, there's my mother," RK suddenly remarked.

"How do you know?" Dan asked. He hadn't heard a thing.

"I recognize everyone's distinct footfalls and the different way they unlatch the door."

"That's remarkable."

"Not really. I have to do something to pass away the time so I've learned to listen very carefully and taught myself to distinguish between different sounds and when I hear a voice I can now attribute particular noises to that person. For instance, I always know when you arrive by the way you wipe your feet as you come in the door, even when there isn't a doormat."

"I'll make a detective out of you yet!" Dan kidded her.

Mrs Dickinson-Bond opened the door. "Oh, you are still here, then. Talked some sense into her and convinced her it's about time she did some work?"

"Not yet," Dan cringed as the woman roughly pulled Robyn to her feet. "I think Robyn needs more practise at getting mobile."

"A kick up the backside, more like."

Dan's hackles began to rise as Mrs Dickinson-Bond roughly manhandled RK across the room. He remembered his manners just in time. "No, I think an extensive physiotherapy session would be just the ticket to get Robyn active again."

"Oh, you do, do you? You a doctor, then?" Mrs Dickinson-Bond let the door slam behind them.

Dan sighed and looked around the ill-kept room in despair. He contrasted it to the clean, welcoming home RK had created at the cottage in Newton Westerby. Like Rev and Mrs Darnell he couldn't understand the Dickinson-Bond's rejection of medical help to speed RK's recovery. *Why won't someone in the family arrange for Robyn to keep the hospital appointments or even contact the hospital and let them organize transport if the Dickinson-Bond's really are too busy on the farm to take time off to convey her? They constantly bemoan the fact that Robyn's recovery is taking too long but refuse to allow her assistance to encourage healing or rehabilitation. I don't understand it.*

Dan winced as he heard Mrs Dickinson-Bond haranguing RK for taking so long in the toilet.

*How degrading! Mrs D-B must know I can hear. The poor girl, I must get her away from here.*

Then he remembered Ben's words, 'Act with your head, not your heart.' *Oh, Lord what am I to do? I am so afraid for her wellbeing.*

Anxiously, Dan rubbed his hands together. He was sitting on the very edge of the chair and realised he was quite tense with agitation over RK's predicament. When he heard RK and her mother returning he jumped up and as he did so his eyes lighted on a pile of paperwork strewn across the table. *Hospital letters*, he thought and at the same time there flashed through his mind the words of the psalmist, *when I am afraid I will trust in You.*

Dan breathed a sigh of relief. *Thankyou, Father God, I will trust You to guide me to make the right decisions.*

Distractedly, he brushed a hand through his hair.

*Hospital letters!*

*Hospital letters means patient's hospital number and clinic name, maybe Doctor's name and definitely telephone number.* Dan quickly secreted the top letter into his pocket just as the room door was pushed open.

"Hello again," he bounded towards the two women with a purposeful step. "Mrs Dickinson-Bond, would you be so kind as to get Robyn's jacket. We're going for a short ride in my car."

The request came so unexpectedly Mrs Dickinson-Bond simply complied and reached behind the backdoor to the coat pegs and automatically handed a coat to RK. Dan detected a frown on RK's face, took her coat and whispered, "Slip your good arm into the sleeve while I hold it for you, please," he carefully cajoled as he observed her stubborn stance and pursed lips.

"I'll leave you to it, then, ducky. While some can go gadding about the rest of us has work to do." Mrs Dickinson-Bond slammed the door and marched stridently across the yard.

"Well, that's me told off," said RK glumly.

"Never mind, now, are you ready?' Dan asked cheerfully as he fastened one button in order to keep RK's coat from falling off her shoulders.

"I don't know what you have in mind, Dan, but I'm as ready as I'll ever be."

"Good! Please sit on this chair," he carefully guided RK. "I'm going to fasten the back door in an open position, unlock the car and move the passenger seat so that it's more comfortable for you. I'll only be a moment."

Within minutes Dan returned, scooped RK up in his arms. "Dan!" she squealed but Dan had gently deposited her into the passenger seat of his car and fastened the seat belt for her before she could catch another breath.

He ran to close the back door of the farm house then slid into the driver's seat and prepared to drive off. Deftly he manoeuvred the car around the farmyard and out onto the country lane. He didn't give RK opportunity to object to his treatment of her but simply stated, "OK, Robyn, I don't know my way around here so I shall need you to navigate."

"But I can't se..."

"No buts allowed and my guess would be that you know these roads like the back of your hand. So, Miss Robyn Keitha Dickinson-Bond, I don't know about you, but I'm starving hungry, it being quite a few hours since breakfast time. Can you suggest a good eating place?"

"You used a but," RK laughed jokingly.

"Allowed in that context. Oh, I do love to hear you laugh, Robyn."

"Good, but why have you stopped the car?"

"Another but? Tut, tut, tut! Well, I'm waiting for directions."

"OK, which way did you turn out of the farm?"

"Right, then I turned left at the T junction."

RK inclined her head then slowly nodded.

"Follow this road for about three and a half miles, take the right fork, then, after about 5 miles take the second right, ur.r.mm, followed by the third turning on the left and then you should come to a roundabout and you need the third turning right off the roundabout. Let me know when you reach that point."

"Well done, I knew you were an excellent navigator. Now, what can you tell about the places we are passing through?"

To Dan's delight RK became quite animated describing what she recalled of the hamlets and countryside plus some history and legend surrounding local notorieties and within thirty-five minutes she had directed Dan to a quaint roadside café called the Haywain.

"I hope you don't mind, this is a lorry driver stop but Joss and Wenny serve the most delicious food."

"Oh, my, another but."

"Stop teasing, Constable Prettyman."

"I'll be happy with anywhere as long as they serve good food with delightful company."

In fact Dan was overjoyed with the response from RK that his impulsive action had evoked.

At the conclusion of their meal Dan persuaded Wenny to accompany RK to the ladies' room. Whilst waiting for them to return Dan's eyes quickly scanned the contents of RK's hospital letter then went outside to ring Doctor Roger Cooper to acquaint him with the information he'd gleaned with regard to RK's hospital appointments.

Roger took down the details.

"I suggest you initially head east towards the Queen Elizabeth Hospital in King's Lynn. I think from the location you've described you are about another 20-30 minutes away. In the meantime, Dan, I will make contact with the hospital and let them know you are on the way with RK. I'll get back to you with further necessary details when I have them."

When RK was ready Dan settled her into the car and headed towards the King's Lynn hospital. As he drove Dan told her what he had done and described the plan of action Roger proposed.

"Dan, how dare you," RK, somewhat taken aback by the way things had happened, shouted angrily at Dan.

After the congenial hour they had just spent together over lunch in the café Dan was astonished at RK's outburst. He braked to slow down the car.

"OK, Robyn, calm down. I can easily turn the car round and take you back to stagnant isolation at the farm, if that's what you would prefer. Or, we can go on and keep these long overdue appointments and see if the doctors think there might be light at the end of the tunnel."

Although she was riled with Dan for taking matters in to his own hands RK recognized it was probably for the best.

"I'm sorry, Dan," RK rejoined in a small conciliatory voice. "Please, keep driving to the hospital I would like to hear what the doctors have to say." The remainder of the journey passed in subdued silence.

Roger called back just as Dan approached the hospital car park. He pulled in to the nearest vacant bay, turned off the engine and answered his mobile. "Make your way to the fracture clinic, they are expecting you. I'm still working on the eye specialists. I'll get in touch as soon as I receive details back from them."

The rest of the afternoon was spent in consultations. The plaster casts were also removed from RK's legs and arm and x-rays taken. RK was then sent for a physio assessment and the staff requested she return the following morning to commence an exercise programme. "Bring a swimsuit with you, hydro therapy may be the best for you at this stage. You can exercise safely in the water while your injured limbs will be supported. It's important that you concentrate on building up your muscles."

Dan tagged along and was encouraging and supportive. The head bandages were removed and stitches taken out. There was a nasty scar down the left hand side of RK's face but Dan wisely refrained from commenting on it although he silently hoped in time it would heal and fade. The eye specialist hummed and aahed and also wanted to see her again the following day for extensive tests. He recommended in the meantime that she retain the eye dressings and dark glasses until he was able to make an informed assessment of the clinical condition of her eyes.

It was late afternoon before they finished seeing all the necessary doctors and Dan felt they ought to let her family know they were on the way home.

"I'll get the number. Do you want to speak to whoever answers the phone or shall I?"

RK smiled. "I'll do it because I'm used to their bad temper."

After so many refusals to leave the farmhouse Dan was glad he had acted on the spur of the moment and insisted on taking RK out for a drive. It had been a good afternoon. They had eventually enjoyed one another's company and at times been on the former friendly, relaxed footing they had shared when she had lived in Newton Westerby.

The ensuing days were spent travelling to the hospital for physio and clinic appointments. When these were over Dan just drove along country lanes. He told RK where they were and it was obvious, from his description and the roadside village signs, he had taken her to places near to her home with which she was familiar and so Dan encouraged RK to share her knowledge of the village or hamlet. He took her to public parks and gardens where she could smell and touch the plants and flowers.

On one occasion they stopped off at the butterfly park for coffee. RK had had a good session in the pool with the physiotherapist; she was relaxed and chatty and enjoying the quick repartee with Dan that had been the hallmark of their friendship in Newton Westerby.

Dan felt they were making progress, be it ever so slight, so much so, he ventured to suggest on his penultimate day, "Why not come back to the village. I believe they've almost finished the extensions at your cottage and I'm told it's lovely, or so Rosie says. She goes in every week to dust and keep it nice, ready for your return. We miss you in the village. Think about it. Much quieter too," he said, as people shouted, phones rang, tractor and lorry engines roared and wooden pallets clattered, as he turned the car into the yard by the farmhouse.

RK sat pensive and subdued long after he had turned off the ignition. Eventually she sighed and spoke quietly from her heart, "Dan, I'm afraid that I may never see again."

# Chapter Six

"Bless the Lord, oh my soul," Dan sang heartily, strumming the rhythm on the steering wheel, as he drove from the hospital along the A17 towards the farm the following day, "and all that is within me bless His holy name."

"My word, you sound happy," RK observed.

"Well, it's been a good day, don't you think?"

"Humph!"

"You seem uncertain."

"No, not really," she replied tentatively.

"Come on, Robyn," he cajoled, "the blessing of God has been tremendous. Don't you dare sit there in the doldrums, count the positives."

"It's alright for you, Dan. You know more about this God thing than I do."

"I'm sorry, Robyn, I sometimes forget how new faith is to you but just think how this week has panned out so far. Call to mind all the good things that have happened to you, if they're not blessings from God I don't know what are."

"Maybe," said RK tentatively, "but I don't have much experience in that area."

"Look, I'll start you off; you were brill in the hydro pool. In just a few days you've come on by leaps and bounds. Movement appears smoother and easier. Aren't you walking so much better?"

"You're right, the physiotherapist pushes me really hard but already I can feel the difference."

"The first time I heard him shouting at you, to put more effort into your movement, I thought he was an unfeeling tyrant. I wanted to biff him."

"Dan," she scolded. "You can't do that. You're a policeman."

Dan grinned, his shoulders quivering as he tried to contain his mirth.

"You're laughing," RK chuckled.

"How do you know that?"

"I've told you. I listen to the silences."

Dan laughed out loud. "Robyn, you're priceless. Anyway, as I studied the physiotherapist working with you, constantly urging you to do more, I realised he knew his stuff. He'd examined you and looked carefully at your x-rays so had a good grasp of your capabilities, as well as your potential, and that's why he was pushing you to achieve the fullest movement in your legs."

"That's true, without his persistence I wouldn't be walking as I am now, and with his expertise I now know what exercises to do to build up the strength of the muscles weakened by the accident and subsequent weeks of inactivity. He's also shown me the correct way to use the crutches."

"What about your arm?"

"That feels really good. The daily workout should gradually improve muscle power there, too."

"So then, another positive on the tick sheet!"

"Yes, in that instance, I have to agree."

"Headaches?"

"Almost gone."

"And your hair looks really nice now that the bandage is off," Dan complemented, more aware than RK how lank and unkempt it had appeared.

"Thankyou, I'm glad you like it. Tina, the hydrotherapist helped to wash and dry it for me after my session in the pool today." Self consciously RK ran her fingers through her hair.

"Therefore, by process of elimination, the comments of the eye specialist must be the reason for your misgiving."

"He certainly didn't give any hope for optimism."

"Neither did he give cause for undue pessimism but recommended patience so tha..."

"Dan, I'm almost out of patience. I want to get my life back on track particularly now we've got the physio sorted out."

"So, thankyou God for progress thus far, please teach me to trust for development in the areas that are still causing me concern. Is that how you feel at the moment?"

"Yes, something like that."

"Actually, the dark glasses are very becoming."

"Oh, Dan, you are funny."

"It's true, Robyn, they suit you. And..., my dear girl, no one is aware of your predicament."

"But..."

"I thought we had agreed – no buts!"

"All the same, the truth of the matter is I can't see."

"Yes, I know, however, you are walking so much better and, if you take my arm for support, no one else will notice anything different about you."

"But..."

"Dear girl, be grateful for what you have. Keep that in mind. Moreover, what else have you already learned through this experience?"

"What do you mean?"

"Well, in the short time I've spent with you, during the past few days, I've noticed you pull on resources from deep within you. This seems to have given you strength and courage that's helped you cope with the recent trauma in your life. True or not?"

"You're right, Dan. At one point, I was so afraid and frustrated I was ready to give up."

"What changed things?"

"All of a sudden, the God person spoke. He told me he had plans for me and to trust Him."

"Wow!"

"Even more astonishing was when Rev Hugh visited he read to me similar words from the Bible."

"That's awesome, Robyn."

"Mmm, I found it startling at first but at the same time it was comforting. It sort of confirmed to me that the words were real and not a figment of my imagination."

"Our Lord does make Himself known in simple yet, sometimes amazing ways!"

"I don't know about that but I shouted at God about my disappointment at the slowness of my recovery. Strangely enough, after I heard Him speak to me, I felt much calmer."

"Peace?"

"Yes, I suppose you could call it that. I do know that the all-consuming irritation I felt about the situation I was in seemed to gradually dissolve. And, you're correct, Dan, about the inner strength to cope. It must have come from God because up to that point I wasn't handling things at all well."

"So, you've discovered God's real and alive, loves you, wants to be involved in your life and you're learning to trust Him."

"Well, I'm not too sure about that, Dan, because I'm still not very well acquainted with Him but the experience is proving a remarkable eye-opener."

"It is incredible how God reveals His presence in most unexpected ways."

"So I'm finding out but because I'm unable to read I talk to Him about everything, my feelings, frustrations and anger. No matter how irritated I am I seem to hear a reply in the quietness though I'm never quite sure if it's in my head or my heart."

The response of his companion churned Dan's heart. He swallowed over the lump that had risen in his throat and said quietly, "Tomorrow, Robyn, I'll bring my Bible with me and read to you from the Gospels."

"That would be helpful, Dan, thanks."

They sat in companionable silence, as each of their thoughts jostled independently, reflecting on the wonder and majesty of a God who concerned Himself about them. Dan couldn't refrain from humming.

"Oh Dan, that sounds good. Do please sing the words then I can pick them up. I don't know any hymns and I would love to learn them."

Unleashed, Dan obliged, his rich baritone voice flooding the car in song, 'Jesus came with peace...' By mutual consent the journey continued pleasurably making music together RK steadily becoming familiar with some of the words and gaining a grasp of the melodies as Dan sang them over and over again for her.

As they approached Sutton Bridge, Dan slowed down, in order to cross the river bridge.

"Hungry?"

"Mmm."

"The Haywain?"

"That would be really nice."

"I like your friends who run it, they're so obliging."

"Wenny was at school with me and studied catering at college. Joss was one of the tutors."

"Well, they're certainly a great combination."

"And the food's not bad."

Dan's spontaneous chortle almost rocked the car, "I'll second that."

---

"Where've you been, Our Kay? Dad's furious with you," Davi called in an exaggerated whisper as she opened the back door of the farmhouse and tip-toed furtively towards Dan's parked car.

"You know where I've been," RK steeled herself to reply calmly, "attending the eye clinic and keeping the physio appointments at the Queen Elizabeth Hospital in King's Lynn. Then, we popped into the Haywain for a bite to eat."

"But this is the fourth day running that you've been late home this week and it was almost dark on some occasions last week by the time you returned from your supposed appointments at the hospital."

"So?"

Dan rapidly scooted round to the passenger side of the car to where Davi appeared to be laying into RK.

"What's this all about?" he demanded, noting the aggressive tone of Davi's conversation. "I wasn't aware Robyn was under any sort of curfew." Dan then gesticulated towards an untidy heap of papers, books and what was obviously female apparel and toiletries scattered about the yard. "And all this?"

"Dad ordered Mic, Mum and me to throw Our Kay's things out of the window. Dad says your week's more than up. I've been watching for you so that I could sneak out and warn you. I'm truly sorry, Our Kay, but he is very angry with you."

"But why?" RK asked, bewildered by this turn of events.

The euphoria generated by the positive progress at the hospital clinics and physio sessions, as well as the more cordial footing their friendship had returned to, evaporated when Dan had to explain to RK that all her personal possessions were strewn in a mindless fashion on the ground below the window of her room.

RK shook her head in disbelief, "Why is he doing this?" Dejectedly she huddled further into the passenger seat of Dan's car.

"Where is your father?" Dan snapped at Davi. His hackles were beginning to rise in defence of RK and the injustice that was being meted out to her by her family. Despite being on holiday, the unprovoked, irrational attack of Mr Dickinson-Bond upon his injured daughter, prompted Dan to assume his policeman's persona.

*Act with your head not your heart.* The words of Ben Durrant came unbidden to Dan's mind well meant words of restraint and caution to guide him in his relationship with RK.

*But this is different. I can't let someone ride roughshod over her, even if he is her father. This sort of treatment is unacceptable. Robyn is in a very vulnerable state at the moment. She doesn't need this. This unfeeling brute of a man has, in one fell swoop, battered the confidence that the doctors and physiotherapist have built up in the last few days. He's a bully. Yet he's a coward who can't even face his blind daughter with whatever it is that's bothering him.*

As the arguing factions in his head persisted Dan was vaguely aware of the conversation between the sisters. Davi, obviously shaken by the ferocity of her father's anger towards RK was anxious to convey, as swiftly as possible, the danger RK was in.

"Dad's anger was triggered off when he saw you walking to Dan's car this morning. He's convinced you were feigning it when your legs were in plaster."

RK shook her head in disbelief. "I can only walk now because the splints are off, my legs are healing, and the physiotherapist is working jolly hard to build up my muscles, though I still need the crutches to balance and steady myself with."

"You know that, and I know that, but Dad, as usual, is being his pig-headed stubborn self and won't accept that."

"I'm sorry you have to bear the brunt of Dad's fury, because of me. I find it hard to understand why he is acting like this."

"Look at it this way, Dad wants you to work on the farm but if you're sick or injured you can't do that so…"

"But…"

"No, Our Kay, hear me out. According to Dad your accident and injuries are all a sham. He's convinced himself if he keeps you locked up in the house long enough you'll soon give yourself away and the charade will be exposed, you'll agree to work on the farm just to get out of confinement…"

RK gasped.

"...and he's adamant you are pretending blindness."

Behind the dark glasses Robyn's sightless eyes teared up, "Oh Davi, why on earth would I do that? Blindness is the most awful thing that has ever happened to me," RK's voice broke as uncontrollable sobs clogged her throat.

"I'm sorry, Our Kay, I can't begin to imagine what it's like to lose your sight."

"DAVI!" A voice thundered from the open window, "stop shirking, come and help finish the job." More things were sent hurtling to the ground.

"There's Dad, calling me, I'll have to go," Davi whispered to RK and scuttled like a scared rabbit through the back door.

Dan stepped forward to touch RK's arm to assure her of his support. Her distress at Davi's revelations of her father's mind-set perturbed him.

*Oh Lord, this isn't right, but what can I do? He* was torn between his role as her friend and his responsibility as a policeman. What would be the best action to take? *Stay calm. Seek advice.*

RK clung to Dan's hand. "Please, don't leave me Dan."

"Don't worry, Robyn, whenever I decide to go I will take you with me." He gently squeezed her hand. "I'd just like to get some answers from your father before we leave."

Dan strode purposefully towards the closed back door, balled his fist and hammered hard.

"Mr Dickinson-Bond, I'd like a word with you, please," Dan's rich baritone voice resonated around the yard. It was firm but non-threatening. *Lord, forgive me, but I'd really like to shake the living daylights out of the man for his heartless treatment of Robyn.*

After what seemed an age the farmhouse back door was flung wide open and George Dickinson-Bond blustered out shaking his fists at Dan.

"You've got a nerve coming back here," George fumed, poking a finger menacingly into Dan's chest.

"I beg your pardon?"

"I wonder what your superior officers would have to say about your behaviour," George sneered maliciously.

"I'm not sure I know what you mean, Mr Dickinson-Bond."

"Oh, don't come the innocent with me, you scoundrel," he ranted and raved, repeatedly prodding Dan in the chest. "You're a liar and deceiver, a charlatan and seducer." George's actions grew increasingly vicious, his speech louder and louder as his accusations became more bizarre. As a thunderous expression ingrained within George's face, and the reddened hue deepened to purple, Dan feared the man was losing control.

"Dad, stop it," RK shouted, "Dan's bosses should award him a commendation for exemplary behaviour." At her voice Dan jerked his head round. "Robyn, be careful."

RK had eased herself from the car and crutch by crutch was making her way uncertainly towards them but her faltering steps only fuelled George's anger.

"See! I was right," shouted George triumphantly. "It was all a sham." He stamped his feet and shook his fists.

"No, sir, you're wrong."

"How dare you," George Dickinson-Bond swung his arms round with force intending to land a blow on Dan but Dan, trained to combat such attacks, put up his arm in self defence to stave off the bombardment.

"Dad! Dad! Listen to me. If Dan had not taken me to the hospital I would still be in my room unable to walk."

"Rubbish! You've been pretending all along, ducky, so's you get out of working on the farm. Then, when your fancy man comes along, hey presto, you can walk. Well, he'd better make an honest woman of you after all this cavorting about," George wildly argued.

"Dad! I can walk now because the physiotherapist has been working hard rebuilding my muscles and gradually my legs are healing. Ring the hospital, they'll confirm my appointments."

Angrily George stomped towards RK. "They're all in cahoots with you and lover boy. I won't get the truth out of them, you slut," he yelled at her furiously.

"You're so wrong, Dad," murmured RK who was quite distressed by her father's wild accusations. "Dan is my friend. He's done for me what you wouldn't do. I think you owe him an apology."

"Don't you tell me what to do, ducky," Mr Dickinson–Bond replied crossly then, raised his hand and hit his unsuspecting daughter with all his might across the face. The unforeseen blow knocked RK off balance. "Ouch!" she yelped as she crumpled on the floor clutching a hand to the side of her face, her crutches clattering in a tangle on top of her.

In one deft step Dan leapt to her aid. "Are you OK, Robyn?" Apart from the point of impact where George's hand had struck, RK's face had lost all colour. He quickly lifted the crutches from her body.

"George, what have you done," a shaken Amy called out to her husband from the back porch where she'd been hovering with Mic and Davi while George's irrational tirade was taking place. As her daughter fell she quickly scurried across the yard to assist RK. Davi reached her sister first and tried to haul RK to her feet.

RK flayed her arms above her head in an attempt to stave off the bevy of well-meaning hands. "Leave me alone, just a minute, please."

"Where do you hurt?"

"My head and left leg."

"Oh, stop the play-acting, Our Kay, and get up," snapped Mic impatiently.

RK cringed at the spite in Mic's voice and tears spilled unbidden from her unseeing eyes.

"If you can't be more sympathetic keep quiet," Davi hissed at Mic between gritted teeth as she bent down towards RK. "Can I get you anything, Our Kay?"

"Who's that?" asked RK anxious to deflect attention from herself. Her mother and sisters looked at her in surprise. Unheard by them a vehicle had pulled into the yard. Mic glanced round. "Oh, it's Neil home from the deliveries." She ran to greet her young man.

With a practised eye Dan observed RK anxiously. The vicious slap from her father had landed across the scar along her cheek and created angry looking weals. The awkward manner in which she fell may have further damaged her healing legs. He was annoyed with himself for not preventing the unprovoked attack on RK, as she stood defenceless, so close to him. The desire to take her into his arms and protect her from her father's unreasonable diatribe surged through him like a whirlwind. He watched apprehensively as George loudly made his way to the house gesticulating fiercely as he went along. At the same time Dan telephoned for professional back-up. "...yes, domestic... I see... Mmm ...paramedics, thanks... we'll wait...I fear we may be looking at a section nine order...if he doesn't burst a blood vessel before you get here...Thankyou, sir."

As Mrs Dickinson-Bond and Davi flitted around the assaulted RK George continued with his unfounded accusations and diabolical outbursts while he proceeded to jettison the remainder of RK's personal effects from the house; the lowering clouds above the farmhouse loomed as threatening as George's glowering mood within it.

Dan recorded notes and took pictures on his mobile phone to present as evidence should they be needed. He then took opportunity to contact Doctor Roger Cooper to acquaint him with the unpredicted turn of events.

"I'll be home tomorrow, Doc, bringing Robyn with me," he concluded decisively.

"Don't be too hasty, Dan."

"Roger, this is really awkward, but I can't leave Robyn here. It's too late to travel home now Robyn is too tired from all the sessions at the hospital."

"I can see you've got a dilemma on your hands."

"I'll try and get her into the B&B but...hmm... Robyn needs help with personal things."

"You get her a bed. I'll see what I can do with regard to assistance."

"We'll need to stay around till the local force and medics arrive. Both Robyn and her father need attention but I'll stay in touch."

# Chapter Seven

Meanwhile, in the fishing village of Newton Westerby, Sunday morning awakened to squally showers. As Emma stepped cautiously out of the house the rain swirled around her skirt and buffeted her upheld arm. In view of the inclement weather Roger had left home earlier with the car to pick up some elderly parishioners for the morning service leaving Emma to walk the short distance to the church on her own. Oh dear, I don't think this brolly is going to give me much protection. It and the wind seem to be at odds with one another about its function. She held tightly to the handle and grasped the fabric attached to the inverted spines with her free hand. I just pray this scuffle isn't indicative of skirmishes of a different nature in what is going to be, for some, an unsettling day.

As she struggled with the elements Emma recalled that late yesterday afternoon there had been intense exchanges on the telephone between Roger and Dan Prettyman. These were closely followed by an equally serious dialogue with Rev Hugh. The vicar had phoned the young Doctor to acquaint him with an early morning call he received from Norwich prison which had resulted in him driving over to Norwich to visit Joe Cook.

..."*Roger, Joe's tried to take his own life. He's full of remorse for all the things he's done wrong and written a letter to Michelle asking for her forgiveness, which he wants me to deliver. I don't know what impact this news will have on Michelle but I thought it might be wise if we saw her together.*"

"*Right,*" Roger absorbed the information for a moment. "*I can leave what I'm doing for a short while but I'll need to check that Dad can cover calls for me, if necessary. I'll meet you on the corner by the Village Stores in five minutes. I'd also welcome the opportunity to chat over a situation that has arisen with regard to two of your other parishioners.*"

*As the two men strode towards the Cook's cottage they spoke of the heartache that had been caused to so many of the villagers because of Joe's criminal activities following his redundancy from the nuclear power station along the coast at Sizewell.*

"*He realises now that what he did was drink directed and is willing to attend classes to retrain while he is completing his time in prison.*"

"*If only he had done that when the opportunity was first offered to him he wouldn't now be in this predicament.*"

"*I suppose we can all look back on things we've done and say 'if only'. I think the attempt at suicide is a cry for help. He desperately wants to see Michelle and the children and has promised he will continue to attend AA sessions to keep the drink issue in check if she will agree to see him.*"

"*Has she never been to see him?*"

"*No, she was so cross that he had involved their children in his criminal activities and, like many others in the village, Michelle suspected he had something to do with the Kemp's deaths."*

*"I understood he denied any involvement."*

*"Yes, there was no evidence against him and today, while I was visiting him, he brought the topic up. He is still adamant he had nothing to do with their accident."*

*"I know Emma believed him when he said that at the trial."*

*"And, having recently spoken with Inspector Ian Capps, I believe an ongoing police investigation may prove that to be the case."*

*"I can understand Michelle believing that if she lets him into their lives again it will 'upset the applecart,' as she puts it."*

*"Yes, the equilibrium of the family seems to be on an even keel at the moment, the younger boys appear to be settled in school, Josh has finally agreed to follow a training programme offered in the young offender's institute, Maxine is doing well in her college course and proving capable in her Saturday job at the Village Stores and Michelle has regular employment which enables her to pay the bills without itchy fingers dipping into the coffers and frittering away their meagre resources."*

*"Rather a tricky situation."*

---

*The Doctor and Vicar were returning from seeing Michelle, who had taken the news regarding Joe more calmly than they had anticipated though she was reticent about committing to visiting him in prison, when Roger received a further call from Dan concerning the altercation with Mr Dickinson-Bond. He lowered his mobile and whispered to Hugh, "I think we're going to need to implement the plan of action for RK's rehabilitation sooner than we'd planned." Roger concluded his call and then explained the earlier dialogue between Dan and himself...*

A sudden gust brought Emma's thoughts back to the present moment and she struggled to hold on to her umbrella as the wind and rain buffeted against it. *Dear Lord, come with Your mercy, peace and love to troubled hearts today,* her heart prayed as she recalled Roger's concerns from the previous day.

*...While Roger had rung his contacts in the mid Lincolnshire area to obtain the medical assistance necessary for RK's personal needs Dan had scooted around collecting together RK's belongings and trying to book her accommodation for the night. However, because it was so late in the day it had been impossible to fit her into an already overloaded nursing schedule or even a local B&B.*

*"I'm sorry, Dan, but social care facilities in Lincolnshire seem to be stretched to the limit so they're unable to help," the Doctor informed him.*

*"No worries, the medics have checked her over and all seems OK so we'll go to the Haywain, a hostelry not too far away. Wenny, the owner and a friend of Robyn's, I'm sure will lend a hand," Dan told Roger confidently.*

*Wenny had other ideas. "Dan, we're not the Ritz or even a Travelodge. We only have basic facilities, no ensuite. We cater for long distance lorry drivers on overnight stops who are looking for a clean bed and a good meal."*

*"Wenny, it's what you can offer or an open field and I know which I would prefer, but Robyn will need help with eye drops and... uhmm... other things."*

*"I see." Wenny stood with her hands on her hips, her head to one side and squinted at Dan with eyes that challenged his daring.*

*"Wenny, please," he implored.*

*In the end Dan slept in the trucker's quarters and RK stayed in the spare room of Wenny and Joss's bungalow where she received more personal care and attention than she'd experienced since being discharged from the hospital. Her father had been sectioned and admitted to a local secure unit pending medical investigation...*

"And now they're on the way here but the time of their arrival in Newton Westerby is uncertain," Emma whispered aloud while her thoughts returned to the present moment in time as she continued her tussle with the elements.

---

"Where's the summer sunshine gone to, Em?" Miranda called out as she stood with Jackie on the Cooper's front doorstep waiting to see if the shower would pass. The sisters had seen Emma cross the road and battle with her umbrella as she walked unsteadily in front of the butcher's shop to enter the lane that led to the church. Her cousin's voice brought Emma's mind back to the present.

"I think you'll find it's hiding behind the clouds. You'll see, by lunch time there will be clear blue skies again."

Miranda laughed, "Are you taking up weather forecasting along with all your many other skills?"

"No. I just listen to the weather report and hope they've got it right."

"Come on Jackie, let's risk it," Miranda cajoled her sister then ran from the doorway pulling her plastic Mac tightly around her to join Emma. Together the young women sprinted briskly across The Green, deftly avoiding the puddles, arriving at the church out of breath but just in time for the morning service to begin.

Their arrival caused a bit of a commotion because still being the holiday season, albeit the final weekend of the school holidays, coupled with inclement weather, visitors had filled up the pews as a means of shelter rather than a place for worship. So, the girls crept into a back pew as the organ commenced the introit.

As they shook their mackintoshes free of surplus water Miranda whispered hastily, "Any more news about RK?"

"Tell you later," Emma mouthed and settled back into the pew. For a moment she closed her eyes to let the notes the organ was playing saturate her heart with the words her mind was identifying with the melody.

> Drop Thy sweet dews of quietness,
> Till all our strivings cease;
> Take from our minds the strain and stress
> And let our ordered lives confess
> The beauty of Thy peace.
> *(John Greenleaf Whittier)*

*That's my prayer for today, relief from stress. I don't know how we're going to solve Joe or RK's predicament, Father God, so I just put everything into Your hands. Thankyou for the promise of peace.* Emma took a deep breath, exhaled very slowly and felt the presence of the Lord envelope her with reassurance.

"Good morning and welcome. You are all here this morning for a reason." Rev Hugh looked directly at his congregation with warmth in his penetrating eyes. "Our Father God is aware of that reason. Maybe simply to get out of the rain..." a titter rippled along the pews ... "or a need to get closer to our Lord but whatever the motive or rationale behind your presence here today God will meet with you in love, if you will let Him."

As the service unfolded the ambience created by the singing, the praying, the silence and the reading of the Word brought balm and comfort, healing and peace, joy and hope, challenge and encouragement to many seated within the embrace of the walls of the church. Even those who had just used the church as a convenience felt an uncharacteristic glow within and were glad they had come.

At the conclusion of the morning service, to the surprise of the local congregants, Rev Hugh took a moment to announce the imminent return of RK to the village. Miranda raised her eyebrows at Emma as they stood for the final hymn. Singing wholeheartedly Emma dipped her head in assent. Tongues began to wag almost before the vicar had pronounced the benediction and the buzz spilled over into the church hall where many of the congregation gathered for the after-church coffee fellowship. Interest from all quarters centred on RK's return.

Young Daniel Catton jostled Adam's arm as he chatted with Ben and Rachel. "Dad, is it really true? Is RK coming home?" The adults smiled at the boy's assumption that Newton Westerby was the place of home to RK. Adam skilfully rescued his coffee cup from spilling. Just as he opened his mouth to admonish Daniel for his carelessness Rachel caught his eye, a quick shake of her head and a calming hand on the shoulders of Mark and Rhoda, who were also brimming with excitement, changed the tone of his remark. "From the statement made by Reverend Hugh it would certainly seem that she is returning to the village."

"Oh, goodie!" Daniel and his sisters had got on famously with RK when she had commenced caring for them after their mother, Laura, had suffered a stroke in the early part of the previous year.

"Yippee!" Mark and Rhoda also danced up and down then together they raced with Daniel to join the animated huddle of village children at the far end of the church hall.

"What's going to happen?" asked Keir Jenner.

"Don't know," said Daniel, "but she won't be bringing her bike, will she?" and he shook his head forlornly.

"That's a shame, it was great. I liked it's roar."

"The old people didn't," put in 13½ year old Lily knowingly. "They always grumbled about the noise it made."

"She was such fun," Kirsty said quietly, "I'm sorry she's been hurt."

Pansy, the youngest of the Jenner siblings, thoughtfully nodded her head in agreement, "She was my friend."

Their parents along with Miranda and Jackie remained clustered around Emma and Doctor Roger.

"This has all happened sooner than anticipated, hasn't it?" Ben asked.

Roger slowly inclined his head. Choosing his words carefully he explained, "It would seem family circumstances have dictated an earlier return."

"Is Dan bringing her home?"

"Yes," he responded briefly.
"When will they arrive?"
"Later today."
"That soon?"
"Where is she going to live?"
"That has yet to be decided."
"Who will look after her?"
"Depends where she's housed."
"Can she walk?"
"Her mobility is improving but she is still using crutches. During his time in Lincolnshire Dan's been able to transport RK to the hospital daily for physiotherapy."
"How will she manage if she can't see?"
"That remains to be seen."
"Is the damage to her sight temporary or perm...?" There was a gasp as Jackie asked the question many of them were thinking.
"It would seem that at present the doctors are unsure of the prognosis."

Adam had been unusually quiet during this exchange. He caught Laura's eye. She gave him a nod of approval.

"Ben, now that your chaps have put the stair lift in place at home Laura is able to manage the stairs, so Doc," Adam shifted his gaze to Roger, "we could easily make the conservatory suite available for RK."

Roger put an arm across Adam's shoulders and guided him nearer to Laura so that he could encircle her too. "My dear, dear, friends, that is such a generous offer. Very, very tempting for me to accept because we all know what a special space Ben and his team created in your home for Laura's rehabilitation, which would be ideal for RK, however, she is no longer in a position to be a carer. In some ways she will need to be cared for, in other ways we have to encourage independence. The one factor that causes me to hesitate in accepting your proposal is her current lack of sight. Although RK is familiar with the layout of your home the unexpected, particularly from boisterous children and scattered toys, are going to be hazards that will make her hesitant and therefore hinder her progress.

"Dear Laura, you are making such fine improvement, for your sake as much as RK's I cannot ask you to take on such a mammoth task, at least, not for the time being."

Speculation was rife not only amongst the young people but also some of the older stalwarts of the community. In other parts of the church hall Bernice and Roy Durrant, the Cooper brothers and their spouses, as well as RK's former antagonists, Jennifer Pedwardine and Lord Edmund were grouped together discussing the implications of RK's return to the village. The Jenner and Darnell families latched on to various conversations around the hall as they moved between the children and the adult groups.

The other astonishing topic of conversation in the church hall, spoken of in hushed whispers, was the attempted suicide of Joe Cook. Raised eyebrows across the room between Hugh and Roger questioned '*How did that leak out?*' This awful news brought again to the surface the fact that Joe was currently serving a sentence in prison for assault and burglary he had carried out against people and property in the Newton villages over a period of time following his redundancy from the Sizewell nuclear power station. Many villagers still blamed Joe and his son Josh for the deaths of Emma's parents in a road accident nearly two years ago.

"No evidence was ever found to support that theory, you know."

"Maybe, but continuing police work suggests the Kemps car may have been tampered with."

"By the Cooks?"

"No, possibly the drug smugglers Mick stumbled over on the back step of the Stores one night in Christmas week as he took out the industrial waste bin ready for collection the following morning."

"You think it was a revenge killing?"

"Could be."

"More likely fear of reprisals if Mick passed on to the authorities what he had seen."

"Do you think Joe or Josh was involved?"

"I doubt it."

"Then why try to do away with himself if he's not implicated?"

"I think the deaths of Mick and Val brought home to Joe the enormity of the crimes he had admitted to, but to be accused of their murder, which he has always denied, has really played on his mind. Prison life has also brought regret that he involved his boys in his criminal activities. It seems he's genuinely sorry his actions have broken up the family."

Breaking away from the pockets of speculative gossip Lord Edmund took hold of Jennifer Pedwardine's arm, "Can I have a word?" Jennifer's knees uncharacteristically were all of a quiver as he drew her to a less populated area of the church hall. Then somewhat bashfully, for a man of his years and experience Lord Edmund blurted out, "My sister Isobel has an evening soiree on the 15$^{th}$ of next month I'd like to invite you to attend with me, if you would be so kind, Jennifer."

Looking up into his kindly face and with her heart all aflutter Jennifer took a deep breath to calm the nerves that seemed to have taken hold of her before replying. "I'd be delighted to accompany you, Sir Edmund. I haven't seen Isobel for quite a number of years. One loses contact particularly when engaged in different fields of work."

"That's hardly surprizing, Isobel was never one to keep in touch. Letter writing was not top of her agenda. They've only recently returned from diplomatic service overseas and Isobel likes to announce their return to society with a splash."

"Will she and ... What is her husband's name?"

"Dobie."

"Oh yes, that's right, I remember now. Do they still have the Red House alongside the river at Newton Lokesby?"

"Yes, when they're abroad they put the house into the hands of agents to arrange long term lets and resume residency on their return to England calling in the decorators for a complete refurbishment."

"I see."

"Our village letting arrangements at Newton Westerby are not sophisticated enough for Isobel though I believe Trixie Cooper and Graeme Castleton have an impeccable record managing the holiday cottages for our community."

"I'm sure they do."

"Dobie is brother to Cynthia Durrant."

"I'd forgotten that."

"It's difficult to keep up with fami..."

"Ur...ur...umm. Excuse me."

Lord Edmund and Miss Pedwardine immediately stopped talking and as one turned to look questioningly and most pointedly in the direction of the voice that had interrupted their private conversation.

# Chapter Eight

❖

Having hovered nervously on the edge of the little tete-a-tete between Lord Edmund and Miss Pedwardine for quite a few minutes, Ellie Darnell straightened her back, lifted her head and drew a deep breath. She had waited all through her Dad's service to approach Lord Edmund and was very keyed up. It was important to Ellie that she present herself and explain her college project to him in the best possible manner. She certainly didn't want to appear rude because that might scupper her proposal before it even got off the ground.

"How can we help, my dear?" his voice boomed out.

"I wondered, sir, if you would give me permission to design and carry out the décor of a room in one of the holiday cottages for my college assignment."

Miss Pedwardine tut-tutted her best headmistress's disapproval, "Surely that's a task beyond a slip of a girl like you..." but Sir Edmund held up a hand to still her tongue. He squarely faced Ellie, his eyebrows raised in amused interest.

"This sounds quite an undertaking. What are you proposing?"

Ellie answered quickly before she got cold feet.

"Access to one of the holiday cottages so that I can get a feel of the place; consultation with you in order to learn what you might have in mind for redecoration; permission allowing me to take measurements and bring swatches of fabrics and colour charts for your consideration. If my design meets with your approval I will carry out the work to the best of my ability," Ellie gasped for breath.

"My, my, my," interjected Miss Pedwardine with annoyance as she clapped her hands emphatically together but Lord Edmund stood silent and still, a frown furrowing his brow. Ellie's heart plummeted to her shoes. *Oh, no I've blown it.*

Then a smile broke across Lord Edmund's stern features. Stepping closer to Ellie he demanded jovially, "What makes you think I would trust you to undertake such a project?"

"I believe I have the capability to create a design that is pleasing to the eye, comfortable to live with, welcoming and easy to keep clean."

"My word, you seem to have tremendous faith in your own ability, young lady. How do I know that it wouldn't cost me the bill of a professional decorator to put it right?" His voice seemed to have modified to a gentle rumble.

"Tantamount to arrogant!" Miss Pedwardine unable to refrain from making comment shook her head in disbelief.

Lord Edmund placed a restraining hand upon Miss Pedwardine's arm and nodded to encourage Ellie to continue.

"My tutor is a stickler for perfection and correctness. I've already had to prove myself and my abilities many times to get this far in my course. If you don't like my design I have to give written agreement before I start the project that I will, at my own expense, revert the room back to its former state."

"I see. Why choose a holiday cottage and not a local home where someone is in need of free redecoration?"

"I thought it would be less hassle because the property would be empty. I want to give it my very best shot because it is for my final exam."

"This is a very ambitious assignment. What would be your time scale?"

"I'm only allowed three weeks from start to finish, another reason why an empty property would be preferable to an occupied one. I can keep to my own schedule."

"Humph! you wouldn't get that luxury in real life. You would have to work around meal times, the cat, the dog, the clutter, the..."

"Lord Edmund," Ellie interspersed before the roar crescendoed to deafening proportions, "I'm aware of the hazards of normal life but for my first project I want to concentrate on design and its execution without those hindrances."

An ominous silence hung between them. Ellie held her breath.

"Aren't you being a trifle over ambitious, Ellie?" Miss Pedwardine asked brusquely.

"I don't think so. I recognize that it will require skill and hard work but creating beautiful homes for people to live in is what I want to do as a career so I am willing to give my very best to achieve that."

"For even a holiday cottage?"

"Yes."

"Humph! You've got spunk and determination, girl. I admire that. When do you have to submit your proposal?"

"On the first day of the Autumn term."

"And carry it out, when?"

"The week commencing fifth October."

"Leave it with me, Ellie. I'll be in touch within the week."

"Thankyou, Sir."

As Ellie walked away from Lord Edmund and Miss Pedwardine she felt she ought to bob a curtsey in thanks for being granted an audience.

*Whew! At least he didn't throw out my proposal. Mum would say give thanks to the Lord.*

A smile of satisfaction slowly tweaked at Lord Edmund's thin lips. Jennifer caught it and the twinkle in his eye.

"Now then, my lord, what are you scheming for that young lady?"

"Aah, that remains to be seen but I've something in mind that I think will challenge our young friend admirably. I'll put it in the hands of Trixie Cooper."

"She certainly doesn't lack self-confidence."

"I liked that," Lord Edmund continued his smile of approval.

Jennifer returned his smile with a knowing grimace for she too had an idea in her head that she had been mulling over ever since the announcement at the end of the morning service regarding RK's impending return to the village. It simply would not go away.

"If you'll excuse me, Lord Edmund, I need to speak with the vicar about a matter of moment."

---

So it was that the answer to RK's rehabilitation into the village came from the most unexpected source and

RK's return also became the surprising answer to Ellie's request to practise her skills at interior design.

As the former headmistress of Newton Westerby Primary school Jennifer Pedwardine had, in her own words, *'taken early retirement to give young blood an opportunity'* but if the truth were known she was finding time hung heavily on her hands. Whilst she revelled in the challenge of her garden there was only so much physical work one could do in a day and it was such a lonesome occupation after the interaction of school life.

She missed people and conversation.

Jennifer had been one of RK's most vociferous critics when she had first come to the village – like many of the older generation – prejudiced before getting to know the person behind the motor bike paraphernalia. However, a friendship of sorts had developed when Miss Pedwardine offered bathing facilities to RK and garaging for the Harley-Davidson after RK moved into the semi-derelict Ferry Cottage.

Jennifer was aware that she had a spacious home and none of the encumbrances that many of the Newton Westerby villagers were saddled with. She had time and she was blessed with resources. It would be uncharitable not to offer to share with someone in need what she had in abundance. The fact that RK was already acquainted with the lay-out of her home was also a factor to be taken into consideration.

So, having reached a decision concerning RK's future Jennifer strode up to the group in the church hall, which included the vicar and Doctor Roger, and in her most forthright manner spoke out at once.

"I can offer peace and tranquillity, bed and board but I'll need medical back-up," Jennifer brusquely announced to the young doctor.

"And you young folk will need to organize youthful diversions," she looked directly at Ben and Emma and the group of younger people gathered around them then, she abruptly turned and began to make her way towards the exit door of the church hall.

Stunned by Miss Pedwardine's pronouncement a pregnant hush pervaded the church hall then everyone began to talk at once about what was going to be necessary for RK's wellbeing. Some had reservations about her moving in with the former headmistress while others saw it as an ideal solution to RK's immediate dilemma.

"Crumbs! Whatever will RK have to say about living with the old battle-axe," muttered Hilary sarcastically behind her hand to those within earshot.

But kind hearted Annette replied, "Miss Pedwardine has a lovely home and it's generous of her to make an offer which RK is bound to be thankful for. I'm certain she'll be comfortable and well taken care of."

"I'm sure you're right," Nicky backed up his sister, "but how will she manage if she's blind?"

"She'll have to be taken everywhere, won't she?"

"And what about steps and stairs if she's struggling to walk?"

"She won't be able to cook, will she?"

"How will she dress herself?"

"A...a...and personal things; it'll be like looking after a grown-up baby!"

"She won't be able to work. Will she?"

"In fact she's going to be quite a liability!"

"Rather you than me, Jennifer," someone remarked as Miss Pedwardine walked passed.

Jennifer's ramrod back stiffened; whether with annoyance or discomfort was hard to tell.

"Let's get her here first," suggested Ben in an effort to calm the heated splat that seemed to be emanating.

"I agree," Roger nodded his appreciation towards Ben. "Over the last week I've been in daily contact with the hospital doctors in order to keep abreast of their findings and recommendations for RK."

"And what is their assessment?" asked Jennifer abruptly as she halted in mid stride.

"Physio, exercise coupled with rest, care and encouragement. However, I want to see for myself what RK's condition is like before passing judgement or making any decisions."

"So, till then we don't really know what the true situation is."

"That is correct."

"And when can we expect RK to arrive?"

"Later today."

"Good gracious, that soon! I must go. I have a lot of preparations to make." Uncharacteristically Miss Pedwardine suddenly became rather flustered.

"Now, Miss Pedwardine, you are not doing this alone. We are all in this with you. I suggest we all go home and have lunch, then decide what needs to be done." Roger laid his hand kindly upon Jennifer's arm then looked around the group of friends gathered closest to him. "Miranda will you act as co-ordinator with, shall we say Ben and Justin for practical matters and link up with Jackie and Annette over girlie things. I have other things in mind for Emma and you, Miss Pedwardine."

"Thankyou, young man, I will see most of you later." Jennifer strode purposefully towards the door.

After a quick word with her husband Emma followed Miss Pedwardine as she made her exit from the church hall. Tentatively she tucked a hand through the arm of the austere lady.

"Miss Pedwardine, do you have lunch ready at home? There are some things Roger would like to discuss with you concerning RK's situation that he doesn't want to be universally known and we would be happy for you to share lunch in our home so he has opportunity to do that."

"Well, this Sunday I planned to have one of Jilly's 'meals for one' from your shop, Emma, but I can easily have that tomorrow. I would enjoy sharing a meal with you and your fine husband, thankyou."

Emma turned to catch Roger's eye in order to convey with a nod that Miss Pedwardine had assented to the proposal she had presented to her concerning Sunday lunch.

"Shall we make our way there now? Roger will come along shortly."

"Of course, my dear," agreed that staid lady graciously.

Together they walked across The Green towards the opening that led down to their cottage on Main Street.

The visit to see RK at home in Lincolnshire, that had been planned by Roger and Emma to assess RK's personal needs ready for when she returned to Newton Westerby, necessarily had to be curtailed in view of Dan's decision to bring her back with him immediately to protect her from her father's unrelenting unkindness towards her. So, much of the conversation and preparation made by the village community was based on assumptions.

Ideas and arrangements flew across the airwaves during the lunch hour as plans were formulated on how best to accommodate RK's supposed needs. Miranda was kept busy ensuring that all aspects were covered tasks not replicated and teams of willing helpers assigned specific jobs.

Following lunch quite a number of volunteers gathered at 'Bakers'. At Roger's insistence Emma and Jennifer counted the footsteps from car to gate, gate to front door and measured out distances inside Miss Pedwardine's lovely house. They paced together to ensure they got it right, from gate to back door from back door to kitchen table, steps up stairs, across landing to bedroom, between bedroom and bathroom. They left no space uncounted and recorded their calculations.

Thankfully, as Emma had predicted, the rain had stopped though the puddles hampered some of their reckoning and threatened to create a dreadful mess on the floors of Miss Pedwardine's home till Ben produced some blue plastic overshoes, which were used by his workers at Durrant's Builders, for the many feet that were traipsing in and out of the house.

The teams Miranda got together moved furniture to different rooms in order to make the house as accessible as possible to RK.

"I would like home life to be as normal as possible, if that is convenient to you Miss Pedwardine. So I suggest we prepare for RK to sleep upstairs with one side of the bed up against the wall," explained the doctor, "and no table lamp. We don't want RK to get entangled with a wire she cannot see."

"Of course, Roger, please do whatever you consider to be necessary for her wellbeing."

"Can she manage stairs?" Emma asked.

"Not sure but I'm presuming that is so."

"We need to be prepared to make adjustments, then?"

"Maybe, in the meantime, may we remove some of your lovely ornaments to protect them, Jennifer, and obvious hazards such as rugs and knee high coffee tables from the hall sitting room area?"

Jennifer nodded then asked, "Shall I put these potted plants on the window sill?" indicating the numerous brass and porcelain plant holders that graced the parquet floor of the hall. The houseplants were arranged attractively in strategic places but they presented danger to a sightless person.

"You do have quite a lot so perhaps some could go in the conservatory? Don't you go humping them about just supervise the removal team."

Again Jennifer acquiesced and Roger inclined his head towards Nicky and Justin who had been assigned the hall sitting room as their area to clear.

"There might be room in the main lounge for the small pieces of furniture and the dining room or the study could be adapted into a downstairs bedroom, if necessary," suggested Jennifer.

"Good, keep it homely, not clinical." Roger strode to the right side of the room and pulled open a door, "Aah, downstairs cloakroom, ideal." He took a quick look. "Mmm, I wonder if the boys could put up a fixed soap dispenser and a towel hook at a handy height. I'll ask Miranda if we have a spare one in the surgery and also get her to arrange someone to put loops onto towels."

"Christina is the one handy with a needle."

Roger dipped his head in agreement. "I'll ask Emma to mention it to her. With all the willing support that's been offered everything's coming together nicely."

"Let's hope the young lady appreciates it," Miss Pedwardine retorted dourly.

Roger raised his eyebrows. "Are you already regretting your offer of hospitality?"

Jennifer shook her head, "No, not at all. I don't want your hard work to be in vain."

Roger laughed, "I hardly think that's likely. After all that I understand she's been through in recent weeks I think RK will be more than grateful to simply have a roof over her head let alone all the extras that have been provided for her wellbeing."

With pursed lips Jennifer replied, "Time will tell."

---

During the hours that the young folk of the village were busily engaged transforming Miss Pedwardine's home into a safe environment for RK Lord Edmund sat alone in quiet contemplation replete from his Sunday lunch. His housekeeper, Lettie Milner, might not match up to the world's Cordon Bleu chefs but her meals were adequate and satisfying although for the most part he just ate what was placed in front of him without giving much thought to what was actually on the fork he put into his mouth. Today, he was even less aware of the content of his meal. His mind was elsewhere his thoughts taken up with other matters in a quite disturbing way. Instead of sitting in the well-worn leather winged armchair that graced the recess in his study, which was his usual abode after a meal, he had wondered into the sitting room and taken one of the chintz covered armchairs that had been so lovingly chosen by Phoebe when he brought her to the house as a young bride all those years ago.

As he sat he leaned his head back and looked up at the portrait above the mantle shelf, painted before Eddie's accident and Phoebe's untimely death. A family complete, bathed in affection, each adding to the joy of the other, he thought.

*Dear Phoebe, how happy we were then and how soon it all changed.* He closed his eyes and let the rhythm of the grandfather clock tick the minutes away. Unmoving he sat. Time seemed to be suspended in space. He tried to empty his mind of all its peripheral clutter and allow only the one matter that craved his consideration to occupy his thinking. It was necessary to be clear headed to broach such a life changing step as the one he was planning. He remained in this position for quite some time. Lettie, opening the door a couple of hours later to enquire if he required tea, believed him to be asleep so tiptoed quietly out of the room but the door catch broke his concentration. He rubbed a hand across his brow and looked again at the family portrait. *How I have missed you both, Phee. Parting is all we can know this side of heaven but I believe one day we will meet again. Since you left me I have kept busy. I believe that was the best way to deal with the pain but now I am in turmoil. Dear Phoebe, I am contemplating change. I have been on my own for so long. The time seems right but I do not feel it will be disloyal to you. This house is too big just for me to be rattling around in it. I feel sure you would approve what I am about to do.*

He rose purposefully from the chair and looked appreciatively around the room. *This is a fine room with a delightful outlook across the lawns to the borders. I ought to use it more often.* With a spring in his step Lord Edmund made his way to the kitchen.

"Ah, Lettie, might I have a cup of tea in the study. I have some papers I need to peruse."

"Yes, certainly, Sir, that will be no trouble at all."
"This is quite a homely kitchen, isn't it, Lettie?"
"Well I think so."
"Well equipped?"
"Oh yes."
"That's good."

*Why he almost skipped across the hallway to the study.* Lettie peeped round the kitchen door to watch him. She was astounded. In all the years she had worked at the Manor she had only ever seen Lord Edmund behave in a sedate and proper manner. She shook her head. *What is the world coming to?* Briskly she set about making the tea.

Lord Edmund picked up a file, took out some papers and placed them carefully on his desk. It was the content of these documents that had set his mind racing. In all directions at first and then back into history, how fascinating that had been. Now, however, his thoughts were primarily projected to the future.

# Chapter Nine

At first, RK loathed Jennifer Pedwardine's regimented daily routine but gradually the disciplined pattern became familiar, less scary and something to cling to. *Dear God, I'm very grateful for Jennifer's kindness but how I long for the day to arrive when the bandages will permanently come off my eyes, I can see and be independent again. I can't wait to get back to my little cottage by the sea.*

As each new day dawned RK prayed this would be the day. The anticipation and impetus of this expectation kept her going. She even felt she could cope with the tedium of Miss Pedwardine's regime if it was only going to be for a limited time. RK recognized she was comfortable and well looked after in Miss Pedwardine's spacious home, so much prior thought having been given to her safety and ease of movement within the house, but being locked inside herself because of her blindness was stifling as was the confinement in unproven surroundings. She itched to be out and about doing things and meeting people. Enforced idleness was anathema to her ebullient spirit. *Not for long, now. Soon I'll be able to see.*

In no time at all RK learned which day of the week it was by the blueprint of activities Jennifer adhered to which had been formulated when she first retired.

One morning when Miss Pedwardine issued very specific instructions to RK before going upstairs to attend to the bedrooms followed by distinct noises outside of the house RK knew it was Saturday.

"Good morning, Nicky," RK called out when she heard footsteps come into the kitchen.

"Hi, RK, how do you know it's me?" Nicky Andaman asked as he lowered the box of groceries onto the table.

"The bang of the back gate and the clatter of tins as you put the box onto the kitchen table gave you away."

"But you can't se... I mean, how can you be sure it's me?"

"You open the door in a particular way and your trainers make a distinctive sound on the kitchen tiles. I know, too, that it's about 10 o'clock on Saturday." RK grinned as her hands guided her into the kitchen. She hadn't yet mastered all the counted steps that Emma and Jennifer had so meticulously worked out just before her arrival, as a result she still felt her way gingerly about the unfamiliar house.

"How can you know that?"

"Deduction, my dear Watson, and strategic use of the little grey cells," RK wagged her forefinger in his direction and put on her best gravelly imitation voice which came out as a cross between Sherlock Holmes and Hercules Poirot. "And Miss Pedwardine did happen to mention it."

Nicky threw back his head and laughed.

"I also know that groceries from the Village Store are delivered at this time on Saturday morning to this address by one called Nicky Andaman."

"You're a joker, RK."

"Am I? I got it right, didn't I?"

"You certainly did, though I still can't fathom how you knew it was me coming into the kitchen," Nicky acceded.

"No one else was expected."

"I see. Is Miss Pedwardine at home?"

"I believe she's upstairs, shall I call her?"

"It's just that she usually likes to pay her bill on delivery."

"Oh, I think that task has been allotted to me."

"But how ca..."

"Now I need you to help me, Nicky, I'm on trial here."

"Right, this is the bill." He put it into RK's hand.

"How much is it?'"

"Oh, er...mm, sorry," Nicky mumbled as he realised his blunder. He twisted his head to peek at the bill in RH's hand and said, "In total the bill comes to £31. 67."

RK felt with her hands along the edge of the kitchen table until she reached a knob jutting out that indicated the position of a drawer. She pulled it open and let her fingers sense the notes and coins that Jennifer had told her were there.

Nicky could see at a glance there was sufficient cash to meet the bill but he waited patiently for RK to pick it up and hand to him what she thought was the appropriate amount.

Cautiously RK fingered the notes. "I'm not sure which is which. I can't tell if this is the £20 or if it's this one." She scrunched them and then laid them flat on the surface of the table, on top of each other and then side by side.

"I'm sure you need both of these, Nicky, but I'm going to have to devise a way of determining the difference. I'll have to work on it."

RK reached for the coins. "I hope this might be easier." She picked them up between her forefinger and thumb feeling them as she did so. "This is a £1 coin and I'm sure this is 20p and this feels like a bigger version so must be 50p." She handed them to Nicky.

"Spot on RK, 3p change and, incidentally, the £20 note is slightly bigger than the £10 one."

"I see," she held out a hand. "Can I have them back? I mean just to practise," she added as Nicky again roared with laughter. He placed the notes into RK's outstretched hand and waited while she repeatedly felt them and put them on top of each other before returning them to him.

"By-the-way, it's good to have you back, RK, how are you managing," Nicky added quietly.

"Fine, thanks, Nicky. How's college?"

"Brill..."

"Is everything alright, Nicky?" Jennifer was watching quietly from the hallway to see how well RK coped dealing with the grocery order on her own.

"Yes, thankyou, Miss Pedwardine, I'm just on my way. Bye, RK." Nicky turned back, looked directly at Miss Pedwardine and murmured hesitantly, "It hasn't been chec..."

"That's fine, Nicky, thankyou," Jennifer replied thinking that learning to deal with household situations in her present condition was a far more important exercise for RK than the checking of the groceries which were generally correct anyway.

Jennifer sensed that RK was exhausted by the physical and mental effort of the task so she reached for the kettle. "I think it's time for coffee."

Miss Pedwardine might be a stickler for order and routine but she was also astute and alert to other people's needs. RK was grateful to her at this moment for her thoughtfulness. With care she felt her way back to the sitting room and eased herself into the high-backed armchair situated to one side of the fireplace with a sigh of relief. Whilst the physiotherapist was pleased with RK's progress there were times when prolonged standing caused her healing legs considerable discomfort.

Throughout the days that followed it almost became possible to forget this moment of caring so caught up in the rigid household routine did RK become. Jennifer left home for the house group at 'Green Pastures' on Monday promptly at 6.45pm. Her visits to the butcher's were timed for 8.45am on Tuesdays and Fridays. The Vicar called in at 9.30 am on Thursday.

At 2.10pm on Wednesday Jennifer made her way to the Women's guild and she caught the bus to Norwich outside the Village Stores every third Friday morning of the month. The washing was done early Monday with ironing tackled on Tuesdays. She hoovered and polished at 8am on Tuesday and Friday; had breakfast at 7.30am, lunch at 12.30pm and tea at 5.30pm each day, if she was at home. She bought fish and chips from Shaun Cooper's mobile fish van once a month when it stopped and parked on the Village Green at Friday teatime and on the alternate fortnight bought wet fish for Friday lunch from the Ransome's fish stall on the quay.

Miss Pedwardine took the Daily Telegraph newspaper which was delivered daily and the local Journal, weekly.

Jennifer wrote two letters a day and visited someone in the village every Tuesday afternoon and had someone visit her alternate Sunday afternoons for afternoon tea. She attended the 11 o'clock Sunday morning service and 6 o'clock evensong.

She pottered in the garden for at least half an hour each day apart from Sunday and the day she went into Norwich. Saturdays she seemed to spend all day out of doors. Jennifer read avidly and frequently lamented the absence of a library in the village. "Stephen, you'll have to do something about it!" she persistently urged Doctor Cooper's youngest son who was a fellow bookworm. As if with all his studying as well as other commitments Stephen had a moment to think about establishing a library let alone doing something concrete about it. She went to bed on the dot of 10.30pm after the 10 o'clock news on TV but was not generally a great lover of the small screen.

At times, although she was some thirty-odd years younger than her hostess, RK felt she was being bulldozed to keep pace with that energetic retired lady, so much so that, even the isolation at her parents farm became attractive and the balm of Ferry Cottage so appealing in preference to the fastidiousness she experienced at 'Bakers'.

"How does she do it?" RK enquired of Emma one day when her friend had called in to see how RK was getting on in her new surroundings.

"Well, I think the busyness simply replaces the rigidity of the school timetable which governed her life for so many years."

"I guess you're right but I do wish sometimes that she wasn't quite so precise. It's very wearing."

The tedium of life at 'Bakers' was only relieved for RK on the days she was taken to the hospital for clinic appointments and physiotherapy treatment. The rest of the time boredom screamed at her over the monotonous routine but fear made her reluctant to leave the house, fear of what people would say, fear of falling over or bumping into something, fear of vehicles hitting her, fear of appearing stupid or inept, fear of not being in control. Till the bandages came off and she could see again RK preferred the seclusion of 'Bakers'. It was a safe haven, of sorts.

Sometimes she stood at the open back door and savoured the fragrance and sounds from the garden. She dare not venture down the step in case she fell. *But one day when the dressings are removed from my eyes I'll see this lovely garden again,* RK promised herself.

One afternoon after a weeding and dead-heading session in the rose beds Miss Pedwardine returned to the house to make a pot of tea. She was laden with lettuce and freshly picked tomatoes from the vines in the greenhouse. As she turned from the pathway onto the patio she caught sight of the wistful expression on RK's face as she stood by the open kitchen door. *Oh how remiss of me, that poor girl.* It suddenly hit Jennifer how claustrophobic the house must seem to a blind girl used to the countryside and wide open spaces.

"How you must miss the bird song and the scents of the flowers, RK." Jennifer quickly deposited her load onto the kitchen table and took RK's arm, "Come on, girl, you can sit in the arbour while I put on the kettle. Do not worry about the counting I will hang on to you." She manoeuvred RK down the step, across the patio and along the crazy paving to the oval lawn. "Now then, two steps up. Good. You sit here and enjoy the sounds and smells. Before long the nights will be drawing in so make the most of this Indian summer. I will be back with the tray and we will take tea together. When we have finished I will take you for a tour around the garden. You will then have news to share with your chauffeur when you travel to the hospital tomorrow."

As she sat waiting for Jennifer to return with the promised tea RK mused for a time on the list of willing volunteers that Miranda had drawn up for her benefit. Each week it was faithfully adhered to so that a number of different drivers arrived to escort her to appointments at the hospital - Miranda, Mrs Darnell, Emma, Roy and Bernice Durrant and sometimes Tessa Jenner with one of the children. Although RK was no longer required to attend daily she looked forward to the break these twice weekly visits gave her, longing for the day when her sight would be restored.

Unbidden her signature quirky grin creased her lips as she recalled the last time Roy had been her chauffeur for when he seated her in the waiting room a screw in his glasses became loose and the lens fell out. He asked assistance from the three other people sat nearby in the waiting room. One responded cheerfully and readily agreed to help look for the lost screw and lens but then he put up a hand and said regretfully, "I'm a bit handicapped at present." He was handcuffed to a dour faced man sitting next to him who turned his head away and ignored Roy's request. A woman on the other side looked on sternly and was also less than helpful so Roy turned and appealed to the receptionist for a piece of Sellotape.

"Why can't yer friend help?" the handcuffed chap shouted out.

"She's blind!"

"Oh, sorry, mate!"

How Roy had enjoyed recounting this story to all and sundry!

*But still no Dan,* RK bemoaned. *He brought me here for safety but seems to have deserted me. I haven't seen him for some weeks. Dear God, please help me understand and give me patience in this situation.*

In fact, the young police constable had not been anywhere near the house since the day he had dropped RK off at Jennifer Pedwardine's home. He had hurriedly deposited her sparse luggage inside the hallway. "I must dash, Robyn, I've been called in to work and I need to report for duty because I'm already a few hours late."

"Thanks for everything, Dan."

"Now you take care, I guarantee you'll be well looked after by Miss Pedwardine. I'll be in touch," Dan called as he rushed out of the door.

*Why hasn't he called to see me? Why hasn't he been in touch? I thought we were friends. We seemed to be so close when he was helping me in Lincolnshire. He stood up for me against Dad's bullying tactics and sorted out my hospital appointments when my family couldn't be bothered. I can hardly wait to hear his voice again and how I long to see his lovely face.*

On the morning of Emma's spell as her driver-escort to appointments at the hospital RK broached the subject of Dan's non-appearance, "Have you seen Dan around the village?"

"Now you mention it, I can't say that I have. He hasn't come into the Stores when I've been on duty and he hasn't done end-of-school road crossing patrol on any day this week." Emma paused for a moment as she manoeuvred the car onto the main road but a frown furrowed her brow as she tried to recall the last time she had seen Dan Prettyman.

"Dan didn't attend house fellowship or music practise, nor do I remember seeing him in church on Sundays. When we get back home I'll make a few inquiries."

"It's so unlike him not to be out and about in the village."

"You're right he's always involved in something in the community. I'm sure Wills or Sgt Catchpole will be able to tell us where Dan is."

"You don't think he's now regretting being overly friendly with someone who is temporarily handicapped?"

"Dan's not like that. I'm sure there's a quite valid reason for him not being around at the moment. Remember it's not just you who's not seen him. He doesn't seem to have been in touch with anyone."

True to her word the very next day Emma strolled up to the police station during her lunch break to make enquiries concerning PC Prettyman's whereabouts. Sgt Catchpole smiled at her beguilingly and chatted in his broad Suffolk tongue, but refrained from giving any facts other than, "I do believe the owd boy left a message for that there young lady on her mobile phone; the one that had short hair that do make her look like a chap."

"Thanks Tom, I guess RK hasn't yet mastered her new mobile," Emma glanced at her watch. "I've got some time before I'm due back in the shop so I'll dash along to Miss Pedwardine's house now and share that news with RK."

Within minutes Emma arrived at the back door of 'Bakers'. She stood for a moment to catch her breath then unlatched the door and walked into the kitchen.

"Hello, RK, it's Emma. I've some good news for you," she called out as she continued to make her way through to the hall sitting room where RK generally sat.

Eagerly RK listened as Emma shared the information from Tom Catchpole.

"You're right about the phone. I really haven't got the hang of it."

"Shall I have a look for you?"

"Please, Emma, it's somewhere on the sideboard."

Emma soon located the instrument and turned on the mobile. When she opened up the voicemail messages a smile tweaked her lips as she heard Dan refer to RK as his 'sweetest songbird.'

"There seems to be quite a few calls. Here, listen to the first one. When it's finished I'll move it on to the next."

"Thanks, Emma."

When they reached the end of the list Emma asked, "Everything OK?"

"Mmm," RK said quietly. "Dan has been seconded to a team in Norwich. He can't say anymore about it in case it compromises the investigation."

Emma rose from her chair. "Well, that is good news. If only you'd known how to use this thing you wouldn't have got into such a stew about Dan's absence from the village."

"You're right. It's one of the frustrations of not being able to do things for myself."

"RK, if you really want to learn to use this mobile phone properly I suggest we ask one of the lads to give you a lesson."

"Yes, this new technology seems to be like a sixth sense to them. But I really don't want to put anyone to a lot of trouble, Emma, I'm sure it won't be long now before the dressings come off my eyes and I'll be able to see for myself."

"In the meantime you're unable to keep in touch with anyone."

"I suppose you're right. Maybe, if I discover how to master this machine I won't feel so isolated." Her face creased into a grin. "You'll live to regret your powers of persuasion, Emma, when I'm calling you a hundred times a day."

Emma laughed. "At least you'll have that choice if you learn how to use it. Now, let me think. The older lads would probably be too technical, anxious to show off their expertise, and I guess Keir and Daniel would have the knowledge but not the patience to teach someone else."

"I suppose the girls would get silly and giggly."

Emma smiled. "The younger ones certainly and I'm sure the older girls would be self-conscious about showing someone of your 'mature years' how to do something that to them is as easy as breathing."

"They probably think I'm of the generation who ought to know how to do it anyway. I feel such a duffer!"

"I don't expect they realise it now requires a totally different approach especially as it operates on voice recognition."

"Because I'm blind?"

"Yes and for that reason I think the ideal teacher would be Gil, nothing fazes him and for one so young he has tremendous patience and sensitivity."

"But Gil seems to live in a dream world all his own." Emma laughed.

"It's true," RK continued indignantly. "He's always got his head in a book and is totally unaware of what's going on around him."

"I still think he's the best one to teach you."

"We'll see."

Frustratingly for Dan he had been unable to share his whereabouts with his friends because of the sensitive nature of the investigation he was involved in. However, following the arrest of the suspects in the case he was dealing with the young constable was reassigned to his normal duties in Newton Westerby.

It was towards the end of the week that Dan returned to the village and, as previously promised, he called in to 'Bakers' to discuss the installation of security locks on Jennifer Pedwardine's windows. RK's heart danced at the sound of her friend's voice. It*'s been ages since I've seen you. I've missed you, Dan.*

Miss Pedwardine noticed RK, whilst quiet in the background, held her head erect and alert and appeared attentive to all PC Prettyman was saying. He had a lovely rich mellow voice which had retained some of his native Suffolk accent.

"It is a disgrace that we householders have to take such drastic measures, particularly in a quiet location like Newton Westerby."

"I'm sorry to say, Miss Pedwardine, this sort of neighbourhood and these types of properties are now being targeted by the burgling fraternity."

"I thought that was taken care of with Joe and Josh Cook behind bars."

"I'm afraid others have jumped on the band-wagon."

Jennifer closed her eyes for a second and had a moment of inspiration.

"Constable, when will you be coming to fix the locks?"

"Oh, it won't be me, Miss Pedwardine. Your leaded lights are a specialist job. We appoint a skilled locksmith to carry out the work."

"I see," Jennifer turned and caught the change in countenance in RK's face.

"In that case, maybe you could return when the job is finished, check that it is completed to the highest specifications and share coffee with us."

"Be delighted to."

Miss Pedwardine smiled her thanks at Dan. Then saw a wistful smile on RK's lips and was satisfied.

*Thankyou, God, a breakthrough!*

"Will you be able to come to the garden party on Saturday?"

"I am on duty but I'll do my best to drop in sometime during the afternoon."

"Good, we look forward to seeing you then."

Dan leaned towards RK and placed a hand upon her shoulder. "Are you going to be there, Robyn?"

*Why is it every time Dan stands near to me I have this inordinate need for fresh air? Is it because I forget to breathe or because his presence sparks a desire for greater closeness?*

"Robyn?"

"Oh, yes, I'll be there," she gasped.

Miss Pedwardine raised her eyebrows in surprise at RK's barely audible response.

"Then I will do my very best to keep crime to a minimum so that I can share a cup of tea with you."

"I shall really look forward to that," RK told him eagerly as colour rapidly warmed her cheeks.

As Miss Pedwardine saw the constable out RK's face was wreathed in smiles.

*We're still friends!*

*Only friends? Anything else is probably out of the question, now.*

RK slowly shook her head and placed a hand across her heart to ease the pain that seemed to lodge there.

# Chapter Ten

❖

Early on the morning of the day of the garden party Rachel Durrant, Newton Westerby's mobile hairdresser, called at 'Bakers' to style RK's hair.

The area by the sink of the downstairs cloakroom had been transformed into a temporary hair salon. RK was sat on a chair in front of the mirror draped in towels and a plastic cape.

"Do you really want to keep it this length?" Rachel asked as she fingered the long, black tresses. It was no longer the lank, unkempt hair that had shocked the vicar and Mrs Darnell two months previously because Miss Pedwardine had asked for Rachel's help when she realised RK was struggling to cope with her growing hair. Initially, Rachel had treated RK like her other home clients, washing, trimming and blow-drying the hair into style. But after a couple of visits she recognized this approach wasn't helping RK's self-esteem. RK couldn't see or appreciate the end result nor understand if this was the case why it was necessary to make such an effort to keep her hair looking nice.

"Why don't you just cut it all off," RK had said crossly, "it will cause less fuss."

So, Rachel changed tack. She collected together some different shaped bottle caps and devised a scheme to enable RK to manage her own hair. Discreetly she drew Jennifer to one side and explained the routine to her while RK was in the shower.

"Miss Pedwardine, would you mind if I asked Ben to put up a shelf in the shower room?"

"No, go ahead. Do anything that will make life easier for RK."

"Would you fill up these caps and place them on the shelf each time RK has a shower?"

"Certainly," Jennifer scrutinized the caps, "but which is which?"

"Dumpy is first and for shampoo, tall and thin is next and for conditioner. The one with a spout is third and to be filled with shower gel."

"Right, so colour doesn't mat..."

Rachel emphatically shook her head. "Shape and order is what matters; dumpy, thin, spout."

Jennifer nodded.

"Now, where is there an easily accessible socket for the hair-dryer and hot air brush?"

Jennifer indicated two possibilities.

"I'll ask RK which position she finds easiest to use?"

RK made her choice and for many sessions Rachel patiently taught her to partially blow-dry her hair and then style it with the hot brush by feeling her way through each movement. Gradually RK felt a sense of achievement and by touch knew how her hair was arranged and draping on her shoulders. After a time Rachel simply called in occasionally to restyle and give her trim.

"Now, how does that feel?"

RK gently shook her head till her raven locks swung gently across her shoulders, and then let her fingers flow lightly through her hair.

"That feels really good, Rachel, thanks."

"Yes, we've got it back to a really excellent condition," said Rachel as she tweaked one or two loose ends. "It has a lovely sheen now and this cut nicely frames your face."

RK laughed. "That's due to your bullying tactics."

Rachel chuckled as she hugged her friend's shoulders. "Not at all, more like your determination to succeed. Look how you mastered the washing regime and persevered to get the hot air brush technique correct."

"No, your constant nagging achieved that."

"It was worth it, wasn't it? You look charming. Have a really good day. Lots of your friends will be here so enjoy their company. I saw a few early-birds walking around the garden when I arrived."

"Aren't you staying?"

"No, I have three more clients this morning but I did promise the children we would come after lunch."

"I see," said RK hesitantly who had hoped to make the entrance to her first public event since her return to the village in company with someone familiar. Rachel sensed a deep reluctance on RK's part to attend the garden party so as she gathered her equipment together Rachel jollied RK along.

"The weather forecast is promising so you make the most of the occasion."

"But I don't know who's going to be there and I can't see the..."

"RK don't be such a wimp," Rachel scolded her friend. "It's going to be a great day, enjoy it."

RK shook her head.

"Emma said she will pop over later this afternoon, work permitting, and I'm sure Mrs Darnell won't be able to resist an opportunity to stroll around Miss Pedwardine's delightful garden. I guess the Jenner and Catton youngsters will be here especially if they know there's a possibility of seeing you. So, you'll have company. I wouldn't be at all surprised if Lord Edmund doesn't come to lend a hand. I also heard that Dan plans to be around sometime during the afternoon."

A smile lit up RK's face as she recalled Dan's promise to put in an appearance. The prospect of the day ahead began to look more promising, though she wasn't quite sure where the importance of Lord Edmund's presence fitted into the proceedings.

---

Miss Pedwardine's Autumn Garden Party was regarded by the majority of people who attended to be a most successful day but Dan thought otherwise. He was desperately disappointed with the discourteous manner Robyn displayed towards her friends that he witnessed throughout the afternoon. Later that evening as they sat together on the rustic bench beneath the majestic chestnut tree in the twilight Dan voiced his concerns.

"Whatever was the matter with you today, Robyn?"

"What do you mean?"

"Well, you were awfully off-hand with everyone."

"You don't know what it's like to be blind. Knowing people are staring at you and not being in a position to respond appropriately is frustrating," RK retorted angrily.

"But you didn't give anyone the opportunity to share your experience," Dan chided, reminding Robyn how churlish she had been to those who simply wanted to chat and spend time with her.

"How can they?"

"The Jenner children wanted to show you the posies they had made for the competition."

"There you are then! How could I see them?"

"You could have felt them and allowed Pansy and Lily to describe them to you." Dan paused to let his words sink in. "Keir had painstakingly included a toy motor bike into his design especially for you. Even if you couldn't see his crestfallen face when you pushed him away you surely must have heard the disappointment in his voice."

"Don't talk nonsense."

"I never had you down as a selfish person, Robyn, but you've allowed this one thing to make you hard and uncaring. You're so absorbed in yourself you're in danger of becoming quite obnoxious."

"Dan, you've no idea what you're talking about."

"Robyn, if I hadn't witnessed it with my own eyes I wouldn't have believed you were capable of such unkindness."

"Don't talk nonsense."

"Stop repeating yourself, Robyn. To deliberately hurt people you were once so fond of, particularly the children, really gets my goat!"

"You're exaggerating, Dan."

"No, I'm not. They just wanted to show they still love and accept you as you are."

"I'm not the same."

"No you're not and that's what disappoints me."

"So?"

"Why on earth couldn't you tell them a story when they asked you?"

"How could I?"

"You haven't lost your memory, have you? The children remembered you couldn't read at the moment so they kindly asked you to do something you could do and always did well, tell them a story."

"But..."

"No buts; Miss Robyn Dickinson-Bond was too wrapped up in herself to think of the generosity of the likes of Keir and Lily, Pansy, as well as, Daniel and Kirsty."

"Were they there, too?"

"Yes, if you had cared to listen, they were also clamouring for their favourite stories you used to tell them."

"Oh!"

"Yes, oh! You've a mighty lot of explaining to do, as to why you treated your young friends so harshly."

"But I couldn't see who was there."

"Does that matter? Lily was trying to describe people and things to you but you wouldn't listen. The disappointment etched on their faces when it was evident you weren't interested was echoed in their voices."

"I didn't notice," RK muttered.

"You'd have heard it if you'd bothered to listen. For someone who, not so very long ago, boasted she'd cleverly mastered the art of listening well you need to give a jolly good reason as to why you didn't listen today. Even Mirry was shocked by your rudeness. It takes a lot to rile her but she walked away from you quite distressed."

"But Dan..."

By now Dan had really got his dander up so raised his arm in a gesture to wave her words away. "Robyn, you're going to need apologies by the bucket load." RK was unaware of Dan's action but she could now sense his displeasure by the tone of his voice.

Fearing he may have said too much Dan rose abruptly and stomped off across the garden without a word of farewell. He caught Emma's arm as she passed by him and quietly said, "Would you stop by Robyn, Em. She's in a bit of a state."

"Sure, Dan."

"We've had words over her irritable manner towards the children."

"I see," Emma glanced across to where RK was sitting then turned back, looked up at Dan, and nodded with understanding.

"I'll just finish helping to put these away then stroll over in a few minutes."

"Thanks, Em."

But RK, shaken and shamed by Dan's words, sat thinking more closely about her attitude throughout the day towards those who had come to speak with her, simply wanted to slouch away to her room and avoid further confrontation with anybody.

---

On her next day off Emma walked purposefully down the lane to 'Bakers'.

"Hi, RK," she called out as she pushed open the back door. "Slip on your jacket, we're going out for coffee."

"Oh, no," RK protested.

"I want to show you my new enterprise," Emma confided excitedly, "and I'd welcome the benefit of your opinion. I won't take no for an answer, so come on, get ready."

After Dan had voiced his concerns to her at the end of the garden party Emma tried to converse with RK but her friend had turned away and clammed up. Emma had discussed with her husband her own misgivings with regard to RK's withdrawn manner and queried how best to tackle it but Doctor Roger appraised RK's condition from a professional standpoint.

"We have a rather unhealthy scenario so we must encourage her to get out and about in the village, mix with people more."

"Yes, I agree, RK's been a recluse for long enough. Her confidence needs a boost."

"It's almost as though her life is on hold till the dressings come off..."

"...when she can see again and everything will be back to normal," Emma finished the sentence for him.

"Sweetheart, why don't you take her shopping or out for a coffee. Prove to her that there are good things she can do, now."

"Mmm, that sounds a great idea. She certainly seems to be in limbo till her sight returns. I'll see what I can arrange."

"Thanks, Carrots," Roger affectionately squeezed his wife's shoulders as he leant forwards to place a kiss on the top of her head. "I'm sure if anyone can entice her out, you can."

Emma laughed as she shook her head, "My powers of persuasion seemed to be somewhat lacking on the day of Dave and Jansy's wedding. RK refused point blank to go."

"That was her loss. It was a really lovely occasion, though not as special as ours," He smiled lovingly at Emma, "and all eyes were on the bride and groom so RK would not have been conspicuous at all though many would have been pleased to see her."

So, it was just a few days later that Emma took RK to the new coffee shop insisting she count the footsteps on the walk between the house and the Stores. RK, clinging to Emma's arm, reluctantly concentrated on her task. Her steps faltered when a vehicle passed them but Emma continued walking so RK had no option but to keep up with her. They passed the bungalow where Emma's sister Alex lived with her husband Graeme and little daughter Bethany.

"We'll stop here," Emma told RK. "How many steps?"

"157," replied RK.

"Now reach out your right hand."

RK complied with the request.

"What can you feel?"

"A fence?"

"Yes, now, run your fingers along the top and round the corner." RK let her fingers explore the criss-cross arrangement of wood.

"We're standing where the two boundary fences of Alex and Graeme's garden meet. So from Miss Pedwardine's gate to the apex of the fence is 157 steps."

RK stood nonplussed by the edge of the fence as Emma continued, "Now take nine strides across the driveway and you'll reach the back wall of the Stores."

Emma stepped to the opposite side but RK remained rooted to the spot.

"Come on, RK, it's all clear."

Still she would not move. Emma purposefully strode back, took RK's arm and guided her across the entrance. "There are no vehicles, no bikes, prams or scooters. In fact there aren't even any people. It's just you and me, so let's try it again, you've nothing to fear." RK bristled.

Emma had unwittingly hit on the nerve of RK's vulnerability.

"I can't do this, Emma."

"Yes, you can. Someone who's got the guts to master a Harley-Davidson can step nine paces across a driveway."

RK shook her head.

"Right," said Emma in her school teacher's no-nonsense voice, "I am going to shout aloud Edward Lear's poem at the top of my voice. Follow the sound. If you don't come quickly you'll soon have an audience. THE OWL AND THE PUSSYCAT WENT TO SEA IN A BEAUTIFU..."

"I made it," RK said breathlessly, reaching out to grab Emma's arm.

There was a clatter behind them. "Just in time by the sound of it," Emma whispered conspiratorially in RK's ear.

Jilly Briggs rushed out of the kitchen door, almost bumping into Emma. "Oh, Em, is everything alright? We heard such a shouting we thought something was wrong."

"Sorry about that, Jilly, everything's fine. RK and I are just coming in for a coffee."

Jilly touched RK on the shoulder. "It's nice to see you out and about, RK, enjoy your coffee. There are scones fresh from the oven, too."

"Than...k...you," RK stammered still recovering from the shock tactics Emma had used to get her to walk the last nine steps.

Jilly returned to her tasks in the Stores kitchen and Emma walked to stand in front of RK.

"Right, we've come 157 steps to the corner of Alex's fence. How many across the drive?"

"Nine."

"With your right hand on the wall you are facing up towards the shop, behind you is 'Bakers'. If you make a 90 degree turn you are facing a lift which will take us up to the coffee lounge. It's four paces to the doors and the controls are on the left hand side."

Tentatively RK followed Emma's instructions. With a hand against what felt like a cool metal surface RK shuffled along the width of the door and groped for the control buttons.

"Press," instructed Emma.

"But it might be the wrong one."

"Try it and see."

"The doors are closed," an automated voice informed them.

RK fumbled till she found another button. "The doors are opening. Enter. Press the button on your left to go up." RK complied. With a faint whirring sound the lift moved to the upper floor. Emma remained silent.

"The doors are opening. Alight and turn right."

"You need to remember to turn round to get out of the lift. Now move forwards using your hands to feel the way. You can't hurt anything or fall over. I'm right beside you." RK stood rigid.

"Come on," cajoled Emma "I'm more than ready for a coffee and I need you to sample the scones and tell me what you think."

"Are there many people here?" RK whispered.

Emma laughed. "Not a soul; just you and me. We don't open for another ten minutes or so. I thought I'd give you chance to get your bearings before other customers come in."

RK relaxed and the relief showed on her face.

"The original dado is still on the wall providing a good marker to follow," Emma explained.

RK nodded and let her hand linger on the waist high wooden guide before allowing it to lead her to the seating area. She cautiously meandered across the floor feeling the backs of chairs. Abruptly she stopped. "Who's that?"

"Oh, it's only Rosie. She's checking the tables are all laid up correctly and ready for customers." Emma smiled across at Rosie and indicated that she should stop by their table when RK was settled. "If you'd like to choose a place to sit she will be over presently to take our order."

Instantly RK ceased mooching about and carefully sat down on the chair she was holding onto hoping she had chosen an inconspicuous spot.

Emma manoeuvred herself onto a chair to the right of RK which gave her a panoramic view of the coffee lounge. In a short while she intended to describe in detail to RK the décor, the furnishings, the layout of the tables as well as the menu. Her objective being to ensure RK felt so comfortable in her surroundings she would be encouraged to venture out on her own.

"It smells nice in here," RK said as soon as she was seated.

"Inviting?"

"Certainly, a warm, enticing aroma of baking that makes you want to sample whatever is cooking."

"That's good. We've really tried to create an appealing atmosphere with the decoration and table settings and if you feel the lingering smell of baking adds to the ambience I think that is something important to focus on."

"Well, I can only imagine what it looks like in here but the smell would certainly entice me to want to come back again."

"I hope the taste is as good and doesn't disappoint you. Here is Rosie to take our order."

For the next half an hour or so, over freshly ground coffee and newly baked cherry scones, the two friends discussed the changes that had been made to Emma's flat in order to create the tea and coffee lounge. They spoke of the purpose built lift to enable the elderly and parents with young children to negotiate the trip from the ground floor to the upper storey to reach the tea rooms as an alternative to the original stairs. Emma described with her artist's eye the rich red and gold décor and RK handled the fabric of the table linen. Then the friends discussed the variety of food that was being offered on the menu throughout the day.

As the coffee shop began to fill with customers one or two of the locals came up to their table and greeted RK with warmth and genuine delight. A number sat and chatted for a while and spoke about what different people had done with RK's best interests in mind.

"I hear Jackie Cooper's contacted the Braille Society on your behalf. I hope they come up with something useful that will help you," said Mrs Saunders.

"Yes, I heard, too, that Dan Prettyman got in touch with the Royal Institute for Blind people and Stephen Cooper picked up some literature from the Norwich library about the Torch trust, whatever that is."

"Gil Jenner has been on the web site of a company in Norfolk who specialise in talking microwaves and clocks and other items you might find useful about the home."

This news and the tenor of the subsequent discussion perturbed RK so she shut herself off from the flow of conversation around her. *They all seem convinced I will never see again.*

"Hope you'll find it all useful, RK. We so want you to do well."

"We're glad you've come back to the village. We missed you."

"We'll be only too glad to ass..."

Bernice Durrant paused in mid-sentence when Billy Knights' mother roughly pushed passed her and came up to Emma's table. She swiped RK viciously with a rolled up magazine. Stunned by her action everyone gasped and for a moment froze but Mrs Knights continued to beat RK around the head alternatively with her handbag and the rolled up magazine.

"So, yew is the hoity-toity Miss who's condemned m'bor to a prison cell."

Emma flew off her seat. "Mrs Knights please stop that." She put out her hands to stop the assault on her friend but Mrs Knights continued her attack and repeatedly hit RK with her improvised weapons. Others came to Emma's assistance but were also caught in the onslaught. The frenzy continued. At a nod from Emma, Rosie picked up the phone and dialled the Police Station House hoping that PC Dan or Sgt Catchpole would be available and not out on another call.

Emma raised her voice, "Mrs Knights, RK can't see what you're doing. She's blind. You're going to cause serious hurt unless you stop."

"What! She can't see? How can she accuse m'bor, then, ugh?" Mrs Knights yelled.

The hubbub in the tea rooms died down. Customers turned their eyes to the table in the corner, held their breath and waited.

The beating stopped but the fury increased. The angry woman bent down and put her face in RK's. "I'll see you rot in hell," she hissed.

# Chapter Eleven

The following Thursday morning Emma's turn on the hospital rota cropped up again. The altercation in the coffee lounge was only mentioned briefly as she assisted RK into the car. Emma was glad the unpleasant incident involving Mrs Knights had been dealt with calmly and succinctly by Sgt Catchpole. It could have turned really nasty. When the Sergeant had explained to RK the relationship of her attacker to the young man RK had identified as the intruder passing on drugs in her garden she was adamant she didn't want the matter taken any further. "Please, Sergeant, let the lady go. She only reacted as any mother would at the imprisonment of her child. I'm fine and I don't want to press charges."

As they travelled, unbeknown to Emma or RK, a decision had been made at the hospital by the eye specialist. This was to be the momentous day RK had been waiting for; the removal of the dressings from her eyes. On arrival at the city hospital this news was imparted to RK as she, accompanied by Emma, was escorted into the consulting room.

RK held her breath in anticipation. A nurse dimmed the lights and the doctor gently removed the remaining layer of dressing from her eyes.

"Open your eyes very slowly. Even though we have reduced the brightness in here it may still be too intense for your sight at this instant."

RK did as instructed but as she gradually raised her eyelids the moment came as a dreadful anti-climax. She couldn't see. The dark curtain was still there. RK clawed at her eyes in disbelief. After closer examination the specialist said quietly, "I'm afraid the condition is likely to be permanent. I'll send my report to your GP. I would like to see you again in 6 months to see if there is any change in..."

RK sat unmoving in the consulting room, stunned.

Emma's ears pricked up. She had been sitting to one side while the procedures had been taking place but after the doctor had pronounced his diagnosis she noticed RK had switched off. Emma rose. '*Your condition has us baffled.*' Seemingly in a world of her own RK was totally unaware of the doctor's explanation and rationale behind his recommended course of action. '*There is no obvious sign of damage, yet the lack of response in critical areas suggest irreversible trauma...*'

RK remained in her seat unable to move.

Emma stepped forward.

"Thankyou for your time, Doctor, as you can see my friend is overcome by the devastating news you have given her. I'll take her home, now. I'll explain what you have recommended and if you forward a full report to her GP, I know he will do the same."

With her friend's assistance RK managed to make her way to Emma's car with tears streaming down her face.

"I'm blind, Emma! Blind!" she spat out. "I'll never see again. I have to live in the dark forever!"

Once inside the car Emma tried to calm RK down but RK was struggling with the warring factions inside her head.

"Blind!" she shouted then angrily clamped her hands over her ears and pulled at her hair as she heard other cars moving about the car park and on to the road. Everyone was going somewhere. They could see where they were going. She just sat and listened and agonized over her condition.

"This is the end, Emma. My life has suddenly come to a standstill and I can do nothing about it. That lorry driver might just as well have run over me. He would have saved me from this agony."

For once Emma was lost for words.

"I feel so vulnerable."

It was a very dejected RK that Emma drove back to the village.

"Emma, what on earth am I going to do?"

"You're going to pray and trust and learn how to adapt," replied Emma with more confidence than she felt, for she, too, had been shaken by the Doctor's prognosis, "and we're all going to help you achieve that."

"That's a very glib response, Emma. How can you expect me to trust God? To me, this is like a death sentence. I really thought it was just a temporary setback. Now, I learn it's to be forever."

"Consider it an unknown adventure."

"More like a catastrophic calamity," RK retorted bitterly.

Against her better judgement the rigid schedule RK had become accustomed to at Miss Pedwardine's became the framework on which to hang her broken life. Doctor Roger constantly emphasized the necessity of routine for RK.

"Please continue the established pattern, Jennifer, because I am hoping familiarity will enable RK to adjust more readily to the permanency of her condition."

So, Jennifer deliberately did not change her routine. RK and her needs were simply absorbed into it. The retired school mistress persisted with the step counting in order to encourage RK's independence. She insisted RK listen for certain sounds and learn to know the time of day or identify an activity or person by what she could hear just as she had on her parents Lincolnshire farm in the early days following her accident. But many times frustration at her sight loss got the better of her.

However, while RK had constant peace and quietness at Miss Pedwardine's she was not recovering as quickly as Doctor Roger had anticipated. She was unwilling to do things for herself when she first moved in to 'Bakers' for fear of making a mistake but to his chagrin following the shattering news from the eye specialist RK withdrew into herself and refused to do anything at all because she felt it was pointless going on with her life. The demons that previously had plagued her threatened to engulf her again.

In spite of this Jennifer's strict schoolmarm regime gradually necessitated RK putting her mind to doing some things in the house by touch, for instance polishing, making her bed and peeling the vegetables. "If you don't, they won't get done. You'll live in a mess and you'll be the one going hungry," was her ultimatum. But it seemed as if RK was not truly coming to terms with the permanence of her condition. She frequently put off doing anything positive in the hope that one morning she would wake up able to see and find that the accident that cost her sight was a bad dream. She refused to go out or meet with people. So, at first, people came to her.

Occasionally, Rachel or Miranda dropped in for coffee and did their utmost to encourage a positive attitude in RK's approach to living. One time, Tessa Jenner visited with her younger children who were so fond of RK hoping they could persuade her to get involved with village life again but to no avail.

Steadily, further variations were subtly thrown in for RK's benefit, for instance, Emma came with Roger when he visited RK and while the Doctor spoke with Miss Pedwardine about RK's progress Emma coaxed RK into the garden. With her artist's eye Emma described the unfolding autumn scene before her and commented on the fragrance of the late flowers, the diminishing warmth of the sun and the increasing breeze from the sea. Emma did all she could to persuade RK to engage with the immediate world around her. She had RK touching the foliage and seed heads as they passed by them.

Similarly, Penny Darnell accompanied her husband to 'Bakers' and whilst Jennifer and Hugh discussed church business Penny took time to speak with RK and tried to get her to talk, acknowledge and share her thoughts and feelings.

On one occasion in exasperation Penny bundled RK through the front door and into her car. It happened so quickly RK didn't have chance to object. Penny simply drove to the Ship Inn car park and had RK walking along the harbour wall before she realised her intent. For some moments Penny let RK listen to and absorb the sounds of the harbour that were precious to her, the sounds that had so captivated her when she first came to the village. Penny Darnell was a no-nonsense type of person and felt there were situations in life that needed dealing with head-on so she spoke directly with RK about her situation.

"You have to put the past behind you, RK, live in the present and look forward to the future ev..."

"But I..."

"...even though it's going to be very different to the one you had envisaged."

"How can I?" RK whined.

"Oh come now, RK, it isn't in your nature to moan or give up on things. It isn't too long ago that you shared with me the moment when God gave you a promise, *I have plans for you*. You were eager at that time to be positive. Do you remember?"

Very slowly RK nodded her head.

"Have you forgotten how special those words were to you?"

"Mmm, I think with everything else that's been going on I've let them slip from my mind."

"Maybe your mind needs to be refreshed so that you can get back on track and make the most of the life you have been given. Give it some thought for a day or two and then if you wish we can get together and consider some concrete ways to make those 'plans' flourish. I think coming to the Sunday service might be a good place to start and possibly linking up with one of the House study groups would also be helpful."

"I would like that."

Penny put the wheels in motion and the following Sunday RK walked with Jennifer to the morning service and on Wednesday evening Graeme Castleton called at

'Bakers' to accompany her to the House group held at their home.

Adam, Laura and the children also came to visit one afternoon during a week-end but it was a disaster. RK hadn't had a good day. At coffee time she dropped her mug which smashed on the kitchen floor and although she had picked up the broken pieces with great care one of the jagged edges had cut her thumb. Then, at lunch time she knocked over her glass of water and spilled food down the front of her clothes. She'd trapped a finger when closing the cloakroom door and as a consequence tripped over the legs of the armchair because she was focussing on the pain in her hand not on counting her steps.

So, by the time her visitors arrived RK was feeling pretty fed up with herself and despite Adam's flamboyance and Daniel and Kirsty's obvious pleasure at seeing her she found it difficult to lift her spirits.

Daniel chatted excitedly about events and people in the village. "A man was poking around in the churchyard last Monday morning..."

"And Mr Peek was very cross," butted in Kirsten.

"'cos he trampled right on top of the graves," finished Daniel.

"Then on Tuesday he was back again with a detective machine..."

"A metal detector, Kirsty."

"That's what I said and Rev Hugh said it was in a prop rate..."

"Inappropriate, Kirsty, dear," corrected Adam.

"I said that."

"This morning when we walked down by the quay we saw him getting on a boat."

"Before that we watched him through the window of Stephen's shop..."

"An' he was pulling all the papers out of boxes and making a drefful mess..."

"Dreadful, Kirsty."

"Yes."

"Stephen looked cross."

"I'm not surprised they were old maps and land documents of the local area. Originals and the only copies in some cases, I guess."

"An' he climbed over Stephen's fence to poke in the smithy with the detective thing.'

"Oh dear!" RK's leg was throbbing where she had knocked it earlier and she was finding it difficult to concentrate on the children's rambling chatter.

Thinking RK look confused Laura asked, "D-did you know about S-Stephen's s-shop, RK?"

RK shook her head. "I know when he wasn't on the sports field or fiddling with bits of wood he always had his head in a book, usually a first edition or something out of print."

"Th-they l-looked h-heavy g-going to me."

"I think Trixie got exasperated with the quantity of books and boxes of books left lying around in Stephen's room when he went off to college," added Adam.

"I b-believe th-there were so many th-they had s-sp-sp-illed over into the s-spare room and also t-taken over what h-had once been Roger's room."

"Doctor John persuaded Trixie it would be a good investment to give Stephen sufficient money for his twenty-first birthday to purchase Kezia's Wood, clear it to discover what building might still be standing amongst the woods, and restore or develop what he found into a store for his books," explained Adam, "but the clearance has revealed far more hidden in the undergrowth than they imagined."

"I-it's been empty and d-derelict for y-years," said Laura.

"All dark and spooky," Daniel croaked theatrically.

"Although unkempt, Doctor John believed it had potential and I think the idea was that Stephen should use the carpentry skills he's acquired at college to renovate the place. With professional advice and volunteer help he's done wonders on the site."

"H-his c-cottage is the one at the end of the s-site."

"Upstairs there is room for sleeping quarters and a sitting room as well as a miniscule bathroom and downstairs he discovered the shop facility with some original fittings. Beyond that, on ground level, he has created a living room cum kitchen and unearthed a scullery with an original leaded stove."

"What a lot of work!"

"Y.yes it was. At first S-Stephen only c-came home at weekends..."

"...but lots of people helped to clear the mess away."

"Yeah, I picked loads of grass and put it in the big bin."

"A skip!"

"It didn't skip," said Kirsten indignantly, "'cos a lorry picked it up with chains."

"Stephen still has to complete his English Degree at the UEA but all his spare time is spent on site. He's discovered a ramshackle smithy along with associated implements and tools and stacks of fascinating records in ledgers and documents which I've had the task of deciphering. They contain valuable information about the history of our village and people who lived here over a hundred years ago."

"He's done up the shop and you'd like it RK 'cos..." said Daniel.

"It's got millions of books."

"That's an exaggeration, Kirsty."

"Well, it's lots."

"It's still spooky 'cos it's got loads of tall, dark shelves all full of books," Daniel spoke with a deep, slow, theatrical voice accompanied by dramatic actions.

"It's got a funny smell, too," said Kirsten wrinkling up her nose, "a bit like the horsey smell at the Beck'nsdale's farm."

"You must go and have a look one day, RK," insisted Daniel, "you'll love it."

"It's not new books but very, very old ones."

"Some are from when Daddy was young."

"Oh, so very old," laughed Adam.

"We'll take you then you can see."

"Don't be silly," hissed Daniel "she can't see."

"Oh, I forgot," tears started in Kirsten's eyes. Startled, she stared at RK and ran to Laura for comfort. Laura put her good arm around her daughter and looked up at Adam.

Poppy started to fidget. She didn't like being confined to one space for so long especially as there was very little to occupy her. Adam swung her up on to his shoulder. Her head almost hit the low ceiling. "Come on, Honeybun, we'll go out and investigate in the garden. Who's coming with us?"

"Me."

"And me."

"You go too, Laura, I believe the garden is looking exceptionally good at the moment even though it is so late in the season."

RK was in a lot of pain and knew she was being particularly bad company and her sense of guilt at letting the little family down threatened to take her back into despondency as feelings of inadequacy overwhelmed her.

A couple of days after the Catton's visit Doctor Roger called at 'Bakers' intent on getting RK to face up to the reality of her condition. He felt, like Penny Darnell, an honest, open and direct approach was required.

"Living with sight loss and coming to terms with the fact that you have a sight problem can be very tough, RK, but..."

"Doc, that is an understatement. I really believed it was going to be a brief inconvenience. How on earth am I going to cope with this for the rest of my life?"

"I agree it's going to take some adjustment but you can do it, RK."

"I can't read, I can't write, I can't ride. I can't see, so how can I do anything else?"

"Hey, RK, slow down."

"Doc, get real! I was expecting to return to the cottage shortly and, when I'd regained my strength, get back to work. There's no way I can do that now."

"Why not?"

"Use your sense!"

"No, you use yours, RK."

"What do you mean?"

"You've been blessed with six senses."

"Six?"

"Yes, sight, hearing, smell, touch, taste and you have an abundance of common sense, or so I'm told."

"And I've been robbed by someone's carelessness of the most important one, my sight," alleged RK bitterly. "My common sense says how can I work if I'm blind? How can I look after children if I can't see them?"

"I recognize that dealing with the emotional and practical impact of changes to your sight can be overwhelming but not insurmountable, and you've still got all your other senses intact."

"It's not the breeze in the park you're making it out to be, Doc. I can't see!"

"Let's change tack. What about the things you can do?"

"Such as?"

"Well, you can talk, you can hear, smell, taste and feel. Your walking is improving daily, so move..."

"Oh OK, but how can I use some of these if I'm unable to see what I'm doing?"

"It will take some adjustment."

"But if I can't cook or wash or iron how can I be independent?"

"You will. It'll be a new learning curve, certainly."

"What do you mean?"

"Consider it a challenge, like learning another language, or a new skill like swimming or cooking, you name it, this is starting afresh."

"Oh yeah! I can't do that."

"I think you can."

"How?"

"I'll be quite candied with you, RK, you have one of three choices. Number one, you can sit and do nothing and as a consequence vegetate, physically and mentally. Number two, I can bully you into doing the things I think you should be doing or thirdly, together we can devise a plan of action that is paced and achievable, using the skills you already have."

"You make it sound so simple."

"It is."

RK shook her head in disbelief.

"I'm not asking you to climb Mount Everest or expecting you to swim the Channel."

"It almost feels like it, Doc."

"Oh, come on, now, RK. How do you manage here at Miss Pedwardine's?"

"Well, as you well know, Emma and Jennifer counted the number of steps between everything before I moved in. In the early days they accompanied me or followed me around like a mother hen constantly reminding me. Now I usually move quite smoothly without banging into anything."

"There you are, a combination of two skills you already have, counting and walking, as well as memory."

RK grinned, "OK Doc, I understand what you mean."

"Good, we'll build on what you already know and at the same time gradually introduce new challenges into the mix."

"Who's the 'we' you keep referring to?"

"Well, I have to work on that but I promise you I will not introduce anyone or anything you are not comfortable with. Initially, if it meets with your approval, I propose involving Miranda."

"Right!"

"She'll be here during her lunch-break."

"Today?"

"Yes, you'll be going out, so please be ready."

"Oh?"

"More walking and counting practise."

"You're quite a task master, Doc."

"I'm determined you're going to succeed."

"Yes, sir!" RK replied jovially but her knees quaked and deep down a sinking feeling churned in the pit of her stomach.

# Chapter Twelve

❖

Miranda called for RK, just after 12.30pm, armed with a spare Dictaphone from the surgery. She placed the instrument into RK's hand.

"We're going to use this, no, you are going to use this, to record the steps you take between various locations we shall visit today."

RK pulled a face. "I really don't want to do this, Miranda," she said reticently, then leaned to her left to pinpoint the position of the sideboard in order to ease the Dictaphone onto it. She had been on tenterhooks ever since Doctor Roger had mentioned the outing with Miranda.

"Why?"

"I don't want every one staring at me."

"No one is going to stare. You haven't got two heads or an extra arm, in fact, you look quite normal to me and everyone, who knows you, will see you as their friend RK walking through the village with me, Miranda Cooper, the Docs' receptionist. Visitors will see two friends out for a stroll."

"I'm sure I'll be conspicuous because I'm not at work."

"What other people choose to think is their affair. We'll go out and enjoy each other's company while the sun is shining. By the way, there's a stiff breeze so you might like to put on a jacket."

Forewarned by Doctor Roger to encourage independence, Miranda refrained from offering to help RK, who got up from her chair and walked resignedly across to the cloakroom door. After locating the handle RK opened the door and reached down her jacket from the hook on the back. When she was ready Miranda placed the Dictaphone back into RK's hand.

"Now what can you feel?"

RK held the machine in her left hand and let the fingers of her right hand flutter over the surface.

"Feel down the side."

"Oh, there's a knob jutting out."

"Press it once."

RK did as Miranda instructed.

"We are going to leave now via the front door. Do you have your keys?" RK nodded as she patted her jacket pocket.

"Good. Now press the knob twice."

"*We are going to leave now via the front door...*" Miranda's voice spoke from the machine.

"Ooo... I didn't expect that."

"You see, it's so easy, press once to speak and record, press twice to listen to what has been recorded," Miranda spoke as she made her way towards the front door. After a few moments she realised RK had not followed her. She turned back to see her friend dithering with uncertainty.

"How am I going to recognize anyone I meet if I can't see them?"

"We'll deal with that situation when it happens, if it happens. You could always use the Dictaphone to familiarize yourself with people's voices. I hope you'll soon come to value it as a useful tool. Now are you all set?"

RK nodded, reluctantly dragging her feet as she followed Miranda through the front door dropping the latch as she passed. She carefully negotiated the step, turned back and reached out to feel for the door knob. She closed the door, felt for the keyhole with her left hand, inserted the key and turned the lock with her right. Miss Pedwardine insisted that for security reasons both locks be turned when the house was left empty.

Before RK could catch her next breath Miranda asked, "How many steps to the gate?"

"Five, I think."

"Right, you lead the way. We'll turn left out of the gate, and then start to count your steps. Don't forget to record the number of steps between each location."

"Can I hold onto your arm, I'll feel more confident? I'm still wary of bumping into things."

"Sure, anything that helps, though I can't think there is anything in front of us that you're likely to bump into. Now then, one, two, three..." *No wonder the villagers say Miranda is the world's best organizer, she's certainly organizing me.*

They set off along the lane, the breeze lifting their hair and rustling the tree branches as they passed. After fifteen more paces Miranda called a halt.

"We've reached the turning to The Close. I'll see us safely across. It will be eleven steps. Don't forget to tell your machine."

"Right!" responded RK voicing the number aloud then she clung more tightly to Miranda's arm.

"Shortly we'll be passing the school."

"It must still be lunch time I can hear the voices of children playing in the playground."

"Yes, I guess the bell will be going soon for them to go in for the start to afternoon lessons."

"Hello, Miranda, RK," a voice called from across the road.

"How many steps?" Miranda whispered to RK.

"Twenty-seven," RK replied.

"Give a wave with your free hand." RK complied.

"Hi, there, Mrs Saunders," Miranda called back.

"Now, that wasn't so hard, was it?"

"No," RK said with a muffled giggle.

"People from the village will recognize you, so consequently speak to you first, giving you chance to identify who is speaking to you. The closeness of the voice will determine if it's to be just a greeting, a brief chat, or a longer conversation."

"You make it sound so straightforward, Mirry."

"Well, I think initially, the length of these encounters will be decided by the person you've met up with but as you gain confidence, as well as recognize voices more quickly, you'll be able to choose the duration of the meeting with whoever you've bumped into."

"You believe self-confidence will give me greater control?"

"I'm sure to a certain extent that is so."

"Right, shall we move on?"

"There now, that proves my point," Miranda laughed. "Encounters in the street have a natural duration that we don't even think about. Gradually you'll learn to deal with them just as you did before you lost your sight. The more you do something the more normal it will become."

"Humph, we'll see."

*You're so sure of yourself, Miranda, 'Bossy Boots' is an apt name to describe you. No wonder you were dubbed with it by your sisters!*

The friends resumed counting their steps as they walked along the lane till RK pulled up abruptly. She yanked at Miranda's arm fiercely, "Was that a car?"

"How many steps?"

"Fifty-two...but was it?"

"Yes, but does it matter?"

"There's not a path here, is there!" exclaimed RK anxiously.

"No, but drivers can see you."

"But I can't see them!" Panic was seeping in.

"If you put your left arm straight out to your side you'll feel the hedge. Walk close to that and you'll be OK. So, there's no need to panic."

"Right," RK released the breath she had been holding in.

*Dear God, will this nightmare never end?*

"Vehicles will always give walkers a wide berth. Shall we continue?"

RK nodded half-heartedly.

"You may not know, as you have been away from the village for a while, but only residents have permits to drive through the village so every vehicle that approaches will be driven by a driver who recognizes you."

"That's a new innovation."

"Yes, brought about because a stranger came to the Village Stores advocating building a supermarket with a car park."

"Oh, my word, I guess that caused a great stir in some quarters."

"How right you are. The PCC were up in arms along with most of the villagers."

"But where did this chap propose to build his superstore?"

"On the site of Kezia's Wood."

"He planned wholesale destruction of the habitat?"

"It wasn't allowed to get that far. When work first commenced on the site there was a lot of rumour and speculation in the village about what was taking place and a great deal of anger was being expressed. However, unbeknown to anyone Doctor John had already bought the site from the de Vere estate convinced there was building of some sort at the heart of the wood. Chit Beckingsdale was commissioned to sympathetically clear the area and Durrant's to carry any restoration that might be required on any property that might remain there."

"It sounds quite intriguing."

"It has been a very exciting project and really brought the villagers closer together. To scotch any unfounded gossip an information meeting was held in the church hall."

"That was a sensible move."

"Yes, it was, because the local people didn't like the cloud of uncertainty hanging over them. Doctor John and Lord Edmund accompanied by Adam presented the facts and answered all questions that were fired at them."

"I guess that proved useful."

"Many villagers feel it is their families' history that is being rediscovered and so want to be a part of it and lend a hand in some way or other. Lord Edmund offered the field that is used on Bank holidays as a permanent car park and burly Harry Saunders applied for and got the job of car park attendant which very nicely solved the problem of congestion in the village."

RK was silent for a time digesting the news Miranda had given to her about the newly built village car park and access permits for villagers. Then she enquired, "What about the car park at the Ship Inn, I'm sure that's where Mrs Darnell took me the other day?"

"Oh, that's still available to patrons, boat owners and other commercial users of the harbour but access is only allowed via Back Lane for people such as the fish merchants which links up with the road to Newton Lokesby. There is a discreet notice on the junction that indicates 'The Ship Inn only'.

"Similarly, on the approach road to the village just past the new car park a small turning has been made which is exclusively for access to Durrant's builder's yard for deliveries, customers and their own vehicles.

"The PCC has worked closely with the highways agency who have been very co-operative and supportive. They have erected a sign where the road to the village leaves the main Norwich road indicating there is limited vehicular access to the village and underneath we've added 'car park available'."

"I seem to have missed so much while I've been away. Are all the trees gone from the Wood?"

"Oh no, Chit was specifically chosen for the task because of his horticultural knowledge and arboretal expertise and he's retained some fine specimens, trees and shrubs, and also quite a portion at the bottom end of the area remains as woodland for the benefit of wildlife. Surprisingly, a row of derelict dwellings has been discovered which will take some time to restore. The only one to have received any attention is the one to the right of the site which is Stephen Cooper's."

"Yes, I heard about that from the Catton children. They want to take me to see it one day."

"It's well worth a visit. Stephen and his team of volunteers have worked tremendously hard. They have made some fascinating discoveries. Did you know he's unearthed the Smithy where Emma and Alex's great, great grandfather worked when he was farrier to the de Vere estate?"

"Adam told me about the Smithy but not its association with Emma and Alex's ancestors. Such a lot of changes in the short time I've been away from the village," RK commented pensively.

For some while the two friends strolled in companionable silence.

"Hi, Miranda, how're yew doin' RK?"

A noisy engine sped by. Miranda called out, "Hi" and waved a greeting to the passing motorcyclist.

RK stood still. "Who was that?"

"Ryan Saunders."

"So, he eventually got his own bike," she murmured.

"Yes, he built it himself from scratch with parts from the scrap yard."

"How resourceful! That's some achievement. I wonder if he'd like the challenge of the Harley."

"You'll have to ask him. Now, ten more paces, turn to the right and stop. We are going to cross this road."

*Oh no, I feel quite sick at the thought of crossing the road without being able to see if anything is coming.*

"From now on I've pre-counted the steps because I want you to concentrate on what you can hear."

"I can't hear anything, apart from the gulls, some trees rustling in the breeze and the sea breaking on the shore."

"Well, that's a fair amount. When you cross the road there is a procedure. Stop, turn to the right, count to five as you listen then turning to the left repeat the procedure. If you cannot hear any approaching vehicles hold your white stick aloft and proceed directly over the road."

"I don't have a white stick."

"We'll soon rectify that. In the mean time, thrust your right hand out in front of you and walk straight across."

Nervously RK stuck out her right hand and stepped into the roadway. *I can't believe Miranda has planned this with such precision.*

"Walk positively, 19 steps. Don't stop once you've started to cross. Good. Well done, RK, keep going," Miranda praised.

Cautiously RK moved towards her friend's voice.

"Oh no," Miranda gasped. "Bradley, STOP!" She yelled and frantically waved her arms in the air.

A screech of bicycle brakes followed Miranda's command.

"You stupid boy! Couldn't you see a blind person was crossing the road?" Miranda shouted at him furiously.

"But it's RK," Bradley retorted back, shaken at being told off so unfairly.

"Of course it's RK and RK cannot see, can she?"

"Oh bl..., I forgot! Sorry, Miranda."

"BRADLEY!"

"Sorry, sorry Miranda, I'm really sorry, I just forgot. Oh boy, I'll be for it now." Bradley hung his head in shame. Miranda looked at the ashen faces of her friend and the distressed boy and thought quickly of a way to rectify the situation.

"RK's learning to cross the road."

"Oh yeah?" the boy said in disbelief.

"It's very different for her now because she relies on sounds. Perhaps you could help us, Bradley."

"Yeah, OK," the youngster agreed reluctantly.

Miranda explained clearly what she wanted him to do. For five minutes or so he rode up and down the road ringing his bicycle bell to warn of his approach as RK practised listening and crossing.

"That's fine. Thanks for your help, Bradley. Please remind your biking friends to look out for RK around the village and tell them what to do."

"Sure, g' bye." Relieved to be let off the hook the boy jumped on his bike and rode away as fast as his legs would pedal.

"I wonder why he's not in school," she mumbled more to herself than RK.

Miranda then turned back to RK. "That developed into a useful encounter. I hadn't given thought to cyclists but hopefully Bradley will soon spread the word."

"I hope they've all got bells!"

"Perhaps Tom Catchpole will do a spot check and information session at the school and youth club. I'll also ask the PCC to display posters on the village notice boards."

"I'm sure Emma would put one up in the Stores, too."

"Everyone will do what they can to help you get around the village safely."

"I truly appreciate their thoughtfulness."

"I deliberately didn't say where we were going to this afternoon because I wanted you to particularly concentrate on counting our footsteps."

"I think after this outing I shall be counting steps in my sleep," RK laughed.

"May be, but I think it is going to be so important to your mobility around Newton Westerby. You're familiar with the village so I hope it won't be too long before you learn to recognize where you are and counting steps will become as natural as breathing."

"You're very optimistic, Miranda."

"Of course, I'm convinced you can do it, RK. Now then, following that little interlude with Bradley can you guess where we might be?"

RK shook her head. "We crossed the road so many times but I think..." she stopped momentarily and listened, then pointed to her right. "I think the sea is over there. I can hear the pounding of the waves on the beach so we might now be standing at the entrance to Ferry Lane."

"Well done! Without counting steps do you think you could take me to Ferry Cottage? You're currently standing on the left hand side of Ferry Lane facing in the direction of the sea."

"I'll do my best. There used to be a lot of ruts and potholes along here. I hope I can remember where they are, I don't want to fall down."

"Take my arm. You guide me in the direction you want us to go and I'll ensure you don't trip."

Within a few minutes RK had them standing outside Ferry Cottage.

"I'm very impressed RK. I knew you could do it."

"I have a picture in my mind of what the area looks like. I've walked it so many times in the past. I just followed the route I could see with my mind's eye."

"That's brill, RK. I've taken the liberty of borrowing the master key for your cottage from Aunt Trixie because I thought you might like to come home; you know, get the feel of the place again."

"Oh Mirry, that is such a nice thought, thankyou. I love this little cottage and you're right it is home."

"Everything is as you had it. Rosie has been meticulous in it's upkeep, especially when the workmen came in to do the alterations. She got really cross with them one day for leaving a mess."

"I'm looking forward to seeing the renovations," RK said excitedly.

"Right. Here's the key, go ahead."

Once the friends were inside Miranda said, "I'll put the kettle on while you get reacquainted. If anything's not as you would like just say so and we'll move it."

"I just want to savour the atmosphere, the quiet, the peace, the tranquillity." RK moved slowly round her little sitting room touching the curtains, moving her fingers along the window sill, finding the ceramic seagull the Catton children had given to her for her birthday. She lifted it carefully to her cheek, felt it's coolness, then replaced it with precision on the wooden sill. Her knees brushed against the chair that sat in the window recess. She leaned over and picked up the quilted cushion Maisie Piper had embroidered for her when she first moved in, blues of many hues shaped like sailing boats appliquéd on the surface. RK shook it then replaced it before stepping towards the alcove to the right of the chimney breast. The palms of her hands glided over the spines of the books that graced the bookshelves erected by Stephen Cooper to house the small collection of favourite volumes as well as a few DVDs that she'd acquired.

"Tea's ready," Miranda called from the kitchen. "How's it going?"

She poked her head around the doorway to see RK reaching up to the picture above the mantelpiece. She appeared deep in thought. Her hands were moving smoothly over the clear pane, as though she was recalling the scene that was painted beneath the glass. Watching her it seemed as if RK was seeing the picture with her fingers. Emma had captured on canvas the vibrancy of harbour activity that had so captivated RK when she first arrived in Newton Westerby. RK's fingers lingered on the spot in the foreground where Emma had positioned RK's Harley-Davidson. Miranda heard RK sigh and saw the droop of her shoulders.

"Do you need a hand?"

RK turned abruptly from the fireplace.

"Ouch!"

"You OK?"

"I've banged my leg on the corner of the coffee table."

"Oh, shall we move it?"

"No, I'd rather keep it where it is. I'll just have to remember it's there." RK moved cautiously around the offending piece of furniture towards the doorway into the kitchen.

"It's so good to be here, thankyou for bringing me, Miranda."

"You're very welcome. Before we go into the kitchen for lunch I want to show you something that Ben had the boys fix up for you. I take it you haven't had lunch?"

"No, I couldn't face anything to eat earlier. My stomach was churning over too much at the thought of you coming and what activity you would have designed for me to accomplish."

"Oh, RK."

"Silly isn't it?"

"Not really. I can imagine it's a bit of an ordeal having to learn different ways of doing things. Anyway, turn and move towards the front door with the sofa on your left."

RK put out her hand to locate the back of the sofa and edged in the direction of the door.

"Two more steps then feel in front of you, below waist height."

"Oh, it's a basket sort of thing fixed to the door." Her fingers explored the wire mesh. "Is it over the letterbox?"

"It is."

RK deftly continued to probe till she found the lid, opened it and drew out the contents. "What a good idea. At least I won't have to scramble about on the floor searching for the post. I'll bring these envelopes through to the kitchen and we can look at them over our cup of tea."

Miranda stepped back into the kitchen and left RK to make her own way. With hardly any hesitation RK reached the kitchen table, drew out a chair and sat down.

"That didn't take too much effort, did it?"

RK chuckled, "Do you know I didn't even think about what I was doing. I was concentrating more on what might be in my post and walked automatically to where I normally sit in the kitchen. I'm glad they kept the furniture in the same positions. It makes being here in my cottage so much easier."

Miranda refrained from comment as RK sat quietly for some while in deep thought. Then she sighed, "I can't believe I did that. It was no problem at all. I just walked from the living room to the kitchen. My feet seemed to know where to go and my mind what to do."

Miranda pushed the mug towards RK's hand, "Don't let your tea go cold."

"Thanks," and she curled her fingers around its shape and lifted it to her lips to drink.

"Because you are so familiar with the village you will soon be moving from place to place with similar ease. It's a case of building up your confidence."

RK shook her head disbelievingly. "I'm not so sure. Out there are things that move, things like bikes, and dogs and people and cars."

"Don't worry your head about things like that at the moment. It will come. Meanwhile, let's eat our lunch. I have to be back at the surgery soon. We have baby clinic at 2 o'clock. Now would you like to stay here for the afternoon or go back to 'Bakers'?"

RK gulped and quickly finished her mouthful.

"That's a surprise, Miranda, but I think on reflection I'd like to spend a little more time here. I love this little cottage."

"I thought you might say that. Now, about your post, I haven't time to open and read it to you now. I mustn't be late for clinic but if you want me to I can do it later. If you would prefer someone else to handle those affairs for you I won't be offended, for instance, Adam or Graeme or even Doc Roger or Mrs Darnell come instantly to mind as people you can trust. I'm used to dealing with matters of confidentiality so can hold my own counsel but it really is up to you."

"Oh, my dear Mirry, I trust your integrity completely. I'll be pleased if it's not too much trouble for you to deal with the post for me. Issues may arise that necessitate involving all the people you mentioned in some capacity at one time or another but I'd rather you helped me on a regular basis."

"That's fine with me. There are also some DWP forms to be filled in to claim the benefits to which you are entitled which will enable you to pay your way. Now, before I leave you can I show you the new conservatory and check you remember where some necessities are but please promise me you won't venture upstairs while you're here alone. I'll give you the full tour when I return."

RK laughed and the deep rich tone seemed to reverberate around the kitchen walls with joy at the return of their fun-loving tenant.

# CHAPTER THIRTEEN

After Miranda had left Ferry Cottage to return to the surgery RK slowly rose from her seat at the kitchen table. Spreading her hands before her she walked cautiously through the cottage intent on exploring her home. Miranda's positive attitude had not only ignited a desire to do something for herself but also prompted a belief that maybe, just maybe, she was capable of managing some tasks on her own.

*Perhaps Emma was right and I must look on my situation as an adventure. I actually walked from the corner of Ferry Lane to the cottage! I didn't trip or bump into anything.*

"Yippee," RK shouted with elation thrusting up her arm to punch the air. *Then, once inside the cottage I moved with ease around the sitting room and from there to the kitchen, on my own.* RK laughed. *I can't believe how simple I found it. Maybe Miranda's opinion is the correct one and that the more I do something the more it will become second nature to me. Doc Roger pointed out I should view it as a new learning curve but I still think some things are going to take a bit more concentration than others.*

For the first time since her accident RK really wanted to learn again about this special place that was her own and how she could adapt her approach to living back in the cottage. She stood still for a moment and leaned against the cupboard she could feel behind her.

*I really can't be dependent on others for the rest of my life. I'm truly thankful for such good friends. Many of them have already done so much on my behalf. In fact, at times it's a bit galling to be constantly told what to do and when to do it. It's frustrating to be so reliant on other people. My circumstances may have changed but I really must stop feeling sorry for myself and learn to be more self-sufficient. At times their generous spirit makes me feel ashamed of my quarrelsome attitude and the way I wallowed in my misfortune. How ungrateful I must appear to Jennifer and Emma and other friends like Miranda who have shown me nothing but kindness!* RK gritted her teeth then, with a determined stance, she declared in a firm voice to the four walls, "I will do it. I'm not a loser. God, are you listening? I hate the blackness I wake up to each morning but I won't vegetate any longer though I just might need your support every once in a while."

'*I am with you always!*'

"Wow! I don't know where that came from but thanks God!"

RK pushed back her shoulders, lifted her head high and started her journey of rediscovery in the kitchen. Moving her hands carefully along the work surfaces she let her fingers feel what she could see in her mind's eye. She came to the toaster and enclosed it in her two hands. She fingered the lead and followed it to the socket in the wall and checked the position of the switch. She reached out to the right side of the toaster and touched the bread bin. She lifted the lid and bent towards the emptiness and sniffed. *Oh good someone's washed it out. Thankfully there isn't the smell of stale or mouldy bread.* For some moments RK continued to renew her acquaintance with the humdrum areas of her little domain, opening cupboards and drawers to jog her memory as to where crockery and utensils were stored.

She proceeded to move carefully around the kitchen using outspread hands as eyes. When she felt a knob she pulled ajar the door that led to the back porch Ben had designed for coats and shoes as well as any other paraphernalia she had cared to store there. Her hands seemed to automatically reach up to the coat hooks then flutter along the shoe rack even though she knew that at present the hooks and bench were empty and bare. RK chose not to open the back door but did unlatch the new door that gave indoor access to the upgraded toilet facilities. A pungent disinfectant smell mingling with bleach and lemon emanated through the open space which suggested that someone had very kindly kept it clean for her. *I think Miranda said it was Rosie who has looked after the cottage in my absence. I must thank her when I next see her. She seems to have been very thorough in her duties. Thankfully, I won't have to worry about creepy crawlies or unwanted furry visitors anymore.*

Carefully she retraced her steps brushing a hand across the backs of the chairs pushed under the table by the kitchen window as she passed by them. When RK reached the wood burning stove she frowned as she gave it a pat and said out loud, "Humph, this might prove a problem." She moved on quickly through the new doorway into the recently built sun room. This was even more difficult territory because she didn't have a memory picture of this particular space that she could call to mind. Miranda had explained that the doorway was in the same position in the corner of the kitchen that had originally been occupied by the pantry. That had been removed although a small broom cupboard had been built ahead into the far right hand corner of the conservatory to house the vacuum cleaner, the ironing board and other appliances that couldn't be kept in the smaller kitchen cabinets.

Miranda had mentioned there was nothing in the conservatory other than an armchair that someone had donated for her comfort. Unsure where it had been placed RK was careful not to stumble over its legs as she let her hands traverse the length of the solid wall towards the cupboard. She turned the corner and explored the windows and wooden sills on two of the sides of the new room, discovered the handle to the patio doors then finger-walked along the house wall picking out the kitchen window on the way back to the arched opening into the kitchen. She retraced her steps, put out her hands, found the chair and sat down. She leaned back, and gratefully sank into the cushioned upholstery, her hands relaxed in her lap. She felt exhausted. *I'm really glad of this respite.* A huge sigh escaped her lips. *I feel as though I have been bulldozed and need to take time to recharge my energy supply. I guess I've accomplished more today than I've done for a long time.*

As she sat in quiet contemplation many different scenes played through her mind such as the fun she had experienced when with the Catton children playing on the beach or sitting on the quay eating lollipops or ice creams as they watched boats sail out to sea or come into harbour escorted by squawking seagulls.

She remembered the impromptu fork and spade supper when her friends had descended on Ferry Cottage with food and implements to tidy up her garden. That was a special evening. It marked a turning point in her thinking towards Christian values and their impact upon daily living.

She recalled the pleasurable drives across the Lincolnshire Fens she had recently enjoyed with Dan learning the songs of worship and praise. Though a frown creased her brow at the fleeting remembrance of her accident and the subsequent days of despondent despair she spent locked in her room at the farmhouse coupled with the anger and rejection she endured at the hands of her family. She shook her head as if to dispel the awful memories.

Her last Sunday in church sprang into her mind when she had made that momentous decision... "*God, we never did get chance to get properly acquainted. I'm really pleased I have the opportunity to go to church again. Jennifer was very gracious letting me walk with her on Sunday. I wonder if Graeme or Alex will call for me to attend their house group this week. It will enable me to ask more questions about You. There's so much I don't know; about You and even about ordinary every day things like...what's the time? I've no idea. A chiming clock might be the answer...I must ask Gil what he found out about speaking clocks... One day I'd like to explore Stephen's shop and smithy and go to the tea rooms and have coffee and scones again...that...aroma was so...oo...*"

The lingering fragrance of baking assailed her nostrils as her eyes closed and RK drifted into sleep. Her thoughts just prior to slumber were of moments filled with happiness and delight rather than of incidents that had been fraught with heartache and pain. This little cottage oozed balm and tranquillity. RK savoured the peace.

Outside, beyond the garden wall, the waves lapped at the seashore, the gulls swooped and called while the village and its occupants meandered undeterred through the afternoon routine.

The early school and shopping bus on its return journey from Norwich stopped at the Village Stores to allow passengers to alight and, by prior arrangement with Emma and Miranda, Gil Jenner was among them. Instead of remaining on the bus till it reached Jenner's Mill Gil got off and sauntered up to Ferry Cottage. Emma had recruited his help, as promised to RK, to explain the functions of the mobile phone that had been acquired on her behalf to enable her to have a degree of independence.

He rapped on the front door of Ferry Cottage, turned the handle and walked in. "Hi, RK, it's only me," he called in a loud voice to announce his arrival. Receiving no response to his shout Gil wandered through the living room into the kitchen calling as he continued his search. Seeing no sign of RK there he looked through the archway into the sun room.

"Hello, who's there?" RK twisted her head sleepily.

"It's Gil, RK. I've come to give you instructions about the new phone," he explained uncertainly.

"Oh, that's kind of you, Gil, I'm really pleased you came. I'm afraid there's only one chair in here so shall we move into the sitting room."

"Yes, if you like, unless you want a cup of tea."

"What a good idea, Gil, will you make it or shall I?"

"Let's do it together," suggested Gil whose tea making skills were somewhat limited but he recognized that a blind RK might be even more restricted in what she could achieve safely. So, while he filled the kettle she found the mugs and located the tea-bags. He poured the boiling water into the teapot and carried the tray into the sitting room while RK followed him with the teaspoons and sugar.

"I don't know if there are any biscuits. Miranda was here at lunch-time but I'm not sure what she's left on the work top. I haven't really moved back in, yet. I'm only visiting today."

"No worries," said Gil as he placed the tray onto the coffee table. He turned towards RK and continued, "As I got off the bus and walked past the Stores Emma came out and gave me some of Mum's stem ginger cookies she knows are your favourites."

"That was thoughtful of her," RK murmured as Gil rummaged in his school bag to unearth the biscuit packet and offer one to RK.

"Thanks," said RK and patted the sofa seat. "Come and sit by me, Gil. I think we make a very good team, don't you? I hope I won't let you down in the IT department."

"I'm sure you'll do just fine. It's a case of re-educating your memory," said Gil with confidence.

"Oh?"

"Yeah, I've been practising and it's quite easy."

"Really? How?"

"By screwing up my eyes and training my finger-tips to do the seeing I can now move around the keypad without really thinking about it and soon you'll be able to do the same. This model also has a voice activated option which you'll pick up easily. After all you have used a mobile before."

"I'm glad you have such confidence in my ability. We'll finish our tea then we can get started."

"Righteo." He took a quick sip of his tea. "Mum was ever so pleased you called in to see us last week on your way back from the hospital."

"That's OK, it was the least I could do to make up for my grumpiness at the garden party."

"Well, the girls were tickled pink that you waited for them to get home from school; they've chatted non-stop about it ever since."

"I guess you need some ear plugs, then!"

Gil laughed. "You are funny, RK."

RK chuckled at his mirth as she reached forward to put her mug onto the tray. "I'm ready, if you are, Gil."

"Almost finished," he gulped down the last mouthful.

"I'm aware of the workings of a mobile phone but not this particular model"

"Sure, it's a different technique but you'll soon get the hang of it."

Patiently, Gil explained the essential intricacies of the new phone, activated the voice recognition mode to make outgoing calls, guided RK's fingers through the keypad and showed her how to identify the answer button. For some while RK practised making calls to a number of prearranged recipients that Gil had instigated. They in turn called back in order for RK to practise her answering skills.

Gil beamed, "You're getting the hang of this remarkably quickly, RK."

RK chuckled, "Did you think I'd be a slow old duffer?"

"No, but from what Emma told me I thought it would take you longer than this to master it."

"It's all down to your expert tuition, Gil. I am really grateful. Now I won't feel quite so isol..." RK broke off in mid-sentence, startled by a persistent hammering on the front door. "Whatever is that?" She clasped her hands to her ears as the pounding increased. "Dear me, what a din!" Gil craned his neck to peer through the window. "There are two big men outside," he whispered.

"Open the door!" bellowed a deep gruff voice accompanied by further banging on the door.

"We know you're in there," shouted a higher pitched voice followed by a vicious kick to the door.

"Is it locked?" RK spoke softly. In a flash Gil was full length on the floor in front of the door pushing the lower bolt across into the locked position. Then, so he couldn't be seen through the frosted glass of the upper portion of the door, he carefully reached up his hand to fix the safety chain into place but flinched back as the letter-box was roughly rattled.

"We require access to your property, immediately," the deep voice yelled through the letter-box. "If you don't open up willingly we'll be forced to break down the door to gain entry."

RK sat motionless on the sofa. She was petrified. *If only I could see I would know what I was dealing with. I can hardly confront unseen assailants.* Her earlier bravado receded like the ebbing tide.

The banging on the door continued. "You ought to comply you're in enough trouble as it is for not responding to earlier visits." RK grew increasingly agitated. *What on earth is this all about? I haven't been here so how could I know about other visits.* She wrung her hands uncertain what she ought to do. *Where was Gil?*

Stealthily Gil had slithered into the kitchen, pulled out his own mobile from his trouser pocket and quietly called Emma to explain their situation and ask for help. Emma immediately dialled the police station house and then the surgery. Fearing the worst she also summoned assistance from Mrs Darnell, who had popped into the shop briefly for grocery essentials, to man the Stores in her absence. "Hugh is just outside if you need him," Penny called out as Emma rapidly exited the shop.

She glanced across to the bench outside the Village Stores where Rev Hugh was chatting with Mr Bracewell. She rushed up to him. "Excuse me," Emma pulled urgently on the vicar's arm. "Please come with me to Ferry Cottage, you may be needed."

"Young people," muttered Mr Bracewell, shaking his head, "allus in a hurry."

"I'm sorry, Mr Bracewell, but this is an emergency."

"It allus is wi' yew young uns," he tutted.

As they hurried along the lane Emma quickly explained to Hugh the little she knew about the state of affairs affecting RK that she had learned from Gil's brief call.

"Bailiffs can't use force to gain entry on their first visit..."

"Bailiffs?" Emma stammered.

"That's what it sounds like but my understanding is that they can only use 'peaceable means' to gain entry to a property."

"But why would they be at RK's door?"

"We'll soon find out," Hugh replied as they strode briskly towards Ferry Cottage. When they turned to cross the lane PC Dan sped by on his police motor-cycle and gave a wave.

He arrived ahead of them at the cottage in time to see a big burly man pick up and use a very large stone to smash the front door window, reach a hand through the gap to remove the door-chain and try to gain entrance. When the door still would not give (because of the lower bolt that Gil had earlier pushed into place) he impatiently kicked at it and shouted, "Open up, now!"

Dan parked up his machine and calmly walked behind the men, who as yet were unaware of his presence, their bellowing and banging was such that it had obscured the noise of the approaching motor-bike. Above their bent heads as they struggled with the unyielding door he caught a glimpse of RK, through the broken glass, cowered in the far corner of the sofa. His heart lurched forward. "Oh, dear God, what have they done to my little song-bird?"

Dan felt at a distinct disadvantage to be entering the cottage behind the breaking and entering men.

So, knowing reinforcements were on the way in the person of Hugh and Emma and not far behind them Sgt Catchpole and possibly others, if he knew the village grapevine, he signalled to Gil whom he could see hovering in the kitchen to open the back door. Still undetected Dan nipped around the side of the cottage, straddled the back garden wall and slipped unseen into the cottage via the sun-room door which Gil had the presence of mind to open.

"Bright thinking, Gil," commended the policeman softly.

"Well, 'cus they've smashed the window right out you'd 'ave been in full view of the front door if I'd let you in through the back door."

"Whatever's going on here?" Dan whispered to the now shaking boy.

"I wish I knew." Gil shrugged his shoulders. "I've never been so pleased to see you, Dan. Those two are madmen. They really scared me and RK."

"No need to worry now, Gil. You've done a great job but we'll take over at this point."

"OK, but I'll just check on RK. It's worse for her 'cus she can't see."

"It might be better if we go together because I think the intruders have finally got in."

"I did my best to keep them out," his voice quivered.

"I'm sure you did, Gil."

"I've also got their pictures on my mobile."

"Well done, Gil! That could be useful. We'll make a detective of you yet." Dan clapped Gil round the shoulders and the boy beamed at the unexpected praise. "Let's go and see what's happening in the sitting room."

"Good afternoon, Reverend, Emma," the Constable said. The two had just arrived at Ferry Cottage. They acknowledged Dan's greeting with a nod as they stood on top of the step by the open front door staring with concern at the cowering RK and the mess created by the intruders. The men who seemed quite unperturbed by the havoc they had caused stood in front of the fire place with clip boards in their hands making notes.

Dan stepped towards the sofa, placed a hand on RK's shoulder, bent down and quietly asked, "Are you OK, Robyn?"

In an almost indiscernible whisper she replied, "Yes."

"Emma, would you sit with RK, please. Take care stepping around the broken glass." Emma swiftly carried out Dan's instruction to be by the side of her trembling friend. She placed a comforting arm around RK's shoulders while Rev Hugh moved to stand by Gil and lend his support.

Dan looked towards the scribbling men who were totally ignoring the other occupants in the room.

"Gentlemen, may I see your break-open warrant?" Dan's raised voice did cause them to look up.

"Aah, Constable, glad you're here. We may need your assistance."

"I asked to see your break-open warrant."

"Well, uhm, the householder refused to give us access and earlier warnings have been ignored, Constable."

"Under section 61(2) of the Taxes Management Act 1970 you require a warrant which permits forced entry."

"Now, Constable, we just gave the door a little help so we could get in."

"I witnessed your entry gentlemen and I would say your action contravenes Article 8 of the European Convention on human rights. Without a warrant you have gained access by illegal means. So, why are you here?"

"To collect payment for rent arrears."

"What rent arrears?"

"From the tenant of the property."

"No one lives here at present," said Dan but his explanation was ignored and the bailiff continued as though Dan had not spoken.

"Once again I ask for payment. If you don't pay my colleague will make a list of your possessions on a C204 Distraint notice and inventory form. Your possessions will be sold to pay what you owe." Without blinking he stared at the blank wall ahead of him. "As you have ignored previous requests for payment you now have 5 days to pay."

"Who are you addressing?" Dan asked.

"Miss Robyn Dickinson-Bond."

Emma gasped.

"Who is serving this notice?"

"The de Vere Estate."

"But that's nonsense," Hugh expressed most strongly. "Miss Dickinson-Bond owes nothing to the de Vere Estate."

"Yeah, that's right," nodded Gil in agreement, having regained his equilibrium.

"Be that as it may, we need to get on," said the bailiff with the deep, loud voice dismissively as he turned to his colleague. "What's next?"

"One TV..."

"The TV belongs to Lord Edmund," interrupted Gil.

"One DVD player..."

"...belongs to Doctor John."

"A radio."

"Oh, that came from Uncle Roy," volunteered Emma.

"...and the curtains all belong to my Mum or Mrs Ransome," shouted Gil to drown the commotion by the front door which announced the arrival of Sergeant Catchpole and Doctor Roger. All eyes turned towards the new arrivals.

"Carry-on owd bor while I 'ave a word with my Constable and Doc here checks over the young lady."

"But Sergeant he wants to take things that belong to someone else."

"Well, you put 'im right owd bor while we 'ave our li'le chat."

"Righteo, Sergeant." Gil looked defiantly in the direction of the bailiffs and continued his explanation of the origin of all the articles the men touched. "The carpet came out of the guest room of the Mill B&B. The three piece suite belongs to Emma's Mum and Dad an' they're in heaven. The big lamp's Mums and the little one belongs to Mrs Cooper. The book shelf was made by Stephen and the little chair by the window was Rachel Durrant's baby bathing chair." Gil paused for breath.

"One picture," The bailiff continued.

"The painting is mine," Emma butted in. "It has my signature in the bottom right hand corner."

"Emma Kemp?"

"Yes, my maiden name."

"The new bathroom and fittings and the conservatory were designed by Ben and built by his builders and belongs to Lord Edmund. So does the house and gardens. Upstairs, the bed in the front room is Mum and Dad's old one. The twin beds in the other room – er – I think one belongs to Mrs Cooper and the other to Mrs Darnell. I'm not sure about the quilts and pillows."

The bailiff with the high squeaky voice sniggered as he fingered the DVDs. His hand then lingered on the seagull standing on the windowsill.

"Don't you touch that," Gil yelled defiantly. "The seagull belongs to RK. Daniel and Kirsty saved up their pocket money last year to buy it for RK's birthday and if you take it their Dad will get you 'cus he's a lawyer." Gil shook his fist angrily at the bailiffs.

"Didn't know we'd have the services of an on-site speaking inventory," mocked the loud mouthed bailiff.

Following his briefing with Sgt Catchpole Dan remained in the kitchen in order to phone Lord Edmund.

"Sir, we have a ridiculous scenario at Ferry Cottage. Bailiffs are issuing a Distraint notice by de Vessey Estates on a de Vessey property."

"What for?"

"Non-payment of rent."

"Which property?"

"Ferry Cottage, former residence of RK prior to her accident."

"What utter nonsense!"

"Quite, my lord! As you know, RK is here today, as agreed by the PCC and Doctor Roger to assess the feasibility of her managing to live independently in the cottage. The only possession remaining in the property belonging to RK is a ceramic seagull given to her by the Catton children and a handful of books and DVD's."

"How is she?"

"Quite distressed."

"I'm not surprised."

"Also, Sir, we shall be arresting the bailiffs. They broke in, contravening the European Act on human rights."

"WHAT!!!"

"Yes, they used bullying tactics and forced entry without a warrant. I witnessed it myself and young Gil Jenner, who was sitting in with RK at the time, captured it on his mobile phone."

"Excellent. Do what you must, Constable, as far as the breaking and entering is concerned, and I'll check with the estate office whose incompetence resulted in such a tactless order being issued."

"Yes, Sir."

"Please, offer my apologies to Miss Dickinson-Bond. I'm sure between us we can get this mess sorted out without any further distress to the young lady."

"With your approval I'll call Durrant's to get the door fixed to ensure the property is secure and we'll keep you informed of developments regarding the bailiffs."

"Very good, Constable."

Dan dealt with the necessary arrangements then strode back into the front room. Emma and Doctor Roger were talking quietly with RK and Gil was hovering by the window keeping an eye on the departing bailiffs who were being escorted to the police vehicle by Sgt Catchpole and Rev Hugh.

"Well, Robyn, trouble does seem to follow you around, doesn't it?" His articulated thoughts came out more curtly than Dan intended.

"What do you mean?" RK murmured.

Dan proceeded to enumerate the different incidents that had occurred in past months, when RK was implicated or present, that had required police intervention.

RK paled. *Why does he sound so distant and aggressive towards me? Where is my warm, kindly friend? I didn't instigate the crimes. I don't even know the people who are involved.*

Emma shook her head at the constable and with pleading eyes looked to Roger for support.

"That's a bit harsh, Dan, don't you think?" The Doctor spoke quietly. "RK happened to be in the wrong place at the wrong time, that's all."

Dan shrugged his shoulders. "That's as may be but it's still a fact. Have you had any letters from the Bailiff's office, Robyn?"

"I'm not sure. Miranda was going to read the ones we found this morning in the letter basket when she returned after clinic this afternoon."

"They're on the kitchen table. I'll get them."

Gil stepped forward from his window gazing and swiftly picked up RK's mail. As he handed the pile of envelopes to the constable he blurted out, "Hey, Dan, you shouldn't be so rough on RK."

"Oh?"

"It's hard being blind, you know. Mum explained it to us when the girls grumbled about RK's odd behaviour at Miss Pedwardine's Garden Party."

"Did she, now."

"Yes! It's like being unable to see the big picture because everyone is clamouring for your attention at the same time, talking at you from all sides, an' because you can't see them, you can't focus on one thing or person at a time and because of all the noise and confusion around you it's almost impossible to know if they're talking to you or someone else."

"I see."

"We didn't understand why RK was different or what she was going through till on Sunday after church Mum made us all wear blindfolds till bedtime so we could experience for ourselves what she meant. It was pretty scary and jolly confusing. You should try it."

RK's eyes teared up as she reached out to grasp Gil's hand. "You are so kind, Gil. I appreciate you all doing that in order to better understand my predicament."

Emma was so choked she was unable to speak but simply tightened her arm around RK's shoulders and placed a hand on Gil's waist to draw him closer towards them in a hug of gratitude. With a grin Doc Roger playfully punched his upper arm, "Well done, lad."

Dan feeling suitably chastened spoke gently to the boy. "Thankyou, Gil, for that insight into Robyn's predicament. I'll remember to be more careful what I say in the future."

A disturbance outside the front door indicated the arrival of the workmen sent by Durrants to carry out the repairs.

"Well, I really must get back to the shop and relieve Mrs Darnell." Emma got up from the sofa. "Will you be OK, RK?"

"I'm fine. Thanks for coming."

"We'll leave you to sort out the repair men, Dan, and as it's getting dusk Gil and I will escort RK to Miss Pedwardine's then I'll see Gil safely home before returning for evening surgery. I'll see you later, Em." Roger patted his wife's arm affectionately as she stepped around the debris.

"Will you let Miranda know what's happened? She was going to show me the upstairs renovations and go through the accumulated pile of post with me after she had finished at the surgery."

"Sure, I'll tell her. Don't fret, those things can be done another day."

# Chapter Fourteen

A misty morning greeted the new day signifying the seasonal change in the weather pattern. Emma, having put the events of the previous afternoon on hold at the back of her mind, sat at her teacher's desk in front of the class marking the register.

"Good morning, Daniel."

"Good morning, Mrs Cooper."

"Well done in your project on fossils. I can see that you put a lot of effort into your research." Daniel beamed.

"Thankyou, Mrs Cooper."

"Good morning, Bradley."

"Good mornin', Mrs Cooper," he sing-songed as is the wont of all school children at register time.

"I understand you were a great help in Miss Dickinson-Bond's road crossing lesson, yesterday." Some of the class snickered but Emma looked straight at Bradley as she spoke.

Colour rose rapidly to his cheeks. He averted his eyes, shuffled uncomfortably and mumbled. "Yes, Miss."

"Well done!" At that unexpected praise his head shot up. He was expecting a rollicking because he'd been absent from school without permission. He looked around his classmates with a smirch on his face, pushed his shoulders back, puffed out his chest and sat up straight in his seat.

Without further comment Emma concluded marking the register. It was her policy to begin each new day with a positive word for every child in her class. She'd discovered early in her career that a little praise went a long way to creating a good atmosphere in the classroom particularly amongst the most unruly of her pupils of whom Bradley was current ring leader. She had also been made aware, by Rosalie Andaman, that he and a couple of boys from the Common had in recent weeks been seen pilfering chocolate bars from the shop.

"This is a tricky problem that really needs stamping on before it gets out of hand but I'm reluctant to bring it up with Bradley's mother, Michelle. She already has enough to contend with."

Since Joe and Josh had been sentenced to prison for burglary and grievous bodily harm against a number of persons in the village Michelle had worked hard to keep the family together despite unkind barbs that had been flung at her by some members of the community who still believed her husband and son guilty of far greater crimes. Her daughter Maxine was proving adept at shop work and knuckling down to her college course with a keenness that was pleasing. The younger boys, Bradley and Thomas had been doing well till Bradley got under the influence of a wilful crowd from the Common.

These were issues that had been brought up at a recent staff meeting. Emma and Jackie Cooper, the deputy head, were looking at ways to address both truancy and shoplifting.

"I think we'll introduce the points system for good behaviour, effort and attendance that seems to have been implemented to good effect in other schools," Jackie stated.

"But what will be the value of collecting points?"

"We'll need to have an award at the end of each school term that will make it a worthwhile goal to aim for. I'll put it before the governors perhaps they will have some useful suggestions."

"Yes, an incentive to improve behaviour and attitude."

"Is it likely to work for the likes of Bradley and co?"

"We can but try."

※

"I won't be in for lunch today, Jennifer," RK announced from the kitchen sink on the following Friday as she washed up the breakfast dishes, a task she was beginning to feel quite comfortable with. "So, there will be no need for you to hurry back from Norwich on my account."

"Oh?" Miss Pedwardine raised an unseen eyebrow as she banged her shopping bags on the kitchen table, but RK's accomplished ear detected a note of scepticism in the tone of her voice.

*Don't be intimidated. Stick to your resolve.* RK carefully placed the mug she was holding onto the draining board and gripped the side of the sink for support.

"Yes, I plan to make my way to the Village Stores for coffee then visit Stephen's bookshop before returning to the coffee shop for lunch."

"I see! You really think you can accomplish all that unaccompanied?" Jennifer asked caustically.

"I intend to try."

"Well, after the various escapades you've been caught up in over the past year that remains to be seen."

"Most of those were not of my making," RK replied defensively.

"That may be so but you're embarking on a mammoth undertaking. I hope that young man knows of your plans."

RK chose to ignore the last remark quite sure that her plans were of no interest to Dan Prettyman. His friendliness towards her seemed to blow hot and cold so that she simply did not know where she stood with him.

"Yes I know, but this will be the first solo outing of many because, as from this moment, I fully intend to get on with the rest of my life even though it will be somewhat different to what I had originally envisaged."

"So, how long will you be?"

"However long it takes."

"Do you have sufficient money?"

"I'll take my bank card. I have savings that will tide me over till the DWP sort out what my allowance is to be."

"I wish you well, girl. I'll be here if you need me and Dan ought to know in case you need him," Miss Pedwardine spoke brusquely as she put on her coat.

"Thankyou. I'm not ungrateful for all you and many others have done for me, Jennifer, but Doctor Roger is right. I must learn to do more for myself. However, I can only gain confidence by actually doing things. So, today's the day I start."

"Humph!" Miss Pedwardine grunted gruffly, briskly gathered her bags and prepared to leave the house. "Make sure you lock the door," she said tersely as she stomped from the room, "and check it," she called back from the hallway.

"Yes, Jennifer," RK sighed. She held her breath as she listened for the click on the front door. Not until she heard it shut did she visibly relax. "Come on, girl, pull yourself together," RK mimicked her landlady. Jennifer Pedwardine rarely showed emotion but RK had learned her off-handed manner masked a gentle, caring nature of which she had been the beneficiary during the last few weeks.

Within the hour RK herself was ready to leave the house and venture out on her own for the first time since her accident. Although the set-to with the bailiffs had shaken her RK was determined to put the episode behind her and carry out her resolve to be more independent. She tried to recall the instructions of Emma and Miranda when they had accompanied her down the lane. She counted her steps and stayed close to the hedge holding the white stick Miranda had acquired on her behalf prominently in front of her. Someone, she had an idea maybe Mrs Saunders, called out to her from across the road. She stood stock still and held her breath while a couple of vehicles drove by and when a buggy pushing person passed quite close to her without speaking she thought *must be a visitor*.

Without further incident RK made it to the lift at the Village Stores though her heart pounded as she crossed the open space of the shop driveway so that she was breathless as she fumbled for the lift buttons.

*Stand still, girl, think straight, stay calm.* Miss Pedwardine's admonitions echoed in her mind. As her fingers searched for the pushbutton RK caught a whiff of smoke and detected a shuffle of feet.

"Hi, RK, how are you? I watched you cross the driveway as I was having my ciggie break. You did well. First time out on your own?"

"Hello, Jilly, yes, today's the start of my new life."

"Good for you."

RK's eyes began to sting. She rubbed them cautiously. 'I'm sorry; I'm not used to being so close to cigarette smoke. I didn't know you smoked, Jilly."

Jilly laughed nervously, "Only when I'm stressed. I'll stub it out."

"But you do all that baking! I can't imagine you being stressed over anything. You always appear to be so organized and in control."

"Oh, I take off my cooking garb and wash my hands thoroughly before starting again in the kitchen. Anyway, it's only the odd occasion that it happens when I'm at work, but there was a bad accident last night at sea."

"Oh, dear!"

"Didn't you hear the sirens?"

"Now you mention it I do remember being woken by some noise but couldn't identify it."

"A charter vessel taking men and supplies to the wind farm en route to one of the rigs burst into flames and sank..."

"Oh no..."

"The lifeboat was launched but the men had managed to get into the inflatable life raft and were winched to safety by the helicopter crew from RAF Wattisham."

"So no life was lost?"

"No, thankfully, though some of the men have burns and other injuries but the worrying thing is that the charter company is the same one Kit travels with to and from the oil rig."

"I guess there'll be an investigation into the incident..."

"It's already started but their findings won't be published for months." Jilly wrung her hands in agitation before continuing, "In the meanwhile, Kit has to get home, and then take a number of trips out to the rig before the cause of the fire is known."

RK reached out to place her hand on Jilly's arm. "I'm sure Kit will be fine. It hasn't happened before, has it?"

Jilly shook her head then blurted out "No" when she remembered RK couldn't see her actions.

"Well then, it was probably a freak accident peculiar to that craft and unlikely to occur in the company's other vessels but I should think they'd be required to run mandatory checks before allowing them out on further trips."

"Yes, that is correct procedure so I know they'll do that as a precautionary measure. I guess I'm just worrying needlessly."

"No you're not. I think it's quite natural to be concerned for the one you love. I've heard text messages don't always get through to the rigs but I'm certain the harbour master would radio a message to Kit if you were to explain the situation to him."

"I'm sure you're right," Jilly nodded in agreement then glanced at her watch. "Ooo, time's running away with me this morning. It's good to see you RK, thanks for listening. I'll take your advice and go up to see Wills, the harbour master as soon as I'm off duty. Now I really must get on. Are you going up for coffee?"

"Yes," RK replied.

"I'll summon the lift for you."

"Thanks."

As she exited the lift when it reached the upper level and stepped into the coffee shop entrance the enticing aroma RK remembered from her previous visit greeted her. *Mmm! Delicious!*

Brisk footsteps came towards her. "Good morning, RK, how are you? Have you recovered from your escapade? Gil said it was dire."

RK turned her head towards the sound of the voice.

"It's you Rosie. I'm well, thankyou, how are you? How's the job going?"

"The job and I are fine."

RK laughed and reached out to hold Rosie's arm affectionately, "That sounds as though you are still enjoying it."

"Oh, I am, loving every minute. I come in early every day to make the sweet pastries and scones and then serve in the coffee shop till about two o'clock. Jilly bakes everything else, though she's got a new College student who seems to be a dab hand at sponges and gateaux that she's encouraging her to develop. I think if Carly's creations prove popular Emma may take her on permanently when she's qualified. Now where would you like to sit, RK?"

"Where would you recommend?"

"How about the table you had before? If you use the same one each time it will become familiar and also because it's behind the screen and by the wall it offers a degree of privacy."

"That sounds ideal. No one will be able to see the mess I make of things," RK chuckled. "Now, Rosie, let me find my own way to it. Just guide me in the right direction so I don't bang into anything that could cause havoc."

It was Rosie's turn to smile. "You won't cause chaos, RK, you always brighten the day with your gaiety. That's why my brothers and sisters liked you so much. You turned everything into fun."

RK wafted a hand dismissively as she felt her way around the backs of the chairs and edged into a space near a table. "Am I in the right place, Rosie?"

"If you feel comfortable there then it's the right place."

"Very diplomatic, Rosie. It seems very quiet this morning."

"It's still quite early."

RK drew a quick breath. "Am I too early?"

"No, I didn't mean that. Friday's always a slow start but it gets busier nearer to lunchtime."

"Oh, I'm coming back for my lunch today. Do I need to book?"

"That won't be necessary. There will always be a place for you."

"Thanks. What delicacy are you going to tempt me with today, a scone, some gateaux or a pastry or even a sausage roll? You choose, so it will be a surprise."

"Now that is a temptation! As it's you, RK, I might be persuaded to make up a plate with a mouthful of each on it."

RK's laughter resounded through the coffee shop. "Now, Rosie, don't be a tease!"

"Me?" she giggled. "You're the one who taught me the art of teasing." Rosie left the table grinning all the way to the kitchen area.

As she sat waiting for her coffee RK thought of all she had heard in recent days concerning the wood clearing opposite the Village Stores and the tales that were being told about former inhabitants of the rediscovered properties.

It would appear that as ledgers and documents unearthed in the front room of the first building in the row were perused, ownership of the property had come into question. Letters, documents, bills of sale and accounts had been discovered from the era when Emma's great, great grandfather was farrier to the de Vessey estate as well as the time, following his untimely death, when his youngest daughter, Kezia, worked hard at establishing the Village Stores. *I'm sure those records will make fascinating reading. I'd love to see the cost of the food items from that generation.* Apparently Kezia's mother had died giving birth to her and she and her two older sisters, Lois and Nesta were subsequently brought up by Granny Bemment, who acted as village 'midwife', layer-out of dead bodies, shop keeper and cobbler and managed her son-in-law's household while he submerged himself in his work at the smithy.

Tinkling of china upon a tray broke RK's reverie. Quickly she shot upright and cocked her head to the right in order to catch any further sounds.

"Here you are, RK." Rosie said with a smile as she set down a tray on the table. "I've done as you suggested, a selection, two sorts of scone and slithers from two of our latest gateaux." She expertly placed all within RK's reach then without fuss picked up her friend's hand to show her the geography of the table. Bending low she whispered, "To your right coffee is poured into a delicate white china mug decorated with red roses, milk no sugar. There's no saucer. Please indicate when you would like a refill. The scones are buttered and placed on the left side of a matching plate immediately in front of you, while the gateaux is on the right, coffee and walnut towards the top and chocolate orange beneath. A desert fork is here on the right should you require it and I will now place a deep red coloured napkin on your lap."

"This is wonderful, Rosie. You were simply superb."

"Not at all, please enjoy, and let me know if you need anything else."

For a moment after Rosie had departed RK felt overwhelmed by her kindness. Then, tentatively she allowed her fingers to reach out in the direction Rosie had indicated. When there were no mishaps and she was able to move within the bounds of the picture map Rosie had created RK relaxed and enjoyed her coffee break. Her mind drifted back to her earlier thoughts about Emma's ancestors.

It would seem from what I've heard that following the death of Granny Bemment, Kezia, who from all reports appears to have been a hard worker, built up the Village Stores. Upon her marriage to John Durrant she and her husband bought the corner property opposite because it provided more room for stock. This is the building that now houses the present Village Stores and Post Office and it's where I'm now sitting.

"Good morning, RK."

RK flinched and dropped the piece of scone she'd been holding. "Oh, Emma, I didn't hear you come in."

"Sorry, RK, I didn't intend to startle you."

"I was miles away wondering what your ancestors would make of their bedrooms becoming a communal meeting place for people to share coffee and scones."

Emma laughed as she pulled up a chair and sat down next to RK. "Well, I think Kezia would have been all for it. She seems to have been an innovative thinker for her generation. Not so her two sisters, Lois and Nesta. They were very set in their ways. They remained in the original property, the one that Stephen's busy restoring, for the rest of their lives neither marrying. They took in washing and sewing and carried on the tradition of midwives and layers-out-of-bodies to subsidize their meagre income. Through lack of use, because of the introduction of steam and subsequently motor power on local farms and the consequent decline in horse power, the smithy fell into disrepair although Lois still cobbled shoes, a skill which she had learned from her father and grandmother. But reading between the lines I don't think they would have approved the change in use of this building even though they never lived here."

"I understand that all documentation points to your family being the true owners of the property Doctor John attempted to buy from the de Vessey estate for Stephen?"

"It would appear so, however, the more people delve into the history of the properties the more it seems a mystery as to how or why the de Vessey estate claims ownership."

"Why's that?"

"Well, the Kemp family appear to be legitimate heirs of Kezia who inherited the estate when her older sisters died within months of one another. Their mother and grandmother had been Kemps. The documents are in Kezia's name. Her father was descended from the Bemment's."

"I hear Adam Catton has been seconded to use his legal expertise to unravel the mystery."

"Yes, that is true. A faded piece of paper suggests Annie Bemment may have been one of the earliest owners of that house. We're unsure how that came about. In the mid nineteenth century because there was so much intermarriage between families relationships seem a little blurred so Adam is meticulously untangling every strand of the family line in order to come to an accurate conclusion with regard to inheritance."

"I don't envy him that task."

"No, it is difficult to get a correct line of succession because most of the village can trace their lineage back to Annie. The property has stood hidden and empty for so many years, in fact, no one living can remember it being the blacksmiths and no one recalls seeing the smithy exposed before."

"I've heard many say that it's always been shrouded by the woods."

"One or two of the most senior citizens have vague recollections of stories told to them by their parents of old ladies living there and Mr Bracewell remembers tales that his grandmother related of the exploits of Lois and Nesta when they were younger."

"This all sounds very intriguing."

"You're right. Tremendous excitement has been generated in the village by the recovery of the artefacts of history. The cameo they present of the sort of life their ancestors may have lived has sparked remarkable interest amongst a cross section of our community. Stephen is particularly anxious to preserve all that has been found however small or seemingly insignificant. To the delight of ladies in the village beautifully hand sewn baby garments as well as gowns and household linen were unearthed in ottomans concealed in the upstairs room, so fragile, they resemble the gossamer lace of cobwebs."

"That's amazing."

"What's even more amazing is that so many want a hand in the restoration of this facet of village life that has been hidden for such a long time."

"I guess they connect with the fragment of history that identifies their own family root..."

"Emma, I need..." RK caught the interruption and heard the scraping of chair legs against the surface of the floor.

"Excuse me a moment, RK, I seem to be needed for something."

RK took the moments alone to reflect on their conversation. She had always been astonished at the tremendous support for a self-sufficient community there was in the village. It seemed whenever a new enterprise was proposed all aspects were thrashed out at parish level as well as on the village grapevine, from her experience generally the village shop. If a proposal was greeted favourably it received unreserved co-operation. In fact, the number of people coming into the new coffee shop while she sat there was evidence of the backing of local people for this scheme of Emma's. Many of them stopped to speak with her and wish her well. So it was no surprise to RK when she learned that Stephen Cooper's venture to open a book shop and carpentry business was given wholehearted approval.

"I'm sure it will not only provide work for Stephen but help the village economy by providing goods and services for locals and visitors alike," she said to Emma who had rejoined her for coffee.

"You may be right though I feel each will have different expectations."

"I think from what I've heard that Stephen is well aware of that and has sufficient vision to cater to the needs of all potential customers."

"That's true. There seems to be no stopping his imagination."

"Apart from funding, I guess."

"Yes, I'm certain that is so, however, although he doesn't have the resources at the moment, he is anxious to locate premises nearby to create a museum to present the artefacts that have been found in Kezia's first village stores and her father's smithy. The discovery of the cobbled roadway behind his property and between the adjoining properties beneath years of overgrown undergrowth has opened up many possibilities, at least in Stephen's eyes, but lack of finance has curtailed further work, in any case, for the time being."

"That must be frustrating."

"It is for Stephen though Lord Edmund has offered the use of a locked barn, pro tem, to house the articles of historic interest in order to keep them together and in a safe place."

"I understand ownership of the neighbouring dwellings has also been looked into by Adam."

"Yes, and although it still has to be confirmed Stephen is already proposing the building adjacent to his be restored and used as a library."

"Oh, Jennifer will be pleased. She has been nagging him for ages to do something about a book lending service so that she and others don't have to travel into Norwich simply to collect and exchange reading books."

"The thing is how long will such a service be viable?"

"What do you mean?"

"Well, with Kindle and such like becoming more and more popular there soon won't be any call for printed books."

"I can't believe that will happen in our life-time, so many people still like to feel a book in their hand and not just the older people but even the children. I remember Daniel and Kirsten enjoyed handling books and being read stories from them."

"I guess you're right. I love opening a new book and can't resist putting it up to my nose and breathing in the delicious scent of its newness."

"According to Kirsty Stephen's old books exude the fragrance of the Beckingsdale's horses..."

Emma burst out laughing, "Trust Kirsty to come up with something like that."

"She always was an original thinker but both she and Daniel think I would enjoy Stephen's shop so I thought I would attempt to get over there today. Then, after exploring his shop I'll make my way back in here for my lunch."

"I should think by then you'll be more than ready to sit down. Don't do too much. Stephen can be overwhelmingly enthusiastic."

"Oh, I don't mind that. He might encourage me in my resolve to be independent."

Chuckling, Emma got up and clapped her friend affectionately on her shoulder, "Good luck and enjoy yourself. Let me know when you're ready to go and I'll see you across the road."

"Oh, that won't be necessary..."

"Ooops," as Emma turned she bumped into Roger who'd just walked into the coffee shop. She put a finger to her lips and shook her head at him, her eyes alight with mischief.

"Well, if I won't do as your escort, RK, how about the handsome man who's your Doctor?"

"Oh, I didn't hear you come in, Doctor Roger."

Roger raised his eyebrows quizzically at Emma but went along with her little ruse because he was so delighted to see RK out on her own.

"Yes, I'm here, RK, and willing to be of service to you, after which I hope my wife can spare time to take coffee with me."

"Oh, don't let me detain you. I'm sure I can make my own way over to Stephen's." RK made to get up from her place at the table.

"Now then, RK, don't be so hasty, you haven't yet finished your own coffee." Rosie, who had been hovering nearby, gently steered RK back down into her seat. "Doc, you and Emma go and have a quiet five minutes together, while you've chance, you're both such busy people. We'll sort out RK's needs when she's ready to leave."

"Yeah, we'll give a 'and."

"O' course."

"It seems as if you have an army of willing volunteers at your command, RK, so for the time being, we'll leave you in the capable hands of Rosie." Before leaving Roger leant forward, touched her arm, and said in a quieter voice, "I'm so delighted to see you out, RK, take care."

# Chapter Fifteen

Some hours later RK realised what Emma had meant about Stephen's enthusiasm; ideas for the future of the rediscovered properties just seemed to flow from him. He had taken her around every inch of his own property, described in great detail all that had been done, what had been found and where and pointed out the possibilities of the other properties. He placed into her hands ancient tools, guided her fingers along the rough hewn walls of the former smithy, the remains of the forge furnace and the wooden panelling in the house as well as encouraged her to bend down to touch the well-worn cobblestones traversed by generations of feet and hooves.

He was anxious she experience the discoveries to the full even though she was unable to see them so constantly persuaded her to "Feel this, RK," or "Explore this with your fingers." Stephen's keenness bubbled over till RK felt she was almost swallowed up with his fervour and excitement. When he led her into the shop part of his domain she was even allowed to hold some of his priceless volumes to experience Kirsty's horsey smell for herself.

"Mmm, a musty sort of smell," exclaimed RK as she poked her nose within the pages. "This aroma conjures up for me a picture of something old, I feel as though I am suspended in the past."

"Back in history, you mean?"

"Yes. It brings to mind the disused labourer's cottage that we played in as children on my Grandfather's farm."

"Were you supposed to?"

"No, it was out of bounds, but that's what made it all the more inviting and my sisters and I pretended we were people of long ago who may have lived and worked there."

"That's the atmosphere I want to create with a living museum."

"The old pump in the yard fascinated me and I spent hours pushing the rusty arm up and down, sometimes being rewarded with only a trickle of water." For a few moments RK was lost in the warm embrace of memories of her fenland childhood while Stephen's thoughts were still engrossed in designs to display village history for future generations and how he could make some of the exhibits interactive.

"I suppose a museum housed in the same building as the library would be best to put on show all the fantastic finds we've made," he mused "but having it up the stairs would not be ideal. Health and safety, you know."

RK laughed. "People like me would prove a liability, you mean."

"Of course," he chuckled, "but this is just a pipe dream of mine at the moment and I would have to find somewhere else to live."

"Have you considered the possibility of using one of the other properties rather than cramming all your enterprises into the same building," suggested RK.

Stephen grasped her arm excitedly, "I think you may have something there RK. Next door but one could well be the perfect venue to develop as the museum but Ben and his team have yet to complete their assessment of the quality of the existing structures. I'm also unsure of the extent of the outbuildings that remain or how much restoration work will be required." He slowly shook his head. "Firstly, I really must concentrate on this property and establishing my own business to build up an income so that I can pay the bills."

"You've certainly got your work cut out for a long time to come."

"That's true and I've also got my eye on the thatched cottage opposite the smithy workshop but ownership of that is in question."

"Good gracious, Stephen, haven't you enough to do?"

Stephen shrugged his shoulders. "Uncle Roy Durrant remembers old Thompson Beresford living there when he was a boy. He feels sure Tom had a daughter but whether she still owns it or not he's uncertain, not seen her here for years but believes she lived Gloucester way somewhere, neglected it somewhat over the years. Be a lovely home if looked after but that's way into the future. Anyway, the coffers are empty so I can't do much about that at the moment." He pulled out the lining of his pockets then grimaced resignedly when he realised RK could not see his actions.

"You've certainly set your sights high and to achieve all that you're going to be working hard for many years to come."

"It will all be worth it," he replied eagerly.

"I'm sure you're right."

"Have you seen the Village Restoration Fund notice boards?"

RK shook her head.

"Of course you haven't. I'd forgotten you weren't here when we commenced this project. I'll take you out to see them now. I'll just put out the closed notice and lock up."

"Are you sure? I've already taken up a lot of your time."

"I will always have time for you, RK, and as you see I'm not exactly run off my feet with customers at the moment."

RK's laughter burst forth, "That time will soon come, I'm quite sure."

Without further ado, he took RK's elbow, guided her through the premises and out into the fresh air. It was obvious that Stephen was thrilled to the core by the transformation of Kezia's Wood and the scope the land reclamation offered. So propelled by his enthusiasm RK was not given a chance to refuse this additional excursion.

They swiftly left the book shop. As they turned right to walk along the lane Bernice Durrant waved and called out to them from across the road as she left the Village Stores.

"Good morning," she quickly bustled over the road to join them.

"How are you getting along, RK?" Bernice leaned forward and touched her arm. "I hope this young man isn't wearing you out."

"I'm fine," replied RK, "and at the moment I'm learning to adapt to my surroundings. Stephen is helping by giving me an enlightening morning explaining all the changes that have been taking place while I have been away."

"I can well believe that. He's such an energetic livewire." Bernice smiled affectionately and RK burst out laughing, "Yes, I've never moved so rapidly through history but I've learned much that I didn't know. It's been a fascinating experience."

"And what about the future? Do you have any plans?"

"Well!" RK sighed, "Doctor Roger has me on a rehabilitation programme. It's supposed to be mutually worked out but at times he pushes me beyond the agreed boundaries. He's determined that I become an integrated member of society as soon as possible."

"That brother of yours sounds a hard task master, Stephen."

"Aunt Bernice, you know as well as I do that when Roger's focussed on something nothing will deflect him from the goal."

Bernice chuckled, "You boys are so alike, 'peas in a pod' as my father would say."

RK nodded her head vigorously, "You're right, Stephen, Roger has a one track mind and really believes I shall succeed in living an active independent life."

Bernice patted her arm, "I'm sure you will, my dear, you're blessed with the same determined spirit that won't give in to defeat. Now, my dears, I mustn't keep you, I have jobs at home needing my attention. Enjoy your journey of discovery, RK. If at any time you need my help just ask. Remember, too, there are lots of people praying for you." Bernice turned, waved her hand in farewell and bustled back along the lane pulling her trolley of shopping behind her.

"I do like Mrs Durrant. I wish my Mum was more like her," said RK wistfully.

"Most people are fond of Aunt Bernice and appreciate her kindliness," Stephen agreed. "Do you miss home?"

"Not really."

"Are you likely to return?"

"Not at all," returned RK sharply.

"Oh!" Stephen, who had only ever shared warmth and affection with his immediate as well as his extended family was surprised at RK's vehemence.

"My family have made it clear that as a blind person I am a nuisance to them, totally useless, so unwelcome at the farm."

"I'm sorry, RK, I can't begin to imagine what it's like to be placed in that sort of position. Some of us did wonder if you would return home to the farm once you'd adapted to your condition."

"No, that's not possible! I've received more kindness and encouragement from my friends in this village than from my own family, apart from my sister Davi, since the accident that I've decided I want to remain here. With help from Doctor Roger and his press ganged volunteers I will settle back into Ferry Cottage in a few days time," she replied with steely grit.

"What about work?"

"That's where Roger and I differ strongly. He's very confident that I will work again."

"And you?"

"Utter nonsense! How can a blind person look after children? Every mother and teacher knows that you need eyes in the back of your head as well as the front when working with active children."

"You're right, that is a difficult one," Stephen said thoughtfully.

"But that's what I'm trained to do, as well as motor mechanics, at the insistence of my father. Ironic, isn't it?

I'm highly skilled and qualified in two areas of expertise but now incapable of doing either." She smothered a choked sob.

"You're a good storyteller," Stephen quickly interspersed.

"Right! I'll put an advert in the Journal, 'Storyteller available, any place any time'. Will that do?"

Stephen laughed and gripped her arm, "I do admire your guts, RK. You don't give in easily, do you?"

"I did at one time till your brother and sister-in-law persuaded me otherwise. They're the ones with spirit who've instilled determination in me. And, after all they've done for me, I won't let them down."

"Good for you, RK. I'm sure when the time is right a job will open up for you. Shall we move on?"

Stephen steered her in the right direction then commenced to regale her with further snippets of news about the progress of the development and his scheme to enhance the enterprise for the future of the village, on the way to the location of the notice board. However, for a time he found it difficult to concentrate because unbidden numerous ideas jostled in his mind, following the conversation he had just shared with RK, with regard to possible job opportunities for her.

In the quiet moments RK's thoughts dwelt on the discovery of the cobbled roadway alongside the property, which seemed to have been dubbed by so many in the village as Stephen's cottage. She tried to picture the adjoining dwellings hidden for so long beneath decades of bracken and brambles, uncontrolled saplings developing into established trees, thicket and thistles, which after the clearance had opened up so many possibilities for Stephen's suggestion for a living museum. "People like authenticity and this certainly dates back to that generation."

"I can almost hear the clippity-clop of horse hooves going out to the fields or pulling a wagon or carriage," RK said.

"I'm so glad you can picture my dream of making history come alive. The uncertainty of ownership of the adjoining property causes concern but I hope it won't be long before Adam has some concrete news for us then with help from volunteers we'll be able to move on to the next phase of restoration." Stephen then went on to describe in detail the next door property that could possibly be suitable as the library.

"It's a pity the archway connecting the two properties has caved in and the room above has been lost."

"How do you know it was there?"

"An old sepia photo has been unearthed which depicts a large gated archway with a room above between the buildings."

"Really?" RK's face brightened.

"In the picture there's a wagon in the foreground with a couple of men loading a sackbarrow so we think it may have been the wheelwrights or saddlers, whichever, the high gate would have opened to allow horse drawn carts and wagons to pass beneath. I don't think it is feasible to rebuild it as it was although the pile of rubble smothered by weeds and brambles suggests there might be sufficient bricks to clean up and reclaim."

"Surely there aren't enough hours in the day to accomplish all that you want to get done and how on earth can you man all the different enterprises on your own?"

"Oh, I'm not doing it alone. We have oodles of volunteers. I simply chivvy them along but Ben and Chit are the true foremen and oversight everything to ensure correct procedures are followed."

"It certainly sounds an exciting project and one that seems to have brought the community closer together."

"Yes, for once, there appears to be harmony between the different neighbourhoods of the parish. They're all keen to restore their heritage."

"That's really good."

Stephen stopped abruptly. "Oh, no! RK, I'm sorry but I've brought you the way by the flight of steps next to the church."

"That's OK," RK chuckled, "I can manage steps."

"But it's a bit of a steep climb," Stephen said apologetically.

"I'm not old and decrepit, yet! Just warn me when we get near to the top." RK reached out to grab the handrail and purposefully climbed the stairway.

"Yes, RK," Stephen murmured somewhat abashed as he hovered behind RK like a mother hen till she safely reached the summit.

"I always used the lane to get to The Green because I generally had Poppy in her buggy," said RK somewhat puffed after her exertions. "I think despite the incline it was less strenuous than the steps."

"Most times I come this way from Mum and Dad's house. It seems much quicker to the Village Stores, the bus stop and certainly nearer to my book and workshop."

"I imagine your long legs fairly skip up and down these stairs two at a time."

Stephen grinned, "How did you guess?" Deftly he manoeuvred RK across the grass.

"Now, here we are RK. I've brought you to the Display Board on The Green because..." he paused, "well... I thought this one was the most accessible." He put his hand under her elbow and guided her towards the board.

"I've done this one in relief so you can feel the different facets of the proposed development. Put your hand up here, RK. See, you can feel my shop and the cobbles alongside. Now, follow along and there are the impressions of the other dwellings as they might be when restored. I persuaded Jilly's brother-in-law to paint the board in bright colours so that they stand out clearly depicting the different stages of the restoration.

"Rob's also designed an information board for the village car park, one side explains the stages of the restoration and the other highlights areas of interest within the village such as footpaths that criss-cross the heath and common, the old smoke houses, the church, the fishermen's hospital etcetera. There's also an additional notice board giving the PCC's reasons for the car park and restriction of traffic through the village, safety, you know, as well as to keep the village unspoiled.

"Various groups within the parish are keen to raise funds for the project and particularly want to capture visitor's imaginations and pockets to support the scheme, so we want to put as much info as possible before them."

"Oh, is this a horse?"

"Yes, and a cart."

"Some trees and a cat, I hope not a mouse."

"No, I'm not Grinling Gibbons," Stephen chuckled. "Actually, I've yet to think of a trademark."

"Surely there's plenty of time for that, though I think among all the artefacts that have been uncovered you'll find something to inspire you."

"You're probably right."

"Possibly a book or a tool?"

"Mmmm, could be!" Stephen murmured thoughtfully. "Although I have a deep rooted love of old publications such as books and maps as well as postcards and have amassed a large collection I recognize that it's my skill as a carpenter that is going to be my bread and butter to pay the bills that suddenly seem to be accumulating at an alarming speed. I'll give it some thought."

"So, you're going to have to knuckle down with the hammer and chisel."

"Too right!"

"And are there plans for the other derelict buildings?"

"Yes, Graeme and Adam have shown a keen interest in one of the properties in the row, as have Stuart Jenner and Rachel Durrant and Lily Jenner has said in no uncertain terms that we must keep one available for her to turn into a flower shop when she's finished school!"

"Really?" RK asked in a surprised voice.

"Yes, they've all been looking to secure premises in order to set up businesses in the village. As you know Adam's been acting window cleaner since your accident and Laura's stroke but feels now is a good time to be considering practising law again, in some capacity. He doesn't wish to return to working in Norwich and his former employers are agreeable to him establishing a branch office in Newton Westerby as he can always be in touch with the main office via the internet."

"That all sounds very good, in theory, but surely it's going to take some time to establish if all these properties still have to be assessed and then restored."

"You're right, RK, it won't happen overnight because there's such an awful lot of work to be done and hence the reason for the restoration fund notice boards to raise awareness for finance to meet the expenses."

"I see and what is Graeme's involvement in all this?"

"Well, Graeme, too, would prefer to be village based rather than city bound in his accountancy business. His association with the village holiday letting business also led to a suggestion that an estate agency could be incorporated in his office; this, the PCC suggests, is to ensure that any vacant premises do not get into the hands of the unscrupulous, either builders keen to knock down and rebuild to make a profit or would be 'second homers' who snaffle up and tie down property. Lord Edmund and those on the village housing committee, like my Mum, are anxious there are always properties available for local people to rent or buy to enable them to live in their home area should they so desire. However, everyone realises the boost to the village economy when holiday makers stay in the area so want to retain a percentage of cottages as holiday rentals."

"When I first came here I thought Newton Westerby was a quiet little backwater where nothing ever happened. How wrong I was!"

"If you delve deep enough our community just brims with activity."

"So I'm finding out but whatever sparks Stuart and Rachel's interest in derelict buildings?"

"Well, they're both looking for premises to develop as permanent bases for their established mobile hairdressing business."

"Really?"

"In fact, if they can find the right property Stuart has suggested they share the space and Rachel is in agreement. They're both looking to take on local apprentices in association with Lowestoft College."

"So, what has for years been an eyesore and embarrassment in the community suddenly emerges as a prominent site with exciting potential."

"You're right, RK and it's all in the control of local people and not some unprincipled builder."

"And I understand from Laura that some of Kezia's Wood has been retained."

"Chit discovered some choice oak and beech and even an avenue of lime trees mingled amongst hawthorn and blackthorn, chestnuts and alder, elder and rhododendrons. He's cleverly cleared the choking ivy, brambles and other weeds as well as self sown saplings and created a managed woodland habitat at the bottom of the very long gardens of the properties."

"I guess not many people garden these days..."

"Apart from Uncle Roy and Aunt Bernice..."

"...and Miss Pedwardine."

They laughed as together they exclaimed, "They are the exception and have very fine gardens."

"Laura was an avid gardener, too, before her stroke and grew a lot of produce for the kitchen. I guess it's not so easy for her now."

"Don't you believe it! Laura's not a shirker and won't give in to the restrictions her stroke placed on her physical activities. She and Tessa Jenner are still keen to promote fresh produce for the table. So, to encourage her Nathan organized the lads in a digging session at the Catton's then Ryan Saunders helped Tessa and Laura plant up the garden. They were the foremost advocates for the preservation of Kezia's Wood for the birds and other wild life usually resident there."

"I can well believe it, and footpaths and benches will make it a park for all to enjoy." RK shifted uneasily before continuing. "Stephen, I do appreciate all the time you've given to me this morning, it's been a fascinating insight into the history as well as the future of this village..."

"But...I know there's a but coming..."

RK's voice boomed out in laughter before she continued..."but I have no idea what the present time is and I'm supposed to be back at the coffee shop for lunch."

Stephen joined her in laughter as he checked his watch, "It is thirty seven minutes past twelve o'clock, so I'll give Emma a call to let her know that you are on your way, then I will escort you back down the lane."

"There's really no need for that, Stephen, just point me in the right direction and I will find my own way there."

Stephen held onto her arm until he finished his call on the mobile phone. "Don't you dare run away from me, RK," he scolded playfully as his companion made to pull away from his grasp, "even if I do begin to bore you to tears. In fact, there's someone coming up the lane to accompany you to lunch far more worthy of your attention than I am." Unseen by RK he raised his arm in greeting to the figure striding his way up the incline.

"Stop teasing, Stephen," RK laughed.

"I've never been more serious and I believe he will escort you by way of the sedate slope of the lane rather than the mountainous descent of the steps."

A few minutes later Rosie glimpsed the pair, en route for their lunch, through the window of the Tea Rooms as she adjusted curtains against bright sunlight for the customers she was serving.

"What a fine couple they make," she thought.

As soon as RK realised her lunch companion was none other than Dan Prettyman her heart somersaulted with delight tempered with apprehension. She kept the tone of their conversation light regaling the young constable with her morning exploits with Stephen Cooper till half-way through their meal when Dan's jocular tone became warm and serious, he clasped her hand and asked RK if he might court her.

"Court me, Dan?" she asked in a bemused voice, "But I feel I never know where I stand with you."

Quite nonplussed Dan sat patiently. He was very sure of his feelings for this lovely young woman and wanted to give her opportunity to express her view on the matter.

"In Lincolnshire we got on so well together, like close friends, you treated me with warmth and caring and I felt definite affection for you BUT since my return to Newton Westerby you seem aloof and detached and positively frosty in your manner towards me."

"That's my job, Robyn. The nature of the work dictates I must be professional in my dealings with the public."

"But I'm not the public!"

"You are if you're present when I'm attending an incident."

"That's my point. There are times when you seem to be wanting a closer relationship with me but there are other times when you are so distant you act as though you don't even know me." She withdrew her hand and deliberately placed it on her lap under the table.

"Robyn, let's get this straight once and for all. I am Dan, your friend who cares for you very much and wants to get to know you better – feel – no buttons, no uniform, you have my undivided attention.

"Robyn, please give me your hand." Dan took it and guided it across his shoulders, "See, no epaulettes." He brushed her fingers across his chest, "Look no pockets and definitely no buttons, just a woolly jumper. I'm off duty – I'm all yours."

"But..."

"Aah, Robyn, you and your buts," Dan chuckled. "When on duty I am Her Majesty's officer of the law and I'm governed by strict criteria."

"But..."

"It's not you or your situation." When RK shook her head and pursed her lips in disbelief he said, "Truly, it's nothing personal. It's just the way it is."

Concerned Dan watched RK's troubled features as she processed his words.

After some moments of silence RK slowly nodded in understanding. "When you're working you speak in a different voice. You sound distant, cold and fierce. I thought it was directed at me, a ploy by you to disassociate yourself from me because you no longer wished to be friends..."

"Well, I'm glad we've cleared up that little misunderstanding because I very much want to be best friends with you, in fact, Robyn, I would like to court you with a view to one day getting married."

Dan stopped speaking. RK hadn't heard a word he had spoken to her. She was continuing along her own train of thought.

"...but now, your voice is warm and deep and almost cuddly. It exudes kindness and gentleness but at Ferry Cottage, when the bailiffs broke in, it was clipped and icy, harsh and calculating. You were very masterly and spoke with authority. I was quite afraid of you."

"Oh, Robyn." Dan reached again for her hand believing that at this moment the physical sensation of touch was the only way to convey the depth of his feeling for her. He held it lightly in his own while he gently stroked the back of it.

"Dan, it's beginning to make sense to me. I expected you to always be the same, well, you know what I mean. You are the same person but you have different roles. Like me when I looked after Daniel and the girls. Sometimes I was firm, at times cross, on occasion gentle, other times we had fun and laughter but I was always me – I simply adapted my role to circumstances. Your job requires the same of you. So, because I can't see you, I must become skilled at listening in order to read situations and by experience learn to differentiate between what are personal meetings between the two of us and those instances when you are on official police business."

The prolonged silence that followed was electric.

RK shook her head. "I guess I'm not explaining myself very well because you are very quiet."

"You are describing your feelings very clearly, Robyn, and I understand perfectly what you're saying. I think it's unfortunate you've got caught up, quite innocently I must add, in a number of cases that have required an official presence."

RK laughed, "And that presence was most officious!"

Dan joined in her laughter. "Can I get you anything more to eat? More coffee? Or shall we make a move?"

"No, I've had sufficient. That was splendid."

Dan pushed back his chair, "I'll settle up with Rosie, then."

"Dan, there is just one thing..."

Dan quickly sat down again, "What is that?"

"You can see me..."

"And what a delightful sight that is."

"Dan, please, be serious. I can't see you. How can I be aware of your feelings if I can't see your expression or look into your eyes. When you're silent how can I know if you're grimacing or frowning, smiling, scowling, winking or pursing your lips, or anything else for that matter."

"By touch?"

"I can't do that if we're not marri..." aghast RK drew back.

"Now, Robyn, you're not to worry about this. I'm sure there's a solution," Dan swiftly butted in.

"See," exclaimed RK tensely, "you know immediately that I'm concerned. How did you know?"

"Your shoulders drooped."

"There you are! I'm not able to see your actions or mannerisms, you know, those tell-tale signs that telegraph unspoken thoughts and feelings."

"Robyn, there's a way through every problem. It might take some time but we'll find that answer." Dan patted her hand affectionately as he rose from the table. "I'll just pay the bill."

"Oh, I've got my card," RK rummaged in her bag but Dan caught her hand.

"My treat, I'll settle up with Rosie then we'll call on Mrs Vicar and ask what she advises, shall we?"

To his relief Dan saw RK visibly relax. "Oh, Dan, that's an excellent idea."

# Chapter Sixteen

❖

Penny Darnell had not long been home from a W.I. planning meeting and only got as far as undoing the buttons on her outdoor jacket when the door bell rang. Responding to the ring she turned to retrace her footsteps down the hallway. She switched on the kettle as she passed, in order to make a pot of tea for her husband who was working in his study, and opened the front door. On seeing her callers she greeted RK and Dan warmly.

"Do come in. Whatever you've called in for I'm sure will go down well with a cup of tea." As Penny hustled her visitors along the hallway she asked, "Now is it a study or sitting room visit?"

"Oh, we don't want to bother the Vicar or put you about, Mrs Darnell, but we would like your advice. I'm sure the kitchen will do fine if that's where you're going to be," said RK following the sound of the vicar's wife's retreating footsteps.

"To be honest, Mrs Darnell, we have in fact only just finished lunch in the tea rooms," explained Dan as he seated Robyn at the kitchen table, "but thankyou all the same."

Penny smiled, slipped off her short outer coat and swiftly prepared a tea-tray for her husband. "I'll just take this along to Hugh, and then I can give you my full attention."

RK looked decidedly uncomfortable perched on the edge of the chair with her back stiff and ram-rod straight so while Penny was gone Dan placed his hands on her shoulders to ease the tension, leaned forward and whispered in RK's ear, "All will be well, my little song-bird."

RK coloured up at his nearness. "How can you be so sure?"

"Trust me I just know it will be so."

On her return to the kitchen Penny joined the young couple seated around the kitchen table and listened as they voiced their concerns. She encouraged them to consider all aspects of their blossoming relationship in an open and honest manner and accept there were bound to be differences in their courtship to what was perceived as the norm because their situation was somewhat unique.

"So there are no hard and fast rules?"

"I don't think so," Penny smiled.

"But..." began RK uncertainly.

"Oh, Robyn, you and your buts!" interrupted Dan playfully.

"But," she continued undeterred, "If people see me touching you they'll think I'm being over familiar."

"Of course they won't."

"The people who matter will see it as a sign of affection and recognize touch is now going to be a vital part of your understanding the world around you and the people in it."

"I really don't want my actions to be misconstrued."

"They won't be," Penny got up as she spoke and reached forward to clasp RK's hand. "Every time I see you I'll greet you like this and I'll ask Emma and Miranda to do the same then, hopefully, others will catch on."

"A hand smile?" Dan grinned.

"Yes, something like that."

"A touch of acknowledgement or agreement?"

"Yes, I think so, a gesture in place of a nod or the shake of the head."

"I like that idea."

"I'm sure that before long it will become a natural action between you and your friends especially when they realise touch simply replaces facial expression and recognition that they take for granted."

"But Dan and me...?

"That, too, will soon be accepted as the norm when word gets round that you are going out together."

---

Not surprisingly, the strolling of Dan and RK back along Green Lane half-an-hour later did not go unnoticed. They were observed by a number of Newton Westerby residents long before the vicar partook of his tea and caused much comment and speculation amongst the onlookers.

The first to see them was Mr Bracewell as he finished a late dinner. He was seated by the window of his cottage which abutted the lane alongside The Green before it turned the corner and sloped down towards the Village Stores. The bow aspect proffered quite a vantage point from which to observe all the too-ings and fro-ings in the village. For someone who didn't venture too far afield these days because of arthritis in his knees it was a good means of keeping abreast of village affairs. "Well, thass a fine kettle of fish!" he muttered to himself as he clattered his cutlery onto his plate and wiped his mouth across a greasy cuff.

His viewing of the couple was closely followed by that of Mrs Jenner who had completed the washing up after her midday meal, fed the cat and opened the door to let her out in response to her persistent mewing, as Dan and RK walked passed. The position of her cottage at the apex of the lane gave her ample opportunity to watch all comings and goings of her fellow villagers. "So, thass how the land lies!" she confided to Kitty who nonchalantly went about her business. Mrs Jenner sagely nodded her head.

As the young couple continued their descent down the lane Cynthia Durrant spied them from the doorway of the butcher's shop as she waited for Billy Cooper to slice up some lamb's liver. Whilst Gordon insisted she buy fresh meat from Cooper's butchers Cynthia refused to go further than the well-scrubbed threshold step.

Cynthia blamed Billy and Pauline for the break-up of their children's marriage and scathingly accused them of believing her handsome boy was not good enough for their daughter. Blue-eyed Matty, the youngest in the Durrant's family of three, had been spoiled from birth and his naughty ways overlooked by his indulgent mother. As he grew into manhood charm masked his deceit and slip-shod working patterns. It was his charm and good looks that had won Miranda's heart. Having been brought up in a home where Christian values, straight talking and honesty were the norm duplicity was foreign to her. After only a few weeks of married life Miranda learned that the outward façade of decency and goodness Matty presented in the public arena was a clever act of pretence. In the intimacy of their own home he was brutally demanding, scornful of her faith and derisive of the naive view of life she displayed when she got upset as he boasted of his female conquests and mocked her when she innocently spoke of loyalty and faithfulness. She couldn't believe that the man to whom she had entrusted her heart and pledged her life was such a charlatan.

Cynthia's response to her son's womanising was, "Well what do you expect? That's what men do!"

But, Miranda couldn't handle Matty's complete disregard of his marriage vows and after five months returned to her parent's home.

Cynthia saw this as a slight on her family and laid blame for this state of affairs squarely at the door of Billy and Pauline because they had accepted their daughter back.

Now, she stood on the butcher's step with her back to the shop and its owners in particular, watching the progress of Dan and RK with interest.

"Well," she exclaimed indignantly, "just look at that! Quite brazen they are, these days."

"Oh, come now, Cynthia, in RK's situation she needs a helping hand. Dan's simply being gentlemanly."

"Humph! Gentlemanly, my foot," snorted the disgruntled Cynthia.

"I agree," remarked someone further back in the shop, "such shameless behaviour among the young uns these days. Dew yew know she spent the mornin' with one young man and is now in comp'ny wi' another this afternoon!" The speaker tossed her head and clicked her tongue in disgust. Others waiting their turn in the queue were of the same mind, "Tittle-tattle seems to follow that young lady around."

Keen to change the subject Billy asked, "You going to Isobel's rearranged soiree, Cynthia?"

"For my sins," she muttered. "Stuck up la-di-da Madame! Everything must be perfect so she can show off her smart house to the village. She's furious with the decorators for being so far behind in their schedule. It happens every time she and Dobi return from abroad. What my brother ever saw in her I'll never know!"

*Oh dear,* thought Billy, *another wrong topic! I wouldn't be surprised if before too long Cynthia's caustic tone doesn't burn her tongue.*

At the bottom of the lane Dan and RK bumped into Cynthia's husband as he waited for his wife to complete her purchases in the butcher's shop.

"Nice day, Mr Durrant," greeted Dan.

"Bound to rain," said Gordon morosely.

*Typical of you,* thought Dan with some amusement. *Nothing ever pleases you, you surly ole sooner!* However, as the young couple passed him Gordon's glum countenance lightened a little. He had a soft spot for the spunky girl who had defied convention by riding a motorbike; a Harley-Davidson, at that! *Pity about the accident - ruined a good machine!* Dan's blood pressure would have risen rapidly had he known Gordon's thoughts mirrored those of Mr Dickinson-Bond, Robyn's father, regarding the demise of RK's former mode of transport.

Only yesterday Miranda had read to RK a letter from her sister Davina with news of her father, which RK had passed on to Dan over lunch.

*"...Dad's been diagnosed with Bipolar. Having started on treatment he's much improved, allowed home and is now back at work, part-time. He's under less pressure because during his enforced absence I've negotiated with the consortium to transport cut flower consignments to Covent Garden and the pre-packed bulbs to distribution*

*centres in Manchester and Birmingham, as well as the beet to the sugar factory in Newark.*

*Thankfully the others, particularly Al and Neil, backed my decisions. When they saw how smoothly the new arrangement worked Mum and the girls also took on board further proposals I presented to them.*

*A local supermarket has contracted to purchase all salad and veg crops on a seasonal basis. Much to my relief they've also agreed to arrange collection and delivery to their other stores in the region as well.*

*Al has taken over production organization and he is revelling in the new responsibility. The new supermarket contract allows him flexibility to experiment on a small scale with crops we've never grown before in addition to the traditional backbone staples of this farm. We've allocated acreage in the home field towards this. Mum and Mic have always wanted to grow tomatoes so the lads have erected a smaller greenhouse on the corner of home field near to the other salad crops for this purpose. They also propose selling salad crops to passing trade from a stall on site during the summer months. Phil's boys are also getting involved in this project which pleases Dad.*

*Neil has agreed to deliver the hydroponics to designated local supermarkets. At the same time he will distribute seasonal bulbs and plug plants to garden centres in East Notts, Lincs and Humberside and North Cambs. They're both delighted they'll have more time at home and opportunity to be more 'hands on' around the farm.*

*I've been able to work out a training programme in conjunction with the local agricultural/horticultural college which will mean we'll have extra hands when we need them. That was certainly a good idea of yours. Grading and quality control is definitely on the student's curriculum so it won't all fall on Mum's shoulders in the future.*

*Dad isn't in a position to quibble. Amazingly, he seems to have accepted change as inevitable. Only the other day I overheard him praising Al for the quality of the hydroponics and you know how much that was his passion.*

*I've also tabled holidays into the schedule for all staff. All work and no play is not good for anyone. Mine starts a week next Thursday. Could you cope with a visitor? I'd like to meet your new friends and see the area that has so enchanted you..."* RK recalled that Miranda had broken off from reading as she butted in.

*"It would be so good to see Davi again. She did her best to support me following the accident despite Dad's anger and irrational behaviour."*

*"At least now that your Dad has been diagnosed you know the reason behind his actions towards you."*

*"I can't help but wonder though, if it had been picked up years ago, how very different life might have been for us all."*

*"You can't keep looking back, RK, life strewn with 'if only' doesn't lead anywhere."*

*"True. I'm learning that I must live in the present, one step at a time – Mrs Darnell's suggestion,"* RK added with a quirky grin.

*"What a great idea."*

*"But I will need to get in provisions for Davi coming and ensure the cottage is spick and span for her visit. Oh dear!"*

*"Now what?"*

*"I've remembered Ellie starts work that week. I can't have decorating mess everywhere."*

*"I'm sure Ellie will ensure that's taken care of and I'm always here with an extra pair of hands."*
*"You are a good friend, Mirry, thanks..."*

⁂

"...not too long. So, what do you think, Robyn?"

RK stumbled and stopped. Had Dan not been holding on to her arm she may well have fallen. For some moments she was completely disorientated. In her mind she was still in the place of yesterday's conversation with Miranda but her ears were hearing Dan Catchpole's voice.

"Dan? Whe...re,...where are we?" RK was totally confused.

Concerned that RK may have been hurt when she tripped up Dan enquired, "Are you alright, Robyn?"

"Yes, yes of course, but where are we?"

"Well, we're actually stood outside 'Bakers'. Did you want to go in and see Miss Pedwardine?"

"Oh no," Quite flustered RK turned round abruptly. "I must go back to the Stores."

*Robyn's quite right about eye contact. It is a problem. She's been miles away on a different plain altogether and not heard a word I've said to her. If we'd been able to look directly at one another we'd have known we were not on the same wave length.*

Dan didn't comment straightaway but took a quick look at his watch then caught RK's hand and drew it back through his arm. "I'll come back with you to the Stores then accompany you home to Ferry Cottage. Time is moving on and I do need to get some shut-eye before I go on night shift."

"If you want to go now I can manage." Misreading Dan's momentary silence RK tried to extricate her arm from his clasp. "Honestly, I can."

Dan grinned. "Miss Independent, as ever, I see, but I'll be pleased to walk with you."

RK collected and paid for the tea parcel that Rosie had prepared for her and Dan cheerily escorted her home. He switched the radio to the channel RK enjoyed listening to, then squeezed her hand in fond farewell before striding briskly to the police house.

After the exertions of the morning RK was pleased to sit down and rest. Her body ached but her mind darted all over the place reliving incidents from earlier in the day linking them with events in the recent past, obscuring completely the voices on the radio. *Dan wants to court me!* Her thoughts skipped to plans she would need to put in place in readiness for Davina's visit particularly in view of the pending redecoration scheme that Ellie had organized. *Dan wants to marry me.* As she sat there her mind took flight...

---

(RK had moved back into Ferry Cottage by the time Ellie had met up with her at the beginning of the new term to discuss the redecorating of the sitting room following instructions she had received from Trixie Cooper. As he had intimated to Jennifer Pedwardine, when Ellie first outlined her college project to him, Lord Edmund had approached Trixie with Ellie's proposal expressing his own thoughts on the matter.

"I would think that RK's home and situation would be a challenging project for that young lady. Put it to her and let's see what she comes up with."

Trixie did just that and without a qualm Ellie accepted the challenge wholeheartedly.

RK was bowled over by Ellie's enthusiasm. She willingly agreed to give Ellie a free hand on design and materials but Ellie wanted input from RK believing it would add clout to her assignment presentation.

The following morning there was a knock at the front door. "It's Ellie, RK," a voice called through the intercom grill Ben had fitted on the outside wall following the episode with the bailiff's men. It had a speaker in the kitchen so that RK could listen and talk with visitors and know who was calling at the cottage. If it was a person she was expecting or someone she wanted to come into her home she was able to press a knob, placed in a position agreed with Ben, which released the lock on the front door.

Ellie had come in and taken measurements, discussed possible colours and themes and also, what was special to RK in the room. She made notes and quick, yet precise, sketches on her drawing pad.

"From what you've told me I think we'll focus the design of the room on Emma's painting of the harbour. I'll source some samples and be back in a few days for you to make some choices."

Over the past few weeks RK had spent less time at Miss Pedwardine's home and more time doing things for herself in Ferry Cottage until she now felt quite comfortable living independently. Doctor Roger met with her frequently and continually enlarged her vision. Her footsteps often found their way to the vicarage where she shared some special moments with Hugh and Penny Darnell learning more about the Christian faith. They linked RK up with the House Group held at Alex and Graeme's which was within easy distance from Ferry

Cottage and was proving beneficial. As Miranda had predicted RK discovered her self-confidence grew as she ventured out more and more on her own.

RK looked forward to walking along to the tea-rooms for her lunch each day; she still didn't feel equal to cooking her own meals on the stove in her kitchen. "That will come with time," encouraged Emma. "In the meantime we enjoy your daily visits to the tea-rooms and it gives you opportunity to meet and chat with friends." As RK left, following her meal, Rosie frequently presented her with treats for her tea. She had learned to prepare breakfast and became adept at making cups of tea.

She and Dan shared precious moments together on his days off duty, walking hand in hand along the seashore or exploring the intriguing villages in the vicinity so well known to Dan. They sang together in the car and RK learned the hymns of worship and praise. They discussed a wide range of topics and always at some point Dan would read to her. As they got to know one another the friendship they had shared in Lincolnshire was rekindled, love blossomed and...)

---

Her daydreaming continued...

*"I can tell you're excited, Ellie."*

*"How on earth can you know that?" Ellie's brow furrowed in perplexity.*

*"Your voice is bouncing up and down as you speak."*

*Ellie burst out laughing.*

*"You're incredible, RK."*

*"So, before you open up your bag of tricks let's have a drink together then you can explain what you've brought for me to see."*

*"I think you're excited too, RK."*

*Ellie followed RK into the kitchen, amazed at her agility at finding her way around. She stood with her mouth wide open as RK adroitly lifted the kettle from its base, walked over to the sink, turned on the tap and filled it with sufficient water for two drinks without making a splash, returned effortlessly to replace it correctly on the base and switched on the kettle.*

*"How do you manage to do that, RK?"*

*"Practise, practise, practise coupled with Doctor Roger constantly nagging me."*

*"I'm sure he's not that bad," Ellie chuckled.*

*"You'd better believe it; He's a real slave driver!"*

*Ellie couldn't stop laughing. "You're such a fun person to be with, RK, no wonder all the little kids like being in your company."*

*RK shook her head in disbelief although a wide grin creased her cheeks.*

*"Tea or coffee?" RK's hands walked across the surface of the kitchen units to the mug tree.*

*"Coffee, please."*

*"Right, perhaps you would serve yourself, spoons are in the second drawer from the right, coffee is in the canister furthest right. I've not quite mastered coffee making. I always manage to spill granules everywhere. I stick to tea, bags are so much easier.*

*"You're a wonder, RK, and an example to us all. I'm sure in time you'll become proficient at coffee making."*

*"We'll see! If you would like sugar, it's in the middle canister that too is a bug-bear."*

*"I've brought some of your favourite cookies from the Stores."*

*"Do you know,"* RK began in a serious voice, *"I'm convinced the whole village wants me to put on weight or else Emma's profits need a boost. She sends biscuits along with everyone who calls to visit me."*

*When her voice cracked Ellie knew she was only joking and joined in with RK's infectious laugh.*

*"I think the cost is being added to your weekly bill!"*

*Between them they carried the coffee things into the sitting room and RK sat down on the sofa.*

*"Now, what have you brought to show me?"*

*"Last week when I called we agreed a colour scheme so, today, I've brought wallpaper and fabric with texture so you can choose which you prefer."* *Ellie pulled the bundles from her bag and placed them on the sofa alongside RK.*

*"Which shall I pass first?"*

*"Paper,"* *RK reached out decisively for the sample to be handed to her.*

*"Remember, we decided that Emma's painting would be the focal point of the room because that is etched on your memory and the chimney breast and alcoves would be painted the palest of sky blues to set it off."* *Ellie leaned forward to put a sheet into RK's hands.*

*"What do you think of this?"*

*"Pebbles?"* *RK's fingers danced across the raised surface 'seeing' through their tips the gravelly seashore situated outside the cottage.*

*"Or this?"*

*Straightaway RK shook her head.* *"Too small and indistinct."*

*Ellie grabbed the sample and let it drop onto the floor.*

*"How about this one?"*

*"Oh no!"* *RK shook her head at once.* *"Too geometrical!"* *That too was consigned to the heap on the floor.*

*"This any better?"* Undeterred Ellie continued to pass the paper sections for RK to check out.

*"Pebbles, again but these are too big."*

*"RK, you're beginning to sound a bit like the three bears, you know, too big, too small, too bumpy, too geometric!"*

*RK's booming laughter burst out again and filled the cottage. Ellie joined in as she passed one more sample to RK.*

*"Mmm, a bit gritty, but possible."*

*"Right, two maybe's and three definite no's,"* Ellie said as she sorted the wallpaper into piles.

*"Yes, that would seem so."*

*"We'll leave the paper samples for a while and come back to them after you've considered the curtain fabric."* Ellie handed the pieces of material over to RK.

*"I know you like the butterflies and flowers on the Meadowsweet Crowson fabric in the kitchen but it's attractiveness is in what can be seen not felt. So, continuing the seaside theme these swatches for the sitting room have a raised weave that you can feel, as well as, highlight the colours in Emma's painting, blue, slightly deeper in colour than the emulsion for the walls, sand, reason obvious, white, reflecting the seagulls plumage and a feint line of red picking out the colour of Dave's boat in the harbour."* Not wishing to upset her client Ellie deliberately refrained from mentioning the red of RK's fated Harley-Davidson depicted in the foreground of Emma's painting. But RK knew the picture like the back of her hand and murmured, *"And the bike."*

*"Yes, of course,"* responded Ellie quickly passing the fabric into RK's hands.

*RK handled the fabrics offered to her in turn scrunching them in her hands then drawing them to her cheeks.*

*"I think I like this one the best," she said running her palm along its surface."*

*"I thought you might. It's a vibrant, striped brocade in the colours I described earlier and has a gold vertical line of embroidery between the sand and white stripes."*

*"I do like the sound of that."*

*"With a lining they will hang beautifully, keep out any drafts and we'll also make a door curtain for the front door ready for winter use."*

*"That's good."*

*"Well, we need to do all we can to keep out those north-easterly gales."*

*RK's rich laughter erupted. "How true, that wind surely finds every cranny it can to invade my space, some days last winter it even sent the post scurrying right across the floor."*

*Ellie tried to suppress a giggle as she took out her mobile phone.*

*"I'll place the order while you finish your tea."*

*"You'd best stop the laughter before you speak to your supplier..."*

*"How did you know?" Ellie spluttered as noise that wouldn't be contained burst from her mouth.*

*"Experience," RK chuckled.*

*"Mr Bracewell would say 'Yew ole sooner.'"*

*"That man is a character of the old school yet can tease as good as he gets not like some sober sides I could mention."*

*Still tittering quietly Ellie made her call while RK sat pensively, conjuring up pictures in her mind's eye of the decor Ellie was planning.*

*"That's done. As soon as the material is delivered Mrs Ransome can get on and make them up."*

*"Mrs Ransome?"*

*"Yes, apparently, she's in charge of all of the soft furnishings in the village housing lets."*

*"I see,"* said RK thoughtfully as she reached out to feel the tray on the coffee table on which to place her empty mug.

*"You haven't mentioned the back wall, Ellie. Are you leaving that as it is?"*

Ellie chuckled, *"Certainly not; that's my 'piece de resistance'."*

*"Really!"*

*"Mmm! Now feel this. What do you see?"*

RK's fingers lightly tripped across the surface of the roll of wallpaper that Ellie placed across her lap.

*"Seagulls?"*

She traced raised shapes which Ellie had cut out and pasted in relief on top of the original design.

*"Sailing boats?"*

Her finger tips nimbly negotiated the paper.

*"Lifebelts, I think."*

Her fingers stumbled over the next shape, then back again. RK paused her forehead puckered. *"Not too sure about this one."*

*"Start at the top."* Ellie guided RK's fingers. RK shook her head. *"Sorry, I still can't make it out."*

*"A seagull on top of a groyne."*

*"Oh, yes, of course,"* her face creased in recognition. *"You know, Ellie, I'm finding this learning adventure is a bit like getting to grips with understanding the Christian faith; the more you search and explore, the more you learn and understand. I am discovering there is so much I don't know and even less that I understand."*

*"Yeah! My Dad would say that it states in the Bible seek and you shall find!"*

*"I'm sure he's right."*

*"Dad's always right!"*

*"In that case, I'll chat to him about that the next time I call into the vicarage,"* said RK decisively as her fingers continued to move across the wallpaper. *"Now, what's that?"*

*"That's supposed to represent waves breaking on the shore but cutting it out and pasting it on will not convey the motion I want to portray so I'm still working on that."*

*"I see."*

*"Anyway, what do you think of my suggestions so far?"* Ellie held her breath.

*"I'm absolutely thrilled with your plans for my living room."*

*"Really?"*

*"Yes, really! You're bringing the view from the kitchen window that I love right into the house. To me that is amazing."*

*Impulsively, for one who so rarely showed her feelings, Ellie threw her arms around RK's shoulders. "Thanks, oh thanks, for your kind words."*

*Some while later Ellie left Ferry Cottage delighted with the outcome of the visit, confident she could achieve a satisfactory presentation for her tutor and hopefully gain a good grade towards her final exam and at the same time create a living space for RK with an ambience that was special to her and meet with Lord Edmund's approval...*

A knock on the door broke RK's reverie. The voice on the radio was still droning on but RK was totally unaware of what time of day it was. Increasingly her hours alone were spent reliving earlier moments or flitting between events and activities from the past until a sound or a visitor brought her back to the present.

*I really must be more pro-active in planning my day or time races by and the day is gone before I realise it. I truly must curb this tendency to daydream my time away.* She got up to press the intercom button.

# Chapter Seventeen

At his earliest opportunity, following the morning he had spent showing RK developments at Kezia's Wood, Stephen Cooper strode purposefully along the lane to 'Bakers'. In the intervening days he had done background research and made useful contacts. He opened the gate and knocked smartly on the front door. Miss Pedwardine was serving up the lunch time meal so asked RK to answer the door. RK had reluctantly returned to stay at 'Bakers' for a few days while Ellie prepared Ferry Cottage for redecoration.

"Give the girl space to work. Best for you both or you'll get in one another's way and in no time be tearing your hair out!" Jennifer had stated. RK had to agree with her logic and moved back into her old room.

Stephen apologized for calling at meal-time, "Hi, RK, I'm sorry to bother you but Emma told me I'd find you here."

"Just temporarily."

"So I understand. This is the only time I have free and I need to talk something over with you and Miss Pedwardine."

"Then you'd better come in, Stephen. We're eating in the kitchen so please make your way through."

Quickly closing the front door RK followed him through the hall sitting room into the kitchen. She reached out in front of her to find her place setting at the table and sat down.

Like a cat on hot bricks Stephen hovered uncertainly from one foot to the other. He had a proposition to present to the ladies with regard to the book shop and was anxious to win a positive response from them both. Without any pre-amble he plunged into his reason for visiting them.

"As you know, I'm attempting to run the book shop alongside the carpentry business and I'm in the final months of study for my English degree at UEA as well as sorting out the property and historical documents we keep unearthing..." Jennifer wafted a serving dish before him along with an enquiring glance stopping him in full flow.

"No thanks, I've brought my own lunch. If I could have a glass of water I'd be grateful. As I was saying..."

"Do stop phaffing about, boy, and sit down." That was definitely Miss Pedwardine's school marm voice. Despite his height and immense muscle power Stephen's knees quaked and the belief that his current course of action was the best to be pursuing began to ebb. *Goodness me! Am I doing the right thing?*

The confidence that had brought him along to see his former headmistress suddenly seemed to desert him.

Miss Pedwardine set down the filled plates on the table having pre cut RK's food as usual. She offered an empty one to Stephen then turned to pour him a glass of water and seemed quite unperturbed by his very obvious hesitancy.

"Can I get you anything else?"

"No, this is fine."

"As you're here perhaps you would like to return thanks."

"Yes miss." The familiar words tripped from his lips.

"For food and friends and every blessing from Your hand, we give You our grateful thanks, O Lord, Amen"

Silence followed grace as they each tackled the food before them.

"Now, what is it you want to discuss with us that is so urgent it can't wait?" Miss Pedwardine's direct approach meant Stephen had to broach the subject full on. So, he proceeded to reveal his aspirations for Kezia's book shop, his plans to establish a library in the village and explain the rationale behind his decisions. Then he dropped his bombshell.

"I would like you to oversight the book shop and help develop the library, Miss Pedwardine, and RK to be your assistant."

"Me?" they both spluttered in astonishment as cutlery clattered on to their plates.

"Why me?"

"Don't be silly!" They spoke in unison at such a preposterous idea.

"I chose you, Miss, because of your great love for books and your desire to make them readily available to all. You see, I did listen to you and this is the first opportunity I've had to do anything concrete about it."

"But I didn't expect to be the one to get it started, young man. I'm retired and I have many commitments..."

"Yes, I know, but if it's to get off the ground I need your skill and experience at least until RK learns a new language and Abi is qualified."

"New language?" Jennifer demanded at the same time as RK blurted out, "What language?"

"Braille!"

"Stephen! What are you suggesting?"

"That you learn Braille. I've been in contact with the RNIB who've put me in touch with some local members of the UK Braille Association who are willing to teach you the rudiments. This is the chap's number..."

"Stephen!"RK almost shouted in exasperation.

"Who's Abi and what has she to do with this?" A frown creased Jennifer's brow.

"Why, Ryan Saunders sister, Abigail, of course. She's at college taking a librarian and business studies course and has offered to lend a hand on Saturday mornings when we're up and running. Then, when she has completed her time at 6th Form College Abi has indicated to me that she may be willing to consider an apprenticeship at our library. I've also been in touch with the chap responsible for library services in the county and picked the brains of a mate in charge of the university library to gather all the info I can about setting up a library in the village."

"I can't believe you're saying this, Stephen."

"Well, it was you who set me thinking about this in the first place, RK."

"Oh?"

"Yeah, when we were chatting about jobs on our walk up to the village sign on The Green, I thought this would be a great opportunity for you."

"But how will it be financed and where will it be housed?"

"And where will the books come from?"

"I haven't worked out the details, yet, but there is a grant available and I've had an offer of free books from a number of sources to get us started. Work is underway on the cottage attached to mine. It's now earmarked as the library and will give the workers impetus and a goal to work towards. So, when you've mulled it over we'll meet up and chat about honing in on your current skills and how to go about developing new ones."

"Has your brother put you up to this?"

"No, I hardly see him these days."

RK cocked her head to one side in disbelief.

"Actually, we're both so busy our paths simply never cross, not even at Mum's for Sunday lunch now that he and Emma are married." Stephen scraped his chair back from the table and got up. "I'm a bit pushed for time so really must be on my way. I have a late afternoon lecture at the UEA so need to get over to Norwich; must catch the 2 o'clock bus."

He turned to Miss Pedwardine. "Thanks for letting me encroach on your lunch hour. Please give my suggestion some consideration, after all it was your idea in the first place, and persuade RK of the potential of my offer."

He placed a hand on RK's shoulder and said playfully, "Fish out that material Jackie requested on your behalf from the Braille association; I bet you've not even opened it! I'm sure Miss Pedwardine will acquaint you with its contents." He almost ran to the front door. "And polish up your story-telling skills. Be seeing you."

"Whew! Was that a whirlwind that blew through here?"

"More like a tornado!"

"That boy never does things by halves, does he?"

"His enthusiasm just blows my mind away. Talk about pie in the sky! How on earth does he think I'm going to handle books and deal with customers if I can't see them?"

"I wonder who is providing the books."

"And how is he going to pay wages?"

"I believe he's looked at this from all angles and certainly appears to have researched thoroughly." When RK simply shook her head in disbelief Jennifer continued, "Don't dismiss his proposal out of hand. Let's wash up, make a cup of tea and take it through to the sitting room so we can think about that young man's suggestion and talk through all the implications it presents."

Reluctantly RK made her way to the sink to commence the task her mind reeling from the proposal Stephen had just outlined to them. Automatically her hands performed their menial chore as arguments pounded to and fro in her head. Her thoughts were in turmoil.

"Whatever possessed Stephen to come up with such a hare-brained idea?" she declared angrily banging a tumbler onto the draining board.

Miss Pedwardine wisely refrained from speaking and in silence cleared away the remnants of lunch, dried up the dishes as RK washed them, prepared to make a pot of tea and pondered on the audacity of Stephen Cooper. She was equally perplexed by such a preposterous plan. Her retirement had been meticulously planned and each day carefully orchestrated. She enjoyed a life that was structured, a throwback to her days as head of the local primary school. Her involvement in the village community and development of new and diverse relationships with local residents were all part of that pattern. She certainly did not want to reschedule the timetable she had developed.

"Tea is ready," barely escaped her pursed lips. With an unseen grimace Jennifer carried the tea tray into the sitting room. When RK did not follow her she returned to the kitchen and found her house guest still by the kitchen sink deep in thought.

Jennifer's line of vision was caught by movement of trees visible through the kitchen window beyond where RK was standing. The gradual glide into glowing gold that personified October was being pushed aside by a harsher reality. Winter was attempting to get an early foot in the door. There were mornings recently when Jennifer was woken by persistent low rumblings as the east wind rocked even the most substantial trees back and forth in her garden and their branches lashed against each other noisily as they were doing now.

"Can you hear the force of that wind, RK?"

In response RK stood stiffly by the kitchen sink at 'Bakers' with arms wrapped around her middle as if to protect herself from the onslaught of noise outside and possibly shield herself from the inner storm that Stephen's ridiculous scheme had stirred up within her. A deepening scowl furrowed her brow.

"That howling wind sounds fierce enough to penetrate or even push out the panes of glass in the kitchen window. I can only imagine what it's doing to the trees and bushes in the garden."

"Somehow branches are still clothed, albeit sparsely, with remnants of foliage." Jennifer Pedwardine leaned uncharacteristically against the draining board. As she looked out of the window to the line of beeches, oak, hawthorn and sycamores that formed the boundary of the garden she noted that what was once a dense wall of green was fast becoming a tattered curtain. Jennifer looked upwards. "There is more sky than leaves in the garden now. Winter seems to be well on its way before autumn has had chance to gracefully bow out."

Jennifer had started to rake up fallen leaves in the garden a few weeks earlier. "I can see it will go on for several weeks to come," she had remarked one day when RK had called to visit.

"Why don't you leave the task until all the leaves are off the trees?"

"Because in shady parts of the garden there would be mounds of them smothering plants that are growing or hibernating till spring re-awakens them into growth. Too many leaves deprive the soil of light."

"But isn't it a natural process? Won't they eventually break down and give nutrients to the soil?"

"You're right, but it takes time and we don't live in a wood, we live in a garden which really doesn't take kindly to such a build-up!"

"Surely raking up leaves should be one of gardening's gentlest pastimes?"

"Yes, but as the trees in the garden grow bigger each year I find there are more and more of them to gather up."

"When I took the Catton children rambling through the woods on the edge of the Common the footpaths were springy."

"That is as a result of the accumulation of foliage and debris building up underfoot over countless generations."

"I know the softness and spongy texture fascinated the children."

"That's fine in the woods but such an accumulation would not be good in the garden; besides, collecting the leaves gives me an opportunity to see how the plants in the surrounding beds are doing as well as providing an abundance of material to add to the compost bins which will gradually break down into friable material to be used elsewhere in the garden next year."

"I'm glad I don't have that hassle in the garden at Ferry Cottage."

"Now, while I enjoy talking about the garden we are skirting the issue we are meant to be discussing." RK shook her head but Jennifer slipped an arm through RK's and steered her in the direction of the main sitting room. "Come on, young lady, we have decisions to make."

"I can't do this, Jennifer, I can't! I can't!"

"Don't be so hasty, RK."

"It is far too ludicrous a suggestion! I simply can't."

"You're not a quitter, RK, I'm sure you'll find a way."

"How? I can't see! How can I read the title of a book?"

"Don't be put off by what is obviously not possible but think of the things you can do. Make a start on your tea while I go and root out the Braille brochures Stephen spoke of." As she reached the door Jennifer slightly turned, "Remember, the leaves may be missing from the trees but the trunk remains solid."

RK sat down with a sigh.

She felt manipulated. Only recently she had begun to take control of her life again and, if she were honest, actually enjoying the independence being back in Ferry Cottage brought her. Now others were attempting to take over once more, making decisions on her behalf. *But I can't work in a shop, let alone a library. It's simply ridiculous!* Almost involuntary RK stamped a foot. *Stephen's not thinking straight! How does he imagine I'll deal with people, especially awkward obstreperous people, if I can't see them? Not everyone is as open and honest as his family.* RK heard footsteps above her head and could envisage Jennifer striding with determination towards her room to find the Braille information material. *Undoubtedly on her return she will badger me into listening to her read the contents and then ensure I carry out all the necessary training. How well meaning she is; still the competent headmistress! I was hopeless at languages when I was at school and I guess this Braille thing will be no different. Despite her teaching skill it won't take Jennifer long to realise my shortcomings in that department.*

Slowly RK took a few sips of tea, replaced her cup and leaned back in the chair. She closed her eyelids. Even with sightless eyes it helped her focus more clearly when the lids were closed. She recalled Mrs Darnell's advice to pause for a moment when she was prone to frustration. Slowly RK counted out loud to 10 then added the psalmist's declaration, which she had recently learned, a number of times. "I will bless the Lord at all times," she recited placing emphasis on different words with each repetition.

The last few weeks had been a tremendous learning curve. *Dan would remind me to count my blessings. I tend to concentrate on trivial inconsequential things. I wonder what he will think of Stephen's harebrained scheme. He will probably suggest this is what is meant by God's plan for me. Dan always looks for the good in every circumstance and persistently reminds me to do the same.* Her mouth curved into a smile. *He truly is a lovely man and keeps me focussed on the important things in life. I believe he really loves me and actually wants to spend time with me. I certainly enjoy being in his company engaging in stimulating conversation and listening to the changing cadences in his voice when he is describing the sea or the shells, the garden or someone's facial expression. I love to hear him sing whether it's hymns of praise or a simple love-song. My heart seems to dance when I hear his voice or he holds my hand. He is such an encourager.*

Once she had decided to stop feeling sorry for herself and view her situation as an adventure RK began to realise the worth of Doctor Roger's words. "Consider it a challenge, like learning another language..." Again a smile came unbidden to her lips. *How did the Doc know I'd soon have to be persuaded to learn Braille?* "...together we'll devise a plan of action that is paced and achievable using the skills you already have." *But read with my finger tips?* However, she had decided to embrace all that the Doctor threw at her in a constructive manner even if it tested her abilities to their limit. Roger believed she was capable of working again and his brother had come up with a solution, albeit a ludicrous one. *I can't believe they haven't colluded! But work in a bookshop and run a library?* Maybe her life wasn't over. Her life still had worth and it was up to her to find its value and fulfil her potential. Like all things worth having it had to be worked at. *I simply have to approach it from a different perspective because I'm now blind. Like my relationship with Dan. That is different but so special.*

She was even beginning to enjoy some of the challenges each new day brought along. *It's all due to the influence of Dan and my other friends here in the village. They constantly encourage me to think and act positively. But Braille?*

She was proved right about Miss Pedwardine's intent. Before the day was through Jennifer ensured RK was fully conversant with the Braille material Jackie Cooper had so thoughtfully sent for on her behalf. As Stephen suspected it had remained unopened gathering dust on the top shelf of the wardrobe. Jennifer read and RK listened. "I've heard of Braille but don't know anyone who's used it."

"It does sound intriguing but I can't imagine how a series of raised dots can possibly make sense."

"It seems the tips of the fingers become the eyes that enable a blind person to read text."

After chatting a while longer about the contents of the package they rang the number Stephen had left to make contact with the Braille instructor. Jennifer insisted RK arrange an appointment at the earliest available date for the first lesson. "He can see me tomorrow morning at 11:30."

By the end of the week it seemed the whole community knew of RK's new venture and were keen to lend their support. "I'm sure they think my progress in Braille will be an asset to the village," she confided to Dan.

"How can that be so?"

"It's almost as though they believe the success of the library is dependent upon my success at learning Braille."

"That's squit!"

"But it's what the villagers think."

Dan took hold of her hand. "Robyn, you're doing this for you. If there is a benefit to the villagers then that's a bonus."

"There's also a tale going round that Stephen will have to close the bookshop if I don't learn Braille."

"That's simply unfounded gossip."

RK remained unconvinced and the assumed expectations of the villagers created tension and pressure within her.

Gil Jenner continued to be RK's main champion in her new endeavours and sent an excited message on her mobile phone. "Meet me on Saturday at 10 o'clock in the Tea Rooms because I have something to show you." Now that really did fascinate her.

She didn't have long to wait to learn of his innovative idea. Sitting in her favourite spot in the Tea Rooms she listened as the young lad explained his brainwave. Gil had enlisted the help of Abi Saunders and together they had devised a book sleeve upon which could be attached a punched out Braille name tape. Enthusiastically he handed his prototype to RK. "See, here it is. You have a go." Gil was convinced it could be adapted for use in the library or Kezia's Book shop.

Tentatively RK took the book that was handed to her. She ran her fingers down the spine and across the flat surface. "I can only feel raised dots. They don't mean anything."

"Once you've learned to read Braille it'll be as easy as pie." Gil's brash youthful enthusiasm frequently triggered fervour in others. Stephen was open to any suggestions or systems if they would make the task easier for RK. He hoped Gil would be able to convince RK she was quite capable of doing the job being offered to her.

However, so many other people were pushing her to succeed that RK's nerve almost deserted her.

On Sunday morning Dan called at 'Bakers' to accompany her to church. "Good morning, Robyn," he greeted cheerfully as RK opened the front door but one look at her face told him she was not having a good morning. Before he'd even stepped over the threshold RK launched into the difficulty that was causing her brow to frown.

"Dan, I'm really going to need some Divine help in this matter if anything useful is to be achieved. This is such a daunting undertaking that Stephen has instigated. These dear people have such high expectations of me but I can't possible attempt it alone."

Dan gently clasped both of her hands in his. "Robyn, don't get so keyed up. You can achieve this. You're not expected to carry it through singlehandedly but with..."

"Dan, the queue of people willing me to succeed is overwhelming. I think before long the whole village will be fluent Braille readers and I'll be lagging way behind. The children are really quick. They know the dots that stand for letters and form the words before I do and Gil is phenomenal. I'm never going to manage to master it," a sob broke in her throat.

"My dear, dear Robyn," Dan stepped closer to her, put his arms around her shoulders and drew her to him. He held her for a moment, his heart thumping at her nearness. In the silence he prayed for wisdom.

"Dearest Robyn, don't get so agitated. I honestly believe you can achieve this, obviously not on your own and certainly not today, or tomorrow for that matter. Don't be rushed. Go at your own pace. It doesn't matter how long it takes; a day, a month, or a year but do accept help. Don't move on until you're sure of what you're learning."

RK pulled away from him. "But Dan, it's all so strange."

"Aren't all new things strange at first? Look at you. Almost the whole village thought you were strange at first."

RK's rich laughter filled the hallway. "They did, didn't they? Thanks, Dan, you always brighten my day and put things in perspective for me." She reached out to grab his hand and squeezed it affectionately.

"What did Bernard, your teacher, say at the last lesson?"

"Practise, practise, practise!"

"There you are, then. You won't know it all overnight so let the stream of helpers be participants in the practising. They'll realise how hard it is for you but also learn something new themselves. And don't forget the verse we read from Philippians in House Group a few weeks ago, 'I can do all things through Christ...' RK repeated it slowly emphasising the word 'can'.

Dan tenderly enclosed her hands in his. Softly he said, "Yes, Robyn, you can," then stretched up with one hand in order to caress the side of her cheek with his forefinger. "You're not doing this alone."

RK smiled. "Thanks, Dan, you're my greatest supporter," and nuzzled her face against his hand.

Still holding her hand Dan pulled it through his arm, "Come, my little song bird, let us make our way to church."

# Chapter Eighteen

Thursday morning saw an influx of villagers call into the Village Stores. Parents who were normally in a hurry congregated at the school gate once they had dropped off their children at the school or drifted home to tackle necessary chores before leaving to get to work on time. Some chatted as they strolled together down the lane. Others entered the shop and gathered round the delicatessen counter waiting till the Tea Rooms opened. Time seemed to pass slowly. Senior citizens wandered through the archway between the Post Office and shop after they had drawn their pensions to pick up essential groceries. The aisles buzzed with pockets of chatter as customers mingled. No-one seemed anxious to be on their way. Many lingered most of the morning reluctant to leave. The question each wanted to ask hovered on the tips of their tongues but remained unspoken.

As the church clock chimed the half-hour Jilly Briggs came through from the Stores kitchen with a tray of freshly baked pasties.

"Just in time for lunch, ladies."

"'ere, what abaht me?"

"Yes, and you Mr Bracewell," Jilly chuckled.

The bell on the shop door jangled. A stranger walked in. Conversation ceased as all eyes focussed on him expectantly as he approached Rosalie at the counter. Maybe he had news.

"Good morning, can I help you?"

"I'm here to see Mr Kemp."

Gasps cut through the silence that followed his announcement.

"That won't be possible, sir," replied Rosalie with incredible composure.

"Nonsense, just tell him I'm here." He banged an overstuffed briefcase on to the counter.

Rosalie shook her head and reiterated, "Not possible."

Murmurings from the bystanders rippled through the shop.

Rosalie's eyes focussed on a grease stain between the first and second buttons on the stranger's suit. "Do you have an appointment, sir?"

"My business is with Mr Kemp. Go inform him I'm waiting to see him."

Rosalie's calm approach enabled her to deal with most situations that arose in the shop. That was one of the qualities that Mick Kemp had really valued in his long time assistant butthe brusque manner of the man before her now caused Rosalie to bristle. She drew a slow, deep breath.

"Mrs Cooper is engaged at present..."

"I don't wish to see Mrs Cooper I'm here to speak with Mr Kemp."

"If your business is to do with the shop perhaps I can help you..."

"You! I'm not talking to a mere cashier."

"I am the manager of the Stores but if your business is to do with the Post Office I suggest you speak with

Mr Andaman, the assistant postmaster. Will you excuse me I have customers who need my attention. When you reach a decision I will still be here." She turned to the queue by the till.

Gossip buzzed.

"The effrontery of the man!"

"How insensitive!"

"Today of all days!"

"Good thing those girls aren't here."

The shop door opened. Rosalie looked up and unbidden a sigh escaped her lips.

"Oh, Mrs Durrant, how good to see you. Is there any news?" Bernice slowly shook her head.

"This gentleman insists on speaking with Mr Kemp." Bernice raised her eyebrows then without more ado walked directly up to the man Rosalie had introduced.

"Good morning, sir, would you like to come for coffee till Mrs Cooper is free?" Undeterred by the man's request to speak with her deceased brother-in-law, in her kindly manner, Bernice hustled the stranger towards the lift and took him up to the coffee lounge before he had opportunity to argue.

The previous day Roy had spotted a Barbour coated stranger from an upstairs window of the property he was working on. He presumed the man to be a holiday maker till he saw him again acting in a manner that could only be described as snooping about the village with a camera in his hand. Roy watched him closely for a time as the man squeezed between the barriers around the reclamation site then walked in a calculated way pausing to take pictures but, when he looked on all sides surreptitiously before pulling a steel rule from his pocket then commenced taking measurements Roy removed his work overalls, donned his overcoat and cap and strode towards the interloper with a precise step.

"It seems he's representing a National Building Company looking to clear the site and build a superstore with flats above and a car park to the rear," Roy explained to Bernice on his return to Green Pastures that evening.

"Not that old chestnut again!" exclaimed Bernice with an exasperated sigh.

"I'm afraid so."

"The girl's really don't want that angst at this moment in time."

"You're right! I'll give Adam a ring to alert him to this new development and see how his investigation is progressing."

When the news filtered through to the village the villagers were up in arms, "Thought that idea had long been quashed." Further pressure was exerted on Adam Catton to speed up his enquiries into ownership of the Kezia's wood properties so that the issue could be unequivocally resolved in the villagers favour so that no outside enterprise could get a foot in.

In the Tea Rooms Bernice slowly sipped the coffee that Rosie had placed before her and calmly explained to her companion that none of the properties he had been viewing were available for sale.

The man looked down his nose at the non-descript pleasant faced, dumpy woman sat at the table opposite him.

"You cannot possibly be party to that sort of information," he retorted sardonically.

Bernice smiled. "Oh, but I can! You see Kezia's wood and all the properties built upon it have been in my family for centuries and I know for a fact that we are not selling any of them. But if you care to leave your business card I will gladly pass on your message when the owner is free." Bernice was born a de Vessey now married to a Durrant so it didn't matter to her which side the legal searches proved in favour of she had a foot in both camps. Her dearest wish was for the matter to be resolved so that everyone could move forward.

Whilst Bernice was explaining to the Barbour coated gentleman that his quest to acquire Kezia's wood was futile Roy was accompanying his nieces Alex and Emma to Norwich Crown Court. Having never attended here before it was with some trepidation that the sisters stepped through the large glass entrance door.

"I'll see you in a moment," said Uncle Roy stepping to one side. The girls were soon ushered into an ante room adjacent to the courtroom and offered a seat. As she walked towards it Emma felt as though her heart was thumping through her rib cage. She had been present at the trials of Joe and Josh Cook but they had taken place at the Magistrates Court. Criminal court proceedings were a different kettle of fish. She glanced about her to take in her surroundings when unexpectedly she saw her brother. Unable to believe what she was seeing she closed then quickly reopened her eyes. Surprised to see Drew coming towards them with Uncle Roy both girls responded with a start. Drew walked over and greeted his sisters warmly. *What a contrast to his attitude the last time we saw him* Emma thought. Drew began to explain his presence there but he was cut short because they received the summons to enter court as proceedings were about to begin. Keen to clarify his position to his sisters he spoke quickly as they walked into the court room.

"Mr Capps-Walker and Uncle Roy persuaded me it was time I addressed my anger. I've come to the trial intent on looking closely at all the issues that bother me concerning our parent's deaths, you know, what actually happened to cause the accident, who was responsible and why, the interpretation of their will etc from the legal as well as the family perspective."

"Oh!" Both sisters stood open mouthed unable to take in this radical turn of events.

"I flew down a day early in order to meet with Mr Capps-Walker and Uncle Roy to thrash out all my angst before meeting with you two today." He smiled.

"A bit of a daunting prospect for I now realise my attitude has been wrong, misguided and very selfish. I'm about to become a father and it made me wonder what my own father would think about my behaviour towards my own sisters."

"Oh Drew, what a joy," Alex whispered.

Emma's eyes widened in disbelief.

"It pricked my conscience because I am quite sure he would not have approved and would have been quite devastated if not appalled at the manner with which I have treated you both." Alex gasped and Emma clasped her hand to her mouth. "Please forgive me."

The bell went for the commencement of the day's proceedings.

"We'll speak later and I hope on a more cordial note than in the past. I lodged in Norwich overnight but will be staying with Uncle Roy and Aunt Bernice at Green Pastures for a few days. Aunt insists we have a meal together this evening so you're invited, with your spouses, to share my company."

"Is Morag here?"

"No – early days- tummy rather unsettled."

"All rise!"

"We'll chat later."

When it began to emerge that it was Billy Knights and not Josh or Joe Cook who may have had something to do with Mick and Valerie Kemp's accident the Police gathered together the available material in order to build up a case against him. However, the CPS threw out the case because of insufficient evidence.

In spite of this, a keen Detective Sergeant convinced of Billy's guilt and also with an eye on promotion trawled through all the material on file pertaining to the activities of Joe and Josh Cook as well as Billy Knights drugs involvement over the past two years, however inconsequential, determined to unravel the truth.

His colleagues jeered at his bull-headedness. "Waste of time, mate. All that info is circumstantial. You'll find nothing concrete! And certainly nothing that will stick."

Undeterred the young man still persisted. He worked in his own time and as the workload increased requested that PC Dan Prettyman be seconded to assist.

Their doggedness unearthed statements that had been made earlier and ultimately discarded as irrelevant in connexion with the previous drugs investigation involving Billy Knights and the Cook burglary offences but which could prove significant in the 'silencing of the shop keeper' enquiry. It exonerated Joe and Josh completely from any involvement in the death of Mick and Val Kemp and pointed unequivocally in Billy's direction. Thus a case was prepared and subsequently brought to court.

As counsel presented their opening remarks Billy sat, for the most part, in the dock with a glazed, bored look on his face. However, at one point his eye locked with Emma's. He gulped. Emma had always been a good mate. Her familiar face jolted memories from the past. She was certainly kind to his Mum since Emma had taken over the running of the Village Stores and always made her aware of special offers in the shop.

His defence lawyer had been talking for a long time, extolling his client's virtues which Billy knew to be totally untrue and fabricated by Mr Farley to make him look good in front of the jury. Unable to sit still any longer Billy jumped up and yelled, "Aw Judge, can't yew stop this squit..."

The guards rushed to quieten him and push him back down into his seat. Judge Brean raised his hand to stay proceedings. "No, let him be. Continue Mr Knights."

"O' course I stitched 'im up." Billy looked across to where Emma was sitting. "I'm sorry about yer Mum, Emma. She were a good sort."

"Mr Knights, please address the court not the public gallery."

"Yeah, well, Mr Judge, Sir, I er...erm, confess I fixed Mr Kemp's car at Christmas so's he couldn't snitch me to the rozzers about seein' me wi' the Docs in the alley at the back o' the shop."

A buzz zinged around the court.

"Silence in court!"

"I see," Justice Brean stroked his chin as he pondered for just one moment.

"In the light of Mr Knights' disclosure you may wish for further conversation with your client, Mr Farley, therefore court will adjourn for one hour."

"All rise!"

Mr Justice Brean nodded towards counsel, "Gentlemen, in my chambers, please."

Stunned, the occupants of the court arose as one and like muted sheep followed one another through the open court room door. Once released conversation erupted.

By the end of the day the verdict was on the tongue of most people in the village, guilty of manslaughter. But the sentence the Judge gave Billy of 10years to run concurrently with his sentence for drug trafficking did not meet with everyone's approval.

"'e should 'a bin sent down fer life."

The family who met that evening at Green Pastures, however, were glad the ordeal was over. Nothing could bring their parents back so together they determined to resolve the long standing issues Drew had with his sisters so that when they waved him off at Norwich airport on his return flight to Edinburgh their relationship was back on more affectionate terms. When Bernice had produced the business card of the Barbour-coated gentleman Drew explained his change of heart and apologised for the angst he had caused his sisters. "I did try to cancel his appointment but his company felt it was too good an opportunity for development and investment to be scotched and decided to go ahead with the survey for their own purposes. Rather than persuade you to sell I congratulate you on creating the perfect meeting place in the coffee shop for locals as well as visitors to the village. From the short time I have been here I can see that the Stores is a hive of activity and the hub of this village community. Dad would be proud of your achievements." That news too winged its way around the village gossip chain.

"A resounding good week for them Kemp girls wouldn't yew say?" remarked Mrs Jenner to RK the next day as she called in to the Tea Rooms for morning coffee after she had picked up her weekly groceries from the Village Stores.

"Doesn't evil usually rebound back on to the perpetrator?"

"Some's think they can do what they likes and get away wi' it. Young Billy's only got 'is just desserts. Jus' sorry it took so long. Yew take care lass, I'm agoin' to sit by the window wi' my coffee."

"Nice to see you, Mrs Jenner, enjoy your coffee," RK replied with a smile knowing full well the window seat gave the old lady pleasure because she had a grand stand view of all that was going on in the village.

"Good morning, RK, I thought I would find you here," Bernice drew up a chair and sat next to RK.

"Hello, Mrs Durrant, how are you after all that has been going on in the family this week?"

"Thankful to God that so many concerns have been sorted out, dealt with and are now settled. The uncertainty surrounding Roy's sister's accident caused unprecedented disquiet amongst the community. We're glad it's over but I am sorry for Irma Knights. Billy has always been such a trial to his Mum. I just pray his spell in prison will help him turn his life around."

"And I hear broken fences have been mended between Alex, Emma and their brother."

"Yes, that is a real answer to prayer. Drew was so angry about numerous matters associated with the death of his parents that for quite some time he wasn't thinking straight. It caused him to make ill-thought out decisions such as attempting to sell the shop and the girls' homes behind their backs. Mick and Val would have been devastated by his behaviour."

"Amazing what brings a change in our lives and in our thinking. For your nephew I understand it was prospective fatherhood and for me it was a bike accident."

"I give thanks to God for the wholeness that has come to your life, RK."

"Yes, and in a way I could never have imagined. I thought my life was over but I've learned new ways of enjoying living. Friends have supported me, persistently cajoled and on occasion dragged me through the difficult stages of rehabilitation but most of all I'm glad they never stopped praying for me and believing that I had a purpose for living."

"Roger and Stephen are both driven young men and seem to take everyone in their wake with them."

"I still can't believe they didn't collude about my future."

"I think you'll find most people believed it was the hand of God directing them to suggest various avenues were open to you."

"Well, thanks to them I have my life back and I have a future."

"With another enthusiastic young man, I understand."

RK blushed. "Dan loves me, wants to court me and when the time is right we plan to marry."

"Congratulations!"

"We have much to learn so we are not rushing into things but taking opportunity to get to know one another."

"Now, my dear, I've heard your sister is arriving later today so I'm here to invite you both to dinner tomorrow, along with Dan, if he's free. I'll be serving up at 6 o'clock and will look forward to seeing you all then."

"Oh Mrs Durrant, thankyou for your kindness." RK was overwhelmed. Apart from coffee and simple lunches at the Tea Rooms she had not eaten out in public since her accident. How would she cope?

Almost as though Bernice could read her mind she said, "Don't worry, it will be something simple and manageable like shepherd's pie or chicken casserole."

Tears filled RK's eyes at such thoughtfulness.

Bernice patted her hand as she got up from her seat. "A new beginning, my dear."

---

Within minutes of Bernice leaving the table RK heard Dan's voice speaking with Rosie in the direction of the cake display counter. A flutter of excitement danced across her stomach. As he drew nearer to her table she wanted so much to feel his arms around her to hear his heart beating beneath her cheek. She longed to reach up and brush her hand through the mob of hair that she recalled in her sighted days. She longed to... "Oh no," she muttered. Such thoughts! She could feel her cheeks flame and it wasn't from the sun or the easterly winds.

RK knew from his footfall when he had reached her chair so was not surprised when Dan bent down and whispered for her ears only, "How's my dearest songbird, this morning?" When his hand touched hers in greeting warmth unfolded itself and stretched deep beneath her ribcage sending wisps of delight right down to her finger tips.

"So very pleased to see you," her free hand affectionately squeezed his fingers, "and all ready to go to the station."

RK clutched Dan's arm as they made their way towards his parked car. She could hardly wait to see Davi and remained perched on the edge of her seat till Dan reminded her with a chuckle, "It might be safer if you sat back with your seat belt on." Excitement rippled right to her toes as together they drove to Newton Lokesby Station.

On the platform RK shuffled about impatiently, "Is the train late?"

"No, I think it's on time."

She stepped to one side then moved back and eagerly grasped Dan's arm, "I can hear it! I think I can hear the train coming." Like a child with a new toy she bounced his arm up and down. Dan grinned from ear to ear. "You're not excited are you, Robyn?"

"Don't be a tease, Dan. I so want Davi to like you."

"As long as you like me is all that matters to me," Dan hugged her to him but as the train pulled in RK shook off his arm and said, "Can you see her, Dan?"

The animated reunion was a joy to behold and incessant chatter accompanied the happy trio all the way back to Newton Westerby. Dan deposited the two ladies at 'Bakers' before making his way to the police station in time to commence his afternoon duty shift. "I'll see you both later. Enjoy the rest of your day, Robyn." Dan's fingers briefly caressed RK's hand after he'd placed Davi's case upon the door step. The tingling made her wish he didn't have to leave.

# Chapter Nineteen

❖

"What a hunk, Our Kay, and so very different to when he visited at the farm," Davi squeezed her sister's arm excitedly as she walked with her along the path the short distance from Dan's car to the front door at 'Bakers'.

"Do you really think so?" RK manoeuvred the bag she was carrying on to the step.

"Of course I do, he is absolutely gorgeous and so besotted with you."

"Dan is lovely," RK agreed dreamily slowly inserting the door key into the lock, "and manly and caring."

"And you're in love with him."

"Yes, I believe I am." As warmth crept from her neck up into her cheeks RK was glad of the task before her.

Davi pushed open the front door when RK had unlocked it.

As soon as she was in the house Davi flung down her case and hugged her sister tightly. "You've changed so much, Our Kay, since Dan took you away from the farm. It's so good to see you, ducky, and you look absolutely fab, longer hair suits you."

Self-consciously RK combed her fingers through her hair. "It took a long while to master it but with Rachel's persistence I learned to manage it. Come through to the kitchen and meet Jennifer. I think she has lunch ready for us."

Flabbergasted Davi watched her sister move effortlessly without bumping into anything.

"Hey, how'd you manage that, ducky?"

RK chuckled. "Friends! Good friends who prayed and constantly pushed me to persevere."

"Hey, what's with this prayer thing?"

"I became aware that life is to be lived yet no one can live my life but me so I decided I'm no longer going to mope or feel sorry for myself but with God's help live it to the full."

"You haven't been brainwashed, have you?"

"Of course not, but I have become a Christian."

"Oh no, Our Kay, that's asking for trouble. Whatever will Dad say?"

"We'll chat later; this is my friend Jennifer."

"Hi, there, I'm Davi."

The discussion over lunch was like a whistle-stop tour for Davi as she learned her sister was no longer a housebound recluse but an active member of the community participating in life in a manner that no one could have been imagined a few months earlier. Conversation moved rapidly from the topic of independent living and the redecoration of Ferry Cottage to RK's job prospects in the book shop and potential involvement in establishing a lending library in the village; her attendance at the house group in the home of Alex and Graeme, her storytelling to the reception class at the primary school, her progress in Braille and her frequent visits to the Tea Rooms for lunch.

"I'm amazed you're able to keep up with such a hectic timetable, ducky."

"I've decided it is best to be busy."

"But you're involved in so much yet you can't see."

"That's the very reason I keep busy. Life needs to have purpose. I have learned that the more I engage with people and their surroundings the more familiar it becomes which builds up my confidence."

After-lunch chores were another eye-opener for Davi as she observed RK effortlessly tackle the washing up.

When the task was completed her astonishment knew no bounds as RK strolled with ease along the lane in order to introduce Davi to her domain at Ferry Cottage.

"Oh, ducky, how quaint! What a delightful home you've created here, Our Kay."

So as not to hinder Ellie's decorating plan they didn't linger long but after a brief tour of the cottage they wandered down to the quay so that Davi could experience for herself the diverse activity in and around the harbour that had captivated RK when she had first come on holiday to Newton Westerby.

As they walked past the harbour master's look-out Titus Wills called out, "Now, yew take care, m'girl, there be a north-easterly a comin' along spiced wi' rain."

"How can he know that? There is not a cloud in the sky, the sun is shining and only a slight breeze is blowing," murmured Davi.

"I guess from experience coupled with instinct and accurate barometers. He's usually right, too."

Davi turned, leaned against the harbour wall and looked out again across the water. "I can understand now your fascination with this place. It's so different to home, very busy but calm at the same time."

"I just love it! I can hear the water lapping against the shore or harbour walls, seagulls squawking overhead, boats rippling through the water and voices and noise of people on the quayside. I can smell the fish, the sea, the diesel and occasionally coffee brewing or a 'fry-up' cooking on a stove. I can feel breezes on my face or enjoy the warmth of the sun. Each encounter unlocks pictures in my mind which I can revel in."

Numerous people called out in greeting as they walked on by.

"So many people know you!"

"Yes, they are all good friends."

The following day the sisters ventured to the Tea Rooms for lunch calling firstly into the Village Stores.

"Hi yer, RK, 'ow yew a doin'?"

"I'm doing fine, thanks. This is my sister who is visiting me for a short holiday. Davi, this is Bradley. He helped me learn to cross the road."

"Hi, there!"

"Shouldn't you be in school?"

"Yeah, but it's lunch-time an' Jilly's pies are better'n school dinners."

"Of course."

"Who do you have with you?"

"Rick and James."

"Hello boys."

"What yer!"

Once again Davi was amazed at the number of people who stopped to chat with her sister.

"Is there anyone in this village you don't know?"

RK's rich laughter reverberated along the aisles causing other customers to smile and join in the conversation.

"Everyone knows RK and we all look out for her."

Davi glanced around the shelves. "What a well stocked shop with incredible variety!" she exclaimed.

"It is very good and much of it is local produce."

"And has excellent staff to serve us," commented Mrs Jenner as she paid for her purchases and passed the girls on her way out through the shop door.

Davi grabbed RK's arm and whispered, "I think they could do with an extra pair of hands or at least another pair of eyes. Those boys are helping themselves to chocolate bars and stuffing them into their pockets."

"Bradley!" RK shouted immediately without waiting for further explanation.

"Yes, Miss," he said defiantly.

"I think Mrs Andaman needs to see you by the till counter, don't you?"

"Oh yeah?" he replied cheekily.

"Yes, and now!" RK responded sharply.

With hands firmly tucked inside his trouser pockets Bradley slouched towards Rosalie who was dealing with the last customer at the checkout. His companions rapidly deserted him darting down the aisle towards the shop door but Davi moved more quickly and blocked their exit.

"Now, boys, do we have a problem," Rosalie calmly asked, "or do you have items you wish to purchase?"

Three pairs of eyes were suddenly glued to their trainers.

"Would you like to empty your pockets onto the counter, Bradley?"

"Aw, Mrs Andaman," he shrugged his shoulders impertinently.

"You, too, Rick and James." The boys shuffled nervously and scuffed their shoes on the floor, arms held rigidly in their pockets defiantly ignoring the request.

Rosalie picked up the phone. An ominous hush pervaded the air.

"Good morning, Constable... ah yes, afternoon..."

A sniff and a gasp broke the silence.

"I have a case of suspected shop lifting... mm... yes... right... thankyou..."

Rosalie was thankful that the shop had emptied for the lunch-time lull meant RK and Davi were her only customers apart from the recalcitrant boys otherwise their misdemeanours would soon have become scandalous gossip.

Within minutes Constable Dan was entering the shop and addressing Rosalie as he cast his eye over the three slouching boys.

"Now, what have we here?"

"Miss Dickinson-Bond saw the boys take chocolate bars from the shelf and stuff them into their pockets."

Bradley's head jerked up. "Doan't be daft, she can't 'ave done. She can't see."

"But this Miss Dickinson-Bond can see," Rosalie pointed towards Davi, "and she is the one who saw your actions."

"Aw no!" Bradley's shoulders slumped even further towards his elbows.

"OK, folks, I need to take some statements." Dan unbuttoned his top pocket flap and pulled out a notebook. "Now who's first? Rick? Bradley? Miss Dickinson-Bond?"

Frightened by the police presence and the belting he would likely get at home when his Dad found out what he had done James burst into tears. His reaction spurred Rick into action. With feet astride and hands on hips he cocked his head in Bradley's direction. "Brad said it would be easy. He allus brings scrumptious pies an..."

"Aw shush, Rick."

"...an' we doan't like school dinners!"

"How many times has this happened, Bradley?"

"Dunnow," he shrugged.

"More than once?"

"Could be."

"Does your Mum know?"

"'Course not!"

"Do you think you would like to tell her?"

"Aw no!"

"So, what do you think we ought to do, then?"

"Dunnow."

"Well, for starters let's see what the damage is."

Dan scribbled on his pad then tore out three sheets of paper.

"Mrs Andaman, would you put three of the cardboard trays on the counter, please?" Into each tray Dan placed a piece of paper.

"Right, Bradley, please empty your pockets into this tray, Rick I'd like you to do the same and James, I'll put your name into this one. Thankyou, boys."

Reluctantly hands emerged with fists full of crumbling pasties mingled with bits of string and rubber bands, scrunched up empty crisp packets along with chocolate bars decorated in the sticky areas with balls of fluff and pellets of paper, one squashed tomato, a bruised banana and a melting chocolate muffin completed the assortment that was put into the boxes.

"OK, Mrs Andaman, would you add up the cost of the items in each tray and write it down on the appropriate piece of paper."

With bated breath the boys waited as, with practised eye, Rosalie quickly totalled up the price.

"Great! Thanks," Dan scanned the figures.

"Now, Bradley, your total comes to £1.79. Are you able to pay for these items?"

"Nah!"

"I see," Dan scrutinized him closely.

"Rick, yours is £1.52. Do you have enough cash to cover the cost?"

Rick pulled his pockets inside out and smirked, "I in't got nothin'".

"James, your total comes to £2.06. Can you pay?"

Once again James burst into tears.

"So, am I right in thinking that none of you can pay for the goods you've taken from the shelves?"

Silence filled the air punctuated by sniffles.

What are you going to do about that?"

"Put 'em back," suggested Bradley cheerfully.

"Do you really think someone will want to buy broken pies, squashed fruit and melting chocolate bars and cakes?"

"'s'ppose not."

"I suppose not, too. So, what other options do you have?"

"Eat 'em up so's they don't go to waste."

RK struggled to stifle a giggle.

"Are they yours to do that with?"

"Well we took 'em."

"But without paying!"

"Yeah! But you know we in't got no money."

"That's stealing."

Bradley's shifty eyes looked up at the shop clock. "'ere we got to get back to school else Miss Cooper'll be mad at us."

"Miss Cooper is already aware that you are not in school and..."

"Aw no!" Rick and Bradley ejaculated loudly. They were unaware that Mrs Scholes, the school secretary, had witnessed the boys exit from school grounds through her office window and notified the police office that the boys had gone AWOL.

"Well, boys this behaviour can't go on. We have to sort it out."

James's howling crescendoed.

"Now would be as good a time as any, don't you think? So we'll go back to school together." Dan turned towards RK and Davi. "Thanks for your help, ladies. Mrs Andaman, would you keep the trays under the counter I'll be back for them later."

Sullenly the boys dragged their feet along the floor of the shop to follow Dan out of the shop, up the lane and straight into Jackie Cooper's office.

"Whatever will happen to them?" Davi asked of no one in particular.

"I believe Emma and Jackie have already discussed how they are going to handle the truancy and shoplifting but were waiting for the boys to acknowledge that their behaviour is wrong and unacceptable before meting out any sort of punishment," Rosalie explained.

"I'm not so sure they will admit they are in the wrong after all one of them wanted to eat what he'd taken even though he couldn't pay for it."

"Bradley still has to get the thieving mentality out of his head that his father instilled in him from a very young age."

"I guess Dan will get the boys to decide what their punishment is to be then arrange a meeting with their parents to discuss how it is to be implemented and supervised."

"That's unusual."

"But effective."

"A type of community service?"

"Something like that. I wouldn't be at all surprised if I don't have one of them in the shop breaking up boxes or stacking shelves."

Davi shook her head in disbelief.

Conversation between the sisters over lunch in the Tea rooms touched briefly on Dan's different methods of dealing with young offenders then focussed on RK's independence in Ferry Cottage and her job prospects in the book shop.

"I'll take you over there as soon as we've finished lunch then you can see for yourself how farfetched Stephen Cooper's ideas are."

"But haven't you got a Braille lesson?"

"I think we'll just have time before Bernard arrives."

As soon as he saw them approaching the bookshop Stephen stepped outside and invited the sisters in. With his usual enthusiasm Stephen regaled Davi with his vision for the bookshop and a library next door; ideas for the restoration of the other derelict buildings in the row; his passion for the history of the village and developing a means to display all the artefacts that had been found in a museum that would portray life as it had been; his desire to establish a carpentry business incorporating woodwork classes to enable him to pay for all that he wanted to achieve.

"Can't you just see RK at the centre of all this activity?"

Davi replied cautiously, "Mm, possibly."

Stephen sensed her disbelief, "But she's brill with people, young and old, they all love her and once she's mastered Braille RK will have everything at her fingertips."

Davi chuckled at his quip but RK shrugged her shoulders.

"Aw come on RK you're getting real good at finding your way around the village." He grabbed Davi's arm, "You must convince your sister of the rightness of her involvement. I honestly believe it's all within her capabilities."

"Hey, Stephen, I'm not miles away so don't talk about me as though I were not here!" RK grinned.

"I know, RK, but your sister is and in the short time she is visiting here I want to win her over in order to persuade you that you would be really good at the job I am offering you."

Davi was no longer listening her attention had been drawn away from the conversation to movement on the other side of the lane.

"Who is that gorgeous man amongst the trees?" Her eyes were fixed on Chit Beckingsdale.

"He's in charge of the clearance of Kezia's Wood. Come outside and I'll introduce you."

The ensuing days were a whirlwind of activity. Davi tagged on to all the visits, classes, meetings and appointments that RK had planned.

At the end of her week's holiday Davi returned to Lincolnshire just as enchanted with Newton Westerby and its residents as RK was with much to ponder about what she had seen and heard and people she had met.

The following weekend was the occasion of Isobel and Dobi's long awaited evening soiree. Most of the village had been invited to attend either as guests, participants or minions willing to jump to Isobel's command for the sake of remuneration. Expectations were high. Evening attire was retrieved from the back recesses of wardrobes and Rachel's appointment book bulged with clients desiring her expertise.

Lord Edmund escorted Jennifer Pedwardine. Dan and RK went together. Harry Saunders had been seconded to Newton Lokesby for the occasion to direct car parking and Justin Durrant invited to act as Master of ceremonies. Lily Piper delighted them all with her exquisite piano playing; Annelie, Dan and Justin charmed the company with trios and duets both classical as well as impish, much to Isobel's chagrin, while Adam displayed his virtuosity on guitar and accordion. Dobi entertained them with his droll monologues and Annette moved them almost to tears by her handling of evocative melodies on the flute. Jilly Briggs prepared and organized the buffet supper and supervised her press ganged helpers with precision to ensure that plates and glasses were never empty.

During the interval friends and family mingled from room to room enjoying the repast and passing comments and pleasantries with each other. Isobel's face reflected the satisfaction she felt at the success of her evening as she glided between her guests gesticulating expansively with her arms to give emphasis to her words. Most people were able to duck or move out of the way to avoid her extrovert gestures. Without looking at all where she was going Isobel knocked into RK and spilled the drink she was holding down her new rather expensive dress.

"You clumsy wench! Why don't you look where you're going?" she screeched. "Look what you've done; ruined my dress." Isobel dabbed fruitlessly at the dampness on her clothing with a handkerchief that was more lace than linen.

"You stupid, stupid girl! You'll be getting the bill to have this cleaned. If the stain doesn't come out I'll expect a replacement." Isobel suddenly sensed she was getting no response from RK. "Don't ignore me, girl. Do you hear me?" Isobel shook RK's arm vigorously. "Why are you wearing those absurd sunglasses in doors? You look ridiculous!" As the incensed woman reached to grab them from RK's face a horrified hush spread across the company.

"Your behaviour sickens me, Isobel." Lord Edmund came alongside his sister and spoke in a quiet, carefully controlled voice. "How dare you blame a guest, who's a friend, for your own appalling behaviour and speak to her in that haughty derogatory manner."

"Be quiet, Edmund, I've a right to be furious. She knocked my arm, spilled my drink and ruined my dress."

"No, Isobel that is not what happened. I witnessed your carelessness. I believe you owe RK an apology." Edmund was seething at his sister's disgraceful behaviour towards RK and working hard to keep his temper under control."

"I refuse to apologise to someone who comes to an evening soiree so inappropriately attired."

Lord Edmund turned towards the bewildered RK and placing a hand gently on her shoulder spoke in a softer tone. "My dear girl, I apologise for my sister's rudeness and ill manners." He motioned to Dan. "I would advise you to take RK home, young man. Treat her with care. Isobel's behaviour has rather shaken her. I'll deal with this here." As the young couple left the subdued gathering Edmund turned back to Isobel and in no uncertain terms told her what he thought of her attitude towards her sightless guest.

"What!"

He ignored the unseemly ejaculation that followed and proceeded to grab Jennifer Pedwardine by the arm and stormed out of the house with pursed lips and stony face. Embarrassed silence followed their exit till one by one others followed in his wake.

"Don't go! Don't go," Isobel wailed but the atmosphere had gone and most had lost the heart to remain.

The abrupt ending to Isobel's soiree was the talk of the village for many days but for RK it was a devastating experience undermining her confidence and self esteem. With all her strength RK fought against the demons of the months before. She no longer wished to cower in fear of the darkness that engulfed her but live in the freedom her friends and new interests had opened up to her. Isobel's uncontrolled outburst had badly shaken her.

"Dear God, please help me." She could barely mouth the words. "Words are simply the garments of prayer. Our Lord knows the deep longings of the heart." Memory of conversation with Penny Darnell flooded her mind. She tried to recall the words of the songs she and Dan had sung together and gain strength from the truth they contained. She whispered the words from that distant Sunday so many months ago, "I believe in Jesus."

In the meanwhile, Dan tightened his features with stern determination and marched up to the vicarage during his off-duty on Monday morning. With quiet resolve he set out his plans to care for his beloved Robyn before Hugh and Mrs Darnell. The episode at Isobel and Dobi Gill's persuaded Dan he should make RK his wife immediately.

By the time he left the vicarage the midday sun had moved on leaving a warm glow that suffused everything with gold picking out the shapes and forms of plants to great effect. That warm glow echoed in Dan's heart distinctly defining the direction he should take. With clarity of mind and lightened step Dan made his way to 'Bakers'. Winter was fast approaching but as late autumn prepared for its farewell seed heads shone in the borders, their delicate forms highlighted with edges gilded by the low light.

Warm reds, yellows, bronzes and oranges illumined every corner of the garden. "If only my little songbird could see the beauty all around her and know that amongst all this loveliness she surpasses it all. I must take a lesson from Emma and learn how to paint pictures in words for Robyn."

Dan drew RK into the garden to explain his intention to bring the wedding forward because he was anxious to protect her from ill-will such as Isobel's but RK was badgered by doubts and worries that Dan only wanted to marry her out of pity.

"My dearest songbird, I love you with all my heart and want to spend the rest of my days making a home and a family with you."

RK's heart did incredible things as she detected the sincerity in his voice. His nearness brought a longing to touch him and be held near to his beating heart.

Boldly she reached to feel his face. As skin met skin a tingling danced throughout her whole being right down to her toes.

"Please hold me, Dan," she whispered.

Gently his arms encircled her till she was enveloped so closely their hearts beat as one. He caressed her cheek and kissed her forehead, the tip of her nose and her upturned lips. Desire surged through them. Tenderly Dan released his hold.

"Robyn..." he began huskily but RK stayed his speech with a finger to his mouth.

"I'll marry you on the beach tomorrow morning."

---

As word travelled rapidly throughout the village concerning the forthcoming nuptials friends had rallied round and pulled out all stops in preparation for RK's big day.

Maisie Piper's fingers flew as she designed and stitched a beautiful gown suitable for wintry weather yet elegant enough for RK to feel special.

Penny Darnell organized the flower club ladies in decorating the church and church hall.

Lily Jenner asked to be allowed to make a posy for RK to carry. "It will be my very first of the many I hope to create when I eventually get my flower shop," she said excitedly.

Jilly Briggs seconded cookery and hostess students from the college to provide a fitting wedding celebration lunch.

Ben recruited graphics students to design invitations and had the youngsters of the village racing round delivering them to all the homes in the community.

Jennifer and Bernice contacted Davi offering accommodation at 'Bakers' or 'Green Pastures'' to any of RK's family who wished to come. Surprisingly RK's parents agreed to attend and were welcomed by Bernice and Roy. Davi stayed with RK at 'Bakers' and along with Emma and Rachel helped to get their friend ready.

Hugh Darnell joined their hands in matrimony on the beach just beyond Ferry Cottage early on Sunday morning three weeks later and incorporated a marriage blessing ceremony into the church service afterwards so that all the church family could share in their joy.

Trixie and Christina spruced up Ferry Cottage in readiness for the honeymooners return stocking the cupboards and freezer courtesy of their friends in the village.

Dan told no-one of their destination but as it was such short notice he was only allowed three days away from work. The couple started life together travelling along the A47 and A17 singing songs of love, faith and assurance. Dan reached for Robyn's hand as they passed the Moulton turning. He squeezed as he whispered, "This is where you were broken but we are going to where our journey of healing and beauty began."

"The Haywain?" RK chuckled.

Dan joined in the laughter then strummed the steering wheel and burst into song, "Beauty for Brokenness..."